Quest Of The Mountain Man

After eleven years in the Rockies, the prospect of free farmland in Oregon makes Beau question his nomadic life as a mountain man.

James Oliver Virmala

Edition 1

Cover Photo By James Oliver Virmala

"Tracks From The Past"

ISBN: 978-1-7340021-0-2

ACKNOWLEDGMENTS

To those who faced the high peaks and created the trails that connected the two coasts of North America. They lived and died cutting the paths of the future, asking for little recognition, just the freedom to go over the next mountain.

CONTENTS

Acknowledgments   i

Chapter One   Pg 1

Chapter Two   Pg 10

Chapter Three   Pg 20

Chapter Four   Pg 42

Chapter Five   Pg 65

Chapter Six   Pg 84

Chapter Seven   Pg 102

Chapter Eight   Pg 129

Chapter Nine   Pg 144

Chapter Ten   Pg 167

Chapter Eleven   Pg 183

Chapter Twelve   Pg 212

Chapter Thirteen   Pg 230

Chapter Fourteen   Pg 246

Chapter Fifteen   Pg 267

Chapter Sixteen   Pg 281

Chapter Seventeen   Pg 304

Cast Of Characters   Pg 328

BOOKS BY THE AUTHOR

Oli's Gold Book One
Search For Oli's Gold Book Two
Return To Oli's Gold Book Three
To Be A Mountain Man
Trouble On The Kansas Plains
Frontier Justice
Return Of The Mountain Man
The Tall Man
The Prospector
The Green Valley
Twilight Of The Mountain Man
The Mother Lode
Quest Of The Mountain Man
Journey's End
Rufus Pike
Rufus And The Pup
The Winding Trail Home
Rufus The Lost Years
The Kankakee Kid
Bogus Island
Tyler Tomas The Brothers' War
War of 1812 The Choice
Kyle Oliver The Next Horizon

CHAPTER ONE

The bright morning sun reflecting off the snow cast dark shadows from the naked aspen trees across the valley floor. To the north side, below a ridge, stood a shanty nestled in a grove of evergreens. A rabbit nibbling on some black cherry bark was startled by the door scraping on crusted snow as a curly-haired mountain man emerged from the dark interior.

Squinting, he raised his bearded face toward the sky and breathed deeply. "By God, it smells like spring is around the corner."

Overnight the wind had become southerly and had brought the smell of the warmer plains air into the mountains. The mountain man was Beauford Levesque, better known as Beau. It was 1849. After the last rendezvous in 1840, marking the end of the beaver trapping heyday, some of the mountain men had continued to live in the Rockies, making a living hunting, trapping larger prey or acting as guides or scouts.

Others had given up the mountain life and

traveled to Oregon, California, or back east to become farmers, tradesmen, and even politicians. Love of the Rockies had kept Beau in the high country.

Tossing the buffalo robe off his shoulders, the bearded man walked around the side of the shanty to relieve himself. Once the spring rains came, the evidence of his winter latrine would quickly be washed away.

After the last rendezvous, Beau had ridden south into Mexican territory with plans of marrying Ana Garcia. It turned out that her need of family had been stronger than her love of Beau. She had left him a letter trying to explain her decision. He still carried the letter with him.

He'd then made plans with a friend, Reiner, to guide travelers over the mountains to Oregon. There was a surplus of mountain men for guides and too few emigrants needing their services, so after two lean years Beau had found himself back in the mountains hunting grizzly, big cats and wolves. He had even done some trapping and buffalo hunting.

Once Beau had the water heating in the fire pit in front of the shanty, he went around back to take care of his sorrel. The horse whinnied from the crude lean-to as it heard the crunch of Beau's footsteps in the snow. Most of the winter the sorrel had shared the lean-to with a packhorse. The packhorse had been attacked two months ago by wolves and severely injured. Beau had brought the animal to a Flathead camp where his friend Elijah lived with his Flathead wife and children. He had given it to them to butcher. The tribe had appreciated the additional food for winter.

After picketing the sorrel in a sheltered area so

it could dig for grass under the snow, Beau ducked back into the shanty and went to the wooden box where he kept his supplies. The winter dwelling was a log structure which measured 10 by 15 feet. There were no windows or fireplace. A stack of spruce boughs along one wall was his bed. A three-legged stool and split log with legs for a table were the only furniture. The roof had sagged under the winter snow load, forcing him to duck when walking near the center.

The firepit in front of the open door provided the only heat in the winter. Beau had been out of coffee, tea, and tobacco for some time. He planned to make a thin gruel of cornmeal and water for his breakfast. While waiting for it to cook, Beau sat on a log next to the pit and soaked in the heat cast off by the flames.

Ringlets of his curly hair hung well below his ears. His beard, showing some gray from the hard mountain lifestyle, was tangled and lay against his faded woolen shirt. He had buckskin pants and calf-high moccasins. Beau had spent two winters in the shanty located in the Big Horn Mountains. The high meadow was protected from the winter winds by steep, granite walls.

The mountain man shaded his eyes and looked to the east of the valley. He saw tracks that had not been there the day before. "Could be a visitor," he muttered to himself, "or could be something good to eat."

Setting the pot down by the fire with enough gruel left for his next meal, Beau went back into the shanty and got his Hawken .53 caliber. The scarred rifle had been with him for the past eight years. He had traded in a flintlock .54 caliber and a grizzly hide for the percussion rifle. In his broad belt he had a knife and a short-handled axe. Slung over his shoulder were his possible bag and powder horn.

He looked over at the sorrel searching under the snow for grass. It had a thick, shaggy winter coat covering the ribs that protruded after the lean feed of winter. The horse looked up in anticipation of going with Beau.

"You just keep on working on that grass," he called to the animal. "If its an elk, I'll be back to get you to drag it back, should I kill it. If it is trouble and it goes bad for me, you can have the shanty."

Beau chuckled at his humor as he headed across the valley toward the tracks. While he was still a distance away, he recognized them as the tracks of an elk. It appeared to have been running. As the mountain man got closer, he saw the sign of the wolves' tracks. They had been chasing the elk and their lighter weight had allowed them to run on top of the crust.

He looked at the direction the elk had gone. "It's headed for the stream, hoping to get away from the cusses," Beau said, talking to himself.

It was a habit he'd picked up over the long winter of isolation. The mountain man saw that there were only three wolves chasing the elk. It was possible that others in the pack were coming after it from another angle. Placing a percussion cap into the rifle nipple, Beau walked briskly, following the tracks.

The stream was a half-mile ahead. It had a thick growth of aspen on the south side, which would give him cover tracking the animals. Eventually the stream wound down from the high meadow and emptied into the Big Horn River.

The sound of the wolves stopped Beau. They had the elk at bay. The thrill of the hunt surged through the mountain man's veins. If he couldn't get the elk, odds were good that he'd come away with another wolf skin. He double-checked the Hawken as he approached the aspen.

Beau headed into the trees, working his way to the left. It led to higher ground and a waterfall. The sounds of the life and death struggle were getting louder. The desperate snorts of the elk could be heard. The mountain man came to the stream at a point above the commotion. Over the ridge in front of him the water tumbled down, its spray freezing onto the rocks and logs below. Just downstream of the waterfall, the elk stood in the middle of the stream, its head stretched out, challenging the five wolves that surrounded it on the banks.

The stream was wider a hundred paces down from the falls. The wolves would not enter the frigid water to go after the elk, so it offered temporary safety. Beyond them the stream narrowed, allowing the wolves to leap across. The elk was trapped and all the wolves had to do was wait until the cold of the stream got to be too much for it and the elk would be theirs.

The mountain man hunkered down behind a windfall and watched the struggle below. The elk would be an easy shot for the Hawken, but getting the meat away from the wolves would be a problem. Then again, Beau could shoot one of the wolves and the sound of his rifle should send the elk running again and take the rest of the wolves with it. He would come away with another wolf skin and could make a few meals from its stringy meat.

The thought of sizzling steaks from a haunch of the elk sounded better. Thinking about the cornmeal gruel waiting for him, a plan formed in Beau's mind. If it did not work, he could still kill a wolf and possibly end up with a hide. As he set up to shoot, snow flakes began to fall. It would take a neck shot, to drop the elk where it stood. He would then reload the rifle before hurrying down and cutting a hindquarter off the downed elk. The wolves should move away long enough to give Beau time to get the meat. Once he had it, they would hopefully go after the downed elk, rather than him.

The mountain man pressed the set trigger on the Hawken. He waited for the elk to lunge toward the wolves near the stream bank, then touched off the front hair trigger. The rifle recoiled against his shoulder and sent a killing ball into the neck of the elk. Its head turned before it collapsed into the shallow water near the bank.

The thundering sound of the rifle sent the wolves running, but not far. His heart pounding, Beau poured a measure of powder into the Hawken and then rammed a ball wrapped in a grease-covered patch down the barrel. While he hurried down toward the animal, the mountain man placed a cap onto the nipple and shouted at the wolves to help his nerves and to try to keep them away.

It would be only minutes before the hunger of the startled wolves would exceed their fear and it would be a fight for the downed elk. Beau leaned his rifle against a sapling and stepped into the ankle-deep water. Pulling his knife, he lifted the leg and frantically cut around the hindquarter as the snow began to fall harder. Then, putting the bloody knife back into its sheath, he pulled the short axe from his belt. Swinging at the hip and leg bone, he separated the two and pulled the haunch loose.

All the while he was doing this, Beau was shouting and cussing at the wolves, making as much noise as he could. Slipping the axe back into his belt, the mountain man swung the hindquarter over his shoulder, clutching the water-logged leg bone just above the hoof. Almost slipping on the fresh snow as he climbed up the bank, Beau grabbed his rifle with his free hand and shouted his goodbyes to the wolves as he moved quickly through the trees.

Blood from the haunch splattered on the back of his legs and the new snow as he hurried to put distance between the kill and himself. Any moment he expected to feel the jerk of one or more wolves latching onto the hindquarter. As he broke out into the meadow he went a few steps before turning to look back.

Sure enough, one of the wolves was following him. The dark-furred animal stopped when he turned. Dropping the haunch onto the snow-covered ground, Beau took a few more steps away. The wolf's eyes were fixed on the meat and never saw the rifle come up. Again, the thunder of the Hawken was heard in the valley. The wolf leaped around with a ki-yi and fell thrashing to the snow.

"By God, one more skin," Beau muttered as he ran back and grabbed the back legs of the wolf and dragged it to the elk meat. Reaching into his possible bag, he brought out some pigging strings and tied the elk leg and wolf together. Then, dragging them behind him, the mountain man headed toward his shanty. Beau was fully aware that he was now carrying an empty rifle.

Panting and sweating, he arrived back at the shanty. The snow had stopped. A spruce near the shanty had a rope hanging over an upper limb. This he had used to keep any meat out of reach of animals looking for an easy meal. He hoisted the hindquarter into the tree and then went back to move the wolf carcass near the fire pit.

The mountain man began to shiver. Under his woolen shirt and long johns, he was covered with sweat. This condition could quickly cause hypothermia and be the death of a man out in the wilds. Beau was well aware of this and, with shaking hands, he added twigs to the firepit. Desperately he blew on the few coals until they caught the kindling on fire. Quickly, he added additional wood to the crackling spruce twigs.

Removing his shirt, he sat on the log and pulled the buffalo robe over his shoulders. Beau sat staring at the wolf near the fire and shaking his head. "You damn fool," he scolded himself. "You had enough grub to make it out of the mountains, yet you had to go after the elk and then get greedy and shoot a wolf. It would serve you right to freeze here on this log for being stupid."

For the next hour, the mountain man continued to reprimand himself as he added wood to the fire. The waves of tremors that started in his chest worked their way up, caused his teeth to chatter. Finally, the chills subsided. The sunshine reflecting off the shanty and the heat of the flames was now almost too much. Beau tossed off the buffalo robe and pulled his knife. It was time to skin the wolf.

Using his razor-sharp knife, he slit the wolf from under its chin to the tail. The winter had been good for this animal. Beau found plenty of fat under the skin. His stomach growled as he worked. Soon he had the skin stretched on a wooden frame to dry. On the rocks, he had place one of the wolves back legs to roast. As he worked he had been turning the meat. While not his favorite, it would make a good midday meal.

CHAPTER TWO

The juicy elk stakes Beau enjoyed that night went a long way at making the mountain man feel that they'd been worth the risk. In the shanty he now had another wolf skin drying, and enough elk to last until he was out of the mountains and back on the plains.

It was early March and he had to get his gear together and head east. He and a fellow hunter had been hired last summer to guide a wagon train from Independence, Missouri to Oregon. As soon as the grass was high enough to provide grazing, they would have to get underway to beat the early winter storms in the Rockies.

It would take just under two months to make the trek from the shanty to Independence. Beau was to meet his friend in the Black Hills near the Six Grandfathers Mountains. It would take him three weeks to reach the Black Hills and Beau would have to take care to avoid the Lakota tribe. Fort Laramie had been built on their lands without permission and the Lakota would attack emigrants and hunters.

The mountain man had planned to ride the sorrel out of the mountains and carry the skins and his gear on the packhorse. Now he would have to lead the sorrel with his packs. It was four days after he had killed the elk when Beau left the shanty. The door was tightly shut and a note was left inside for anyone who should decide to spend time in the valley.

There had been no sign of the wolves. The elk would satisfy their hunger for over a week and it would take additional time before they were hungry enough to tackle large prey. It felt good to be heading east. Beau loved to see new country. He had never been to the Black Hills. He'd listened to others talk of the beauty of the Dakotas.

It was two days before he reached the plains. They were still snow-covered, but it was not nearly as deep as in the mountains. The sun was just about to go behind the mountains when Beau caught sight of a campfire. Stopping a distance away, the mountain man observed the camp. A single man was moving around, taking care of his horses and stirring something at the fire.

Prior to walking up to the camp, Beau called out. The man ducked behind cover and called back, "Who's out there? Show yourself."

"I'm Beau Levesque," the mountain man called out. "It just my packhorse and me. I'll be stepping out now."

Being cautious about strangers, Beau kept his horse close for cover. As he approached the camp, the man stood up holding a Kentucky Long Rifle in front of him. He was wearing well-worn, and stained buckskins. "The name's Claude Dingle," the man called out. "Come on in."

Stepping clear of the sorrel, Beau led it into the camp. "I got no coffee or tobacco to share, but I do have some elk."

A gust of wind brought the smell of what Claude was cooking. It was coffee. Along with the smell of coffee came the rotten, sour smell of Mr. Dingle. "Let me take care of my animal here and I'll join you in a cup of that brew."

Beau pulled the packs off the sorrel. They included the results of his winter hunt: Two grizzly skins, nine wolf skins, two big cat skins, and an assortment of smaller pelts. His food pack was nearly empty. The personal items didn't amount to much. Most of these he carried on himself. There was enough of the elk left for one good meal for the two men.

Claude reached out his hand when Beau came from taking care of the sorrel. "It's good to meet a fellow traveler. I met a fellow that had coffee three days ago. Swapped three fisher pelts for a bag of beans and some tobacky. He was a nice fellow, but didn't even want to stay the night."

Shaking the man's hand, Beau stepped back as the breeze brought the awful smell to him again. "Some folks just aren't sociable," the mountain man replied.

Beau had his own cup and frying pan. Claude poured the coffee while the mountain man sliced the elk into the pan. He added a dab of fat gotten from the wolf. Soon the grease was snapping around the meat. The man made a good pot of coffee, but every time he came close to Beau it almost made his eyes water.

While they were chewing on the elk, Beau asked, "Where you headed?"

"Montana territory," Claude replied. "They say there is some mountains toward the north that has winter all year round. On a hot summer day there is ice for the taking to make a cold drink."

"I'm heading for the Black Hills," Beau said.

"Wouldn't catch me there," Claude told him. "The Lakota lift your hair before you see them."

"I appreciate your warning," the mountain man said. "I'll take care going through there. I'm meeting a friend who's got a cabin in the Black Hills. We spent last summer hunting buffalo."

"You don't say," Mr. Dingle said, breaking into a big smile. "I hunt buffalo most every year. I am a skinner. Taking part of this year off to go north. I hope to be back hunting by late summer."

Beau smiled at the man, thinking, *That's it. You smell like a hide wagon.*

The two men enjoyed a smoke after the meal and talked of hunting buffalo, trapping, and mountain life. When Claude suggested Beau roll his blankets out near the fire, the mountain man told him he needed it cool to sleep well and then rolled out his blankets well away from Claude and up wind.

The next morning, Beau had the sorrel packed by sun-up. Claude sat near the fire, mixing up some dough. The Dutch oven was heating on the fire. As he shaped the bread, he left dirty hand prints in the dough. Looking up, he saw Beau with the horse. Setting the dough on a rock, he got up and came over with the steaming pot of coffee. "You best have a cup before leaving. I'm making a fine breakfast of side meat and sourdough."

The sour dough almost got the mountain man to change his mind about leaving early. But another whiff of Claude and the memory of the hand prints reminded him of the urgency. "I'll have a cup, but then I need to go. It's a long way to the Black Hills and I'm walking."

As Beau hurriedly sipped the hot brew, Mr. Dingle complained, "Folks is always in too much of a hurry. I just don't understand it."

As he led the sorrel away, Beau waved and called back, "Maybe I'll see you on the plains someday. I'll take you up on the sourdough."

Headed in a southeasterly direction, Beau walked through calf-deep snow, pacing himself so he wouldn't overheat. The high plains were over 4,000 feet and spring was another month away. The bitter cold of winter was over, but one could still expect a good snow storm.

His first goal was the Tongue River. There was a trading post there, along with a few settlers who'd built cabins. The owner of the trading post was Tolliver. He had come from England on contract with the Hudson Bay Company. Eventually he had gained free man status, moved south and started the trading post. He was married to a Cree woman and had four grown sons and two daughters. Furs that Tolliver purchased were still sent north by boat or packed on caravans led by his sons.

The trading post was a welcome sight. Beau planned to spend a couple days enjoying some Scottish whiskey and company while the sorrel got fed grain. He could get more for his winter's work if he brought the furs to Independence, but it would be lots of wear and tear on his horse. Plus, it would keep him on foot.

One of Tolliver's sons was splitting wood, and the owner was carrying an arm load into the post. The old owner recognized Beau and gave him a shout out. "Bring your pack and hoss to the stable. I'll get out a bottle and have the missus warm up some stew."

Tolliver was a slimly built man, stoop-shouldered, with thinning, gray hair. His leathery, wrinkled features showed the years of hard work in the high plains. One of his sons named Ecgbert assisted Beau with the packs. The dark-haired boy smiled and said, "I'll give your horse a good brushing and fill it with grain, Mr. Levesque."

"Thanks, Ecgbert," the mountain man replied. "The two big packs got some furs to sell. Got the heads and paws of the grizzly's also. Have your pa look them over."

"I can do that for you," the boy said proudly. "Father has put me and Randolph in charge of buying furs."

Ecgbert and Randolph were the youngest of the boys. Old man Tolliver was finally sharing some of the load with his sons. "Just remember, you and your brother are going to be looking at a couple of the finest bear skins in the mountains."

Smiling, Ecgbert said, "Yes, sir," as he took the lead rope.

Beau headed for the trading post and the bottle of whiskey, knowing that the sons would be just as hard to deal with as their father. The old man had taught them well on all parts of running a trading post.

The post was a low, log building with four glass windows to help brighten the dim interior. The smell of new rope and leather goods mingled with the gun oil, spices, and wood smoke. Barrels of goods lined one wall and wooden boxes of items were stacked against another. Shelves were filled with canned goods, tin items, lamps, shooting supplies, bolts of cloth, bags of coffee beans, white beans, corn meal, cold flour, and leather bags of pemmican.

For a remote post, Tolliver's was well-supplied. A couple of times a year items were brought in by boat along the river. Other items were brought back by his sons returning from packing out furs. Right now, Beau's main interest was the plank bar and counter in the back, which held a bottle of whiskey and a glass.

Old man Tolliver pushed through a curtained doorway that led to his living quarters in the back. "Let me pour you the first one," he said, smiling. "Emma is warming your supper."

He had given his Cree wife the name Emma in honor of his own mother. She was a short, plump woman, her hair streaked with gray. She had a wide smile, which exposed missing front teeth that had been knocked out while she was helping her husband shoe a cantankerous horse.

Beau was on his second drink when Emma emerged through the curtain with a steaming bowl of thin stew and thick slices of bread. "The meat is bear," she said. "The rutabaga make it taste good."

The mountain man thanked her as he slid the bowl closer. The whiskey had already made him feel a glow. Plunging a slice of bread into the juice, he took a large bite, the stew juice dripping into his beard. Beau would enjoy the next couple of nights. Just behind the curtain was a hall with a small room on each side. Each had a comfortable bed. A hot bath would be required before Emma would let him sleep there. Even now the daughters were busy heating water for the bath.

* * *

The next morning, Beau awoke with a headache and dry mouth from putting a dent in the Scottish whiskey. He was wearing new long johns, a new green woolen shirt, woolen pants, and high-cut boots. His hair was cut, and the beard was trimmed to about three inches long. All in all, he felt like a new man. The mountain man could be sure that Tolliver would keep track of all expenses, but Beau knew the comfortable bed and bath would be complimentary.

The sun had the icicles dripping. While the potbelly stove kept the coffee hot, the trading post door was left wide open to let out the bad air and allow the good in. Beau sat at a small table with old man Tolliver and Ecgbert. The discussion was on the price of furs. Naturally the demand was down for the ones Beau had brought in, but the young son would try and do everything he could to give Beau a good price.

The old man never said a word, but the mountain man was sure that some type of signal was given when an acceptable value was reached. Lying on the table next to Beau's coffee cup was a list of the items he owed the trading post. Some were supplies he was taking with him, some were consumed at the post.

The owner offered Beau a cigar once the dickering was done and brought out the remainder of the bottle of whiskey. "My son is too generous with you," the old man complained.

"You are right," the mountain man said. "If he had done his job, I would leave here owing you money." There was a moment's hesitation, and then both men laughed.

With business taken care of, a deck of cards

was taken out and the two men spent the afternoon playing poker. The bidding was kept low so neither could be hurt too much. By the time Emma announced that supper was ready, the two men had just about broken even.

The next morning, it was time to leave. Two days in the comfortable bed had almost spoiled Beau. During the nights he'd had company, but he had been sworn to secrecy about letting her father know. Over the past several years of stopping at the trading post, he had gotten to know the eldest daughter, Ellie. Her husband had been killed from a fall from a horse. She had not remarried and looked forward to Beau's visits.

The care and grain had the sorrel looking much better. While putting his supplies into the saddlebags, he noticed two twists of tobacco that he hadn't had to buy. Ecgbert also gave him a sack with grain for the horse. Without the packs of furs, Beau could now ride the sorrel part of the time.

As Beau rode away from the trading post, the old man stood in the doorway calling goodbye. Around the corner of the post the eldest daughter stood with a blanket around her shoulders. Smiling, she watched the mountain man as he disappeared across the Tongue River.

The spring thaw hadn't started in the north and the rivers were easy to cross. Ice along the edges was the only thing Beau had to watch out for. The horse could break through and injure its legs, or flounder and spill Beau into the water. Each evening, he gave the sorrel a portion of grain. It would be gone within a week, but in the mean time it would help keep the horse's strength up.

CHAPTER THREE

It was the end of March when Beau entered the Black Hills. He was headed for a cabin near the Six Grandfathers Mountains. His friend, Jocko Wells, had wintered there. Jocko was barely over five feet-tall, with broad shoulders and thick, muscular arms. He had straight, brown hair that he kept close-cropped. He was a crack shot with the Hawken and could out-skin most other buffalo hunters.

The two men had spent time at Fort Laramie before winter and heard talk of all the wagon trains heading west to Oregon. A portly gent with a large goiter was looking for men to guide wagon trains next spring. He bought Beau and Jocko drinks while offering them work.

Both men had traveled the route years back and decided that it would be good money leading the wagons and they had made arrangement with the man to guide one in May. Each was promised $150 with their supplies provided, along with a wagon and a team which was theirs to keep. Beau would be leading the train while Jocko would be scouting the trail.

Beau was leading the tired sorrel as he approached the mountains. The snow-covered ground was crusted over, making walking through the knee-deep snow difficult. After a few steps on firm crust, the mountain man would break through. Finally, he just stomped hard enough to bust the crust as he went.

Smoke was drifting up from the fireplace as Beau approached the cabin. Jocko liked things in their place. There was no debris around the cabin and the wood was neatly stacked near the door. A gray and two brown mustangs were in the corral next to the cabin. A partial haystack remained near them. A deer was hung in a tree cooling, its back legs spread with a stick to let the air circulate through the body cavity.

The mountain man was relieved to reach a path in the snow leading to the cabin. There were bits of blood and hair in the path, letting Beau know it had been the route taken back with the deer. As he approached the cabin, Beau hollered out. Around from behind the cabin came his stocky, broad-shouldered friend.

"It's about time you showed up," Jocko called back. "I was thinking I'd have to go without you."

"The snow made travel a bit slower and I spent a couple of nights at Tolliver's," the smiling mountain man said.

"Still chasing that daughter of his, ain't you?" his friend kidded him.

Blushing under his beard, Beau made no reply as he pulled his saddle bags off the horse.

"Put your animal in the corral and pitch it some hay," Jocko told him. "I was about to skin out the deer. It'll be venison steaks for supper."

Beau had pulled the saddle off the sorrel and was giving it hay when he saw Jocko carrying the skinned deer carcass into the cabin like it weighed nothing. *Damn, that man is strong*, he thought.

The mountain man followed his friend into the cabin carrying his gear. While they had no idea who had built it, the cabin was well-built. It had a dirt floor and a small table with a couple of stools. The shelves on the walls had once held supplies. The fireplace at one end provided heat and a place to cook. Jocko had a pot of coffee ready and an iron skillet heating for the venison.

"If we leave in the next day or two, we should be in Independence by the 1st of May," Beau told his friend.

"I see you ain't got no pack horse," the stocky man said.

"Wolves got it," Beau replied.

"I got an extra," Jocko told him. "I won it arm wrestling after you left the fort."

"The man was a damn fool that challenged you."

Changing the subject, the mountain man asked, "Have you seen any sign of the Lakota?"

"Too early for them," his friend replied. "They'll be in winter camp for another month, maybe more."

"I guess it depends on how hungry they are by now," Beau guessed.

The next few days the two men were busy getting ready to go. Some of the venison was dried over a fire near the cabin. Unnecessary gear was discarded to allow fast travel. Their Hawken rifles were boiled out and oiled. Extra balls were cast and greased patches cut. Both men enjoyed the tobacco Tolliver have given Beau. They either smoked or chewed it, depending on how busy their hands were.

A light snow was falling when the two men rode away from the cabin. Their supply packs were split between the two mustangs, making each load easy to carry. Jocko had some wolf and cat skins, and pelts from fisher and mink.

It would take most of a month to make the 750-mile trip to Independence. By trading off riding the mustangs some of the time they could cut off several days, depending on the weather. Jocko liked to cook, so each night Beau would take care of the animals while the stocky man got a meal together.

By the time they reached the Missouri River the snow was completely gone. Due to the condition of their weary animals, they were still a week out of Independence. Beau noticed that the grass was up and would give fair grazing for the wagon trains.

* * *

It was April 25th when they reached Independence. Beau had not been there since 1838, when he and a black friend, Elijah, were fugitives. One had been running from the law, the other from slave hunters. That was lot of years ago, and Beau had little to fear anymore. But just in case there was a dusty old poster, or someone with a long memory, he wouldn't be spreading his name around the town.

Independence had grown over the years. The town had stately buildings, several church steeples, an expansive waterfront industry, and to the west a scattering of camps with clusters of wagons. That night Beau and Jocko set up camp just outside of Independence. They were able to see hundreds of campfires to the west.

While they picked up a few supplies, Jocko traded his furs and Beau looked at a newspaper. The bold headlines read, GOLD IN CALIFORNIA!! The mountain man had been aware of talk of gold over the years in one place or another, but had never had the burning desire to chase the yellow metal. Jocko had been drawn to a couple of strikes only to find out very few got rich and many left poorer than when they came.

The next morning, Jocko stayed with the horses and gear, while Beau walked into town to find Robert Finlay, the man who was setting up the wagon train. Finlay's office was in a weather-beaten clapboard building near the waterfront. He was the plump man with a large goiter. While the weather was cool, his face was red and he mopped sweat from his brow.

"You're late," Finlay said.

"We were supposed to be here by the end of April. It's only the 26th now," Beau argued.

"The train I had you scheduled to lead left a week ago. They are off to the gold fields in California," the man stated.

The mountain man felt heat rising in his neck. "California? I was to lead a train to Oregon."

Robert snorted. "These folks don't want to go to Oregon. There's gold to be had and they want it."

Suddenly, Beau felt desperate. He and Jocko had planned their whole year on guiding the wagon train. "Well then, me and my partner will take a train to California."

"I got trains scheduled every week for the next

six weeks," Finlay informed him. "I got guides hired, sitting around eating my groceries, waiting for their turn. Folks are paying high prices to get their wagons on a train. Supplies and stock are getting scarce. By mid-June it's too late to get through the mountain passes before the snow. If you're willing to hang around town until then, I might be able to get you a train. You'd be taking the folks to the mountains and then winter there. Once the passes opened up, you would guide them to the gold fields. You'll have to get your own wagon, supplies, and stock."

"Why would people be willing to leave late and winter on the plains?" Beau asked.

"Why hell," Robert exclaimed. "To get a jump on next year, and they'll pay good money to do it."

"What would you pay me and my partner to guide them?" the mountain man asked.

Robert Finlay hefted his stocky frame up out of the chair and turned to look out the window. "By rights, I should charge you the same as the rest of the wagons." Hearing Beau's audible gasp, he continued, "Seeing how we had a deal, even though you come here late, I will give you and your partner $100 each. That is if I can put at least a forty-wagon train together."

Beau was seeing red by this time. What the man was offering was no deal at all. It was hard enough for one man to survive the winter out on the plains with game being scarce. By spring those who didn't freeze would have eaten all their stock. If he and Jocko were able to get the train over the mountains, they would have worked over a year for a measly $100 each.

Frustrated, Beau turned to leave the man's office. Stopping at the door, he said, "I'll talk with my partner."

"Don't be sitting on your decision," Robert warned him. "I got men waiting in line for the chance to guide a train."

As Beau walked back to bring the bad news to Jocko, he looked around. From every direction there were wagons, two-wheel carts, and riders with pack animals coming in. Much of the plain around Independence had been trampled into mud by all the traffic. The mountain man knew that Robert Finlay wasn't his only option to get a train west, but with the fever for gold, he could expect the same story from all the others.

Jocko was putting a meal together when Beau got back to camp. "I've been watching wagons come in ever since you left. Makes me wonder which ones will be going with us."

"I got bad news, Jocko," he replied. "The man said we were late and lost our train."

The stocky man quit stirring the bean pot and looked up. "Late? We ain't late."

"People are paying big bucks to go west and aren't willing to wait," Beau said, clenching his jaws, breathing deep before continuing. "He said our train left for California a week ago. They are all headed for the gold fields in California."

Jocko's face paled. "We're going to Oregon, not California."

Shaking his head, the mountain man replied, "There ain't no trains going to Oregon. The gold has them all going to California. Tomorrow we can go into town or Westport landing and see if we can find someone else that needs a guide and scout to the gold fields."

"No!" Jocko shouted, throwing the stirring

spoon on the ground.

Surprised at the outburst, Beau countered, "No? The man said the wagons are all going to California. We may not even be able to hire onto a train going there."

The stocky man's face was red and veins in his temple were pulsing. "I wasted a lot of miles coming here. Tomorrow I am heading for Oregon. I can't wait. You're welcome to come with me if you want."

Suddenly, Beau's expression changed to one of confusion. "I'll go with you to Oregon, but is there a reason we need to leave tomorrow? Can't we do some checking around?"

Picking up the spoon, Jocko carefully wiped it clean with a handful of grass and squatted next to the pot of beans. "I got a reason. Last summer I was injured while hunting buffalo. A greenhorn wounded a buffalo and it come after us. I was loading my Hawken and the kid took off, climbing into some boulders. I tried to leap out of its way, but the shoulder sent me rolling. Another hunter got a killing shot into the buffalo before it could turn and come at me again."

The stocky man paused as though reliving the attack. Finally, he continued, "They didn't know if I'd live or die and couldn't have me laid up on the hunt, so a couple guys brought me to the Mormon Ferry. I was there until my ribs and whatever else inside mended. While I was there I met this lady. She helped nurse me back to health. We kind of liked each other and when I headed back to the hunt, she said she was going to Oregon."

"Wait a minute," Beau interrupted. "You met this lady and she went someplace in Oregon and you plan to go and find her?"

"Its more than that," Jocko said. "I know where she is and she's waiting for me."

"Why didn't you just go with her?" his friend asked.

"I was broke. I had money coming from the hunt, but I had to finish it to get paid," the stocky man explained. "I had to help haul the hides back here to the Westport Landing. I was coming from here when we met at Fort Laramie and talked to the man about wagon trains. His talk made sense. I had to stay over winter before leaving anyway, and if I could make money going to Oregon, I would arrive in better shape."

"You will probably spend whatever you have now to make the trip," Beau pointed out. "You will be broke again."

"That just might be," Jocko said, finally smiling, "but I'll have Lisa."

"I'll tell you what," he told his stocky friend. "Give me two, maybe three days to find us a job going west. Even if it is California, after we get there you can take the Siskiyou Trail north and be in Oregon three weeks later."

"That's almost another month," Jocko pointed out. "It would be November by the time I got to Willamette Valley, too late to help with harvest."

"You hope to make money hiring on to harvest for farmers?" Beau asked.

"I kind of have a farm in Oregon," the stocky man explained.

"Who's working it?" his friend asked. The mountain man hadn't been aware his friend already had land in Oregon. Beau headed to the packs to get their tin plates and cups.

"The lady at the Mormon Ferry," Jocko explained. "She and our baby are on the farm."

The mountain man stopped in mid-step. "Your baby!"

Jocko blushed deep red. "I got word from her last year when I got to Westport Landing. She said she was with child and wanted to marry me. She said she had some land in our name and was starting to prove it up. I sent back that we'd get married as soon as I got to Oregon."

Finding it awkward to talk of such things, the two men fell silent and began eating the meal. Once the plates and pot were wiped clean, they sat around the fire drinking the last of the evening's coffee. Beau sat there grinning as he tamped tobacco into his pipe.

Watching his friend, Jocko finally blurted out, "What the hell is so funny?"

"You somebody's pa," Beau chuckled.

Frowning for a moment at his friend, Jocko suddenly broke into a smile, "Yep, me a pa."

"Why didn't you leave from Fort Laramie last fall?" the mountain man asked. "Or at least have stayed there until this spring and left from there?"

"We met the man that talked of us getting paid to go to Oregon." Jocko stood up and tossed the dregs out of his cup. "Too bad it didn't work out."

The next morning, Beau was able to convince Jocko to give him a couple days to find a wagon train west. He told the stocky man that if he was only able to get one to California, Jocko could head for Oregon at the South Pass and he'd take the wagons the rest of the way to California by himself. Nobody would know the difference.

Riding the sorrel, he left to check with others

setting up wagon trains. Jocko had to stay in camp to prevent his horses and their gear from being stolen. Beau traveled west 10 miles to Westport Landing, passing dozens of emigrant camps. He saw three wagon trains leaving with over 40 wagons in each. He found only two additional offices that were putting wagon trains together. None of them had a need for a guide this season and all required payment from Beau and Jocko to join them.

Disappointed, the mountain man rode back toward the camp in Independence. He saw a few small groups of wagons leaving. Unwilling to wait for their turn and the safety of a larger wagon train, some struck out on their own, thinking only of the riches in California. A plan started formulating in Beau's mind. He just might be able to band a few of them together and form his own train.

Beau found Jocko anxiously waiting for him. "Your mood has certainly improved since I left," he told his friend.

The stocky man was beaming. "It has indeed," he replied. "A couple of hours ago six wagons stopped to cook at our fire. They had just come from Robert Finlay's. They were supposed to be part of our wagon train going to Oregon. They had been delayed due to illness. He told them that the only ones available were wagon trains going to California."

"He told us the same thing," Beau replied.

"These folks still want to go to Oregon," Jocko said. "They got family they're going to join."

Looking at his friend, the mountain man stroked his beard. "I was just thinking about finding some folks that would be willing to band together for the trip to California, or now maybe Oregon."

That evening the two men went to talk to the Oregon bound folks. Beau was pleased to find out that there were eight other wagons that were looking to go to Oregon. A grizzled, older man named Otto Graf spoke for the wagon folks. He and his two sons, Beck and Ludwig, had one of the wagons. The man seemed to stiffen a bit when the talk of money for leading the wagon train came up.

"We would only be looking for a few suggestions once we left Fort Hall," the old man said. "We were kind of thinking of you and your partner as one more wagon."

Beau figured this was not the time to discuss the value he and Jocko would provide. First off, he was hopeful that nothing would change the minds of these emigrants. Three of the additional wagons were already in the area and the other five were a day behind this group. It was decided that there would be another meeting as soon as the other wagons arrived.

On the way back to their camp, Jocko said, "The old man wants to be the leader."

"If that's the case, we'll ask for a vote of the wagons," Beau replied. "If they want to follow him, we ride west, the two of us."

The mountain man knew the dangers they would be facing on the trip west and had followed the complete trail in the past, and much of it more than once. He hoped everything would work out and in the next couple of days they would leave with 14 wagons.

The two men were just finishing their breakfast the next morning when two burly men rode up. Beau smiled at them and called out, "We got some coffee left."

"Finlay wants to see you." With that said, the

men rode back toward Independence.

"You think he has a wagon train for us?" Jocko asked.

"I'll go find out," Beau replied. They were just a quarter-mile from Finlay's office, so rather than saddling the sorrel, the mountain man wiped his mouth on his sleeve and headed into town.

The robust Robert Finlay was sitting at his desk, lighting a cigar. He offered one to Beau. Accepting the smoke, the mountain man took a splinter from the spill vase and caught it on fire in the lamp to light the cigar. Finlay motioned to a chair and Beau sat down.

"I had a visit from Otto Graf this morning," the man said, brushing some cigar ash from his shirt. "He said you offered to guide their wagons to Oregon. He wanted to know if you were reliable."

"I talked to them," Beau replied. "Nothing has been decided, yet."

"Well, let me help you decide," Robert said. "I run wagon trains out of Independence. If they want to go, you work for me. Send them here and I'll make the deal."

"I don't know if I can do that," the mountain man said, trying to explain. "I believe they want to set up their own wagon train."

The man's round face turned even redder. "You just stay away from the bastards!" he snapped. "I'll be talking to them."

Shocked at the change of attitude, Beau stood up to leave. "Mr. Finlay, me and my partner are going to Oregon. If someone wants to join me on the trail, I won't tell them no."

The fat man glared at the mountain man as he

left the office. Beau was sure he'd just made an enemy. It was evident that Finlay expected money from every wagon leaving Independence and wasn't willing to let any of it get by him.

Walking back to the camp, Beau realized that it was Otto Graf's checking on him that had alerted Finlay. It bothered the mountain man that he hadn't been taken for his word. A man's word was very important in the west and an easterner like Graf might not realize that.

By the time he reached the camp, Beau had pretty much decided that he and Jocko would be going west on their own, unless his partner objected. The stocky man was gone to water the horses when Beau got back. There was a stream nearby, but the water had waste and debris in it from the many camps upstream. The best water was a mile south.

When Jocko got back he told his friend about going alone. "Would you be going to Oregon or California?" the stocky man asked.

"Oregon, I have been thinking about settling down in Oregon," Beau let him know.

Jocko went to picket the horses. Beau thought about what he had just admitted. For the past couple of years, he'd been re-thinking the life he'd been living. He was 33-years old and hadn't left his mark anywhere. There was still free land in the Willamette Valley of Oregon.

The sound of a wagon going by caught Beau's attention. It had four men sitting in the back plus a driver. It was headed for the six Oregon-bound wagons. The driver was one of the burly men who had brought the message this morning. The unsuspecting emigrants were sitting near the fire, eating their midday meal.

"Hey, Jocko!" Beau called to his friend. "It looks like trouble for Otto and his people."

The mountain man stuck his short-handled, single-bit axe into his broad belt. He grabbed his Colt Paterson .36 caliber revolver from his possible bag. It had four of the five chambers loaded. Clutching the revolver, he ran for the covered wagons. Behind him he could hear Jocko's short legs pumping to catch up.

As Beau ran, he realized that he didn't have percussion caps in the revolver. The attackers wouldn't know that, so the Colt might still be useful. Sticking it behind the belt as he ran, the mountain man pulled out the short axe.

The men in the wagon were focused on the emigrant wagons. They leaped out, clubs in hand, and went past the wagons, beating on them and creating whatever damage they could. One man tossed a lit lamp into the back of a wagon as he passed it.

The emigrants turned toward the attackers just as they were rushed. Some attempted to defend themselves with pieces of wood near the fire, while others tried to run, protecting their heads with their arms. In an attempt to defer the attackers, Beau and Jocko shouted at the top of their lungs as they bore down on the melee.

The mountain man swung the short axe, striking flesh and bone with the blunt side of the blade. The five attackers, caught by surprise from behind, turned in a feeble effort to defend themselves. Overwhelmed, they scattered onto the plain, abandoning the fight.

One of the attackers lay near the fire, unable to get up. The emigrants move to converge on him with blood in their eyes. "Stop!" Beau shouted. "He's done. We don't want to kill anyone here."

Jocko joined his friend in protecting the downed man. There was blood running down the side of the stocky man's face from a scalp wound. Several of the folks from the wagons were also bloodied. Suddenly, attention went to the burning wagon. Buckets of water were scooped from the dirty stream and thrown onto the flames.

Otto came up to Beau, who was trying to help the downed attacker to his feet. "They had no right to come at us," the old man said with rage in his voice.

"They only came because you made Finlay aware that we were putting a group together and he realized he wasn't getting any money for it," Beau informed him. "I'll bring this man back to Finlay. You and your people best be ready to move out tomorrow if you want us to lead you west." Then the mountain man added, "And that can be with or without the other eight wagons."

Jocko helped Beau get the man back into the wagon. His shoulder was injured and he was bleeding from a gash on his back. The mountain man was pretty sure it was the work of his short axe.

"I'm coming with you to see Finlay," Jocko said.

"You best stay out here and help these folks get ready to leave," Beau suggested. "There is a chance I might not be coming back and you'll have to lead them west by yourself. Both Finlay and I might be dead before the sun sets. I hope it doesn't come to that, but there is no way he is going to stop you from seeing Lisa."

Beau climbed into the wagon and drove it to

their camp. Jumping down, he grabbed his possible bag and put caps on the nipples of the Colt Paterson. Glancing back at the wagons, he saw one of the women putting a bandage on Jocko's scalp.

The mountain man's plan was to try and reason with Robert Finlay. If that was not possible, he would have to put the man out of action by injury or death. If it did come to that, Beau would again be a fugitive and have to head for the mountains alone, drawing pursuit away from Jocko and the emigrants.

The man in the wagon groaned at the wheels hit the rutted streets of Independence. Beau had seen a building with a doctor's sign. He drove to it and helped the injured man into the office. The front was empty. From the cubicles in the back, there were the sounds of the doctor working on somebody.

The slamming of the door closing alerted the sawbones. He pulled back a curtain and looked out. "I got my hands full with a couple of hombres that took a beating." Looking at Beau and the injured man, he continued, "Unless he's bleeding to death, make him comfortable on the chair over there and I'll be with him as soon as I can."

"Don't be too long, Doc," Beau replied. "He's hurting pretty bad. Maybe some broken bones and a pretty bad cut."

"Damn fools get into a brawl and then the son-of-a-bitches expect me to work on all of them at the same time," growled the doctor. He then pulled the curtain shut and went back to the men behind it.

"I done what I could," Beau told the man. Helping him to the chair, he took a pillow and put it against the gash on his back and leaned him against the back of it. "Sit still. It should stop the bleeding until the doc can see you."

Leaving the doc's place, Beau looked up the street toward Finlay's office. He took a deep breath and walked towards it. The next few minutes would determine the rest of the mountain man's life.

He looked back towards the wagon in front of the doc's office. "That will be my way out of town if necessary," he muttered.

His first impulse was to crash through the man's door and go at him. Stopping just shy of the office, Beau decided to try and reason with Robert Finlay first. After checking the revolver in his belt, and without knocking, the mountain man opened the door and stepped in.

Finlay was working on his books. He set his pencil down and leaned back in his chair, his face showing little expression. "You raised hob with some of my boys."

"I just brought another to the doc's," Beau replied, making every effort to keep his voice calm. "Most should be back working in a week or so."

"I'm a reasonable man," Finlay said. "I don't plan to press charges if you and your friend leave Independence, alone, by sundown."

"You can't press charges against folks protecting themselves from an unprovoked attack." Beau replied, his stomach tightening.

"Oh that," Finlay replied, a grin on his face. "I have no intention on pressing charges for what happened to my men."

Before Beau could say anything, the fat man continued. "I was a deputy before getting into the business of setting up wagon trains. For a while now, there's been something nagging at me. You know what

I mean. Something familiar but just not coming to mind."

With that, Finlay reached back to a shelf and pulled out something and slapped it on the desk. It was an old wanted poster for Beau and Elijah!

"It was the last name, Levesque," the fat man said. "I had heard it before, but just didn't place it. Then after your last visit, it came to me. I went down to the sheriff's office and dug through old posters and there it was."

After the initial shock of seeing the poster, and the explanation of Finlay's recollection, Beau got his thoughts together. "That poster means nothing. I was blamed for defending myself against the assault of a cruel man. Your sheriff has no jurisdiction on something from Arkansas and I have nothing to worry about."

"You are quite right, Mr. Levesque. Nobody wants you for assault here in Missouri, but our laws are very clear about assisting runaway slaves." Finished with explaining the charge, the fat man's face twisted into an evil smile. "You, my friend, might just be hung for this."

Thoughts of Elijah during their trip through Missouri in 1838 flooded back to Beau. He had assisted the friend through this state. Unsure of his next move, the mountain man watched as the fat Mr. Finlay carefully put the wanted poster back on the shelf.

"Now then. By the end of the day," the man instructed, "you and the other fellow will leave Independence without the folks in the wagons. I will make sure they go west in their turn."

"You have no right to choose when and where

people go west," Beau retorted, getting angry. "The slave on that poster had been given his freedom by Horst Weber, before he died. The man that spread those posters destroyed the papers and lied to the sheriff in Arkansas."

Standing quickly and knocking his chair over, the fat man slammed his fist on the desk. He stepped around the desk with fire in his eyes. Beau tensed. He knew the fight was coming and one of them would not be able to walk out of this office. From somewhere a club appeared in Finlay's hand and he attempted a savage swing at Beau's head.

Ducking to the side, the mountain man tripped over another chair and fell against the wall, striking his head. Dazed, he tried to roll away while grabbing for the Colt in his belt. Something large fell beside Beau. His arm with the Colt was trapped! Anticipating a blow from the club in the next instant, the mountain man struggled to pull his arm loose, feeling nauseous from striking his head against the wall.

Pulling himself free, Beau began to heave as he crawled away through his own vomit. He had lost hold of the Colt. His eyes were blurry and watering, Beau turned, grabbing for the knife in his belt. Blinking rapidly to clear his eyes, he saw the unmoving Robert Finlay lying on the office floor.

Disbelief on his face, Beau wondered if had he fired the Colt during the struggle? He remembered cocking the revolver as he'd grabbed it. The trigger had no guard and could have been pulled. He had been struggling, dizzy and throwing up. Was it possible he'd not noticed the gun firing? Scrambling back to Finlay, Beau rolled him onto his back.

He pulled away at the horrific sight of the

man's face. The left side stared at him with hate and anger. The right side sagged, looking almost dead. The man was babbling incoherently, saliva seeping from the right side of his mouth. The left arm and leg floundered while the right lay uselessly.

Beau's head still ached, but the nausea and dizziness had subsided. He wiped the vomit off his beard and, using the side of the desk for support, he stood up. After kicking the club away from the side of Finlay, he noticed the Colt lying on the floor, still cocked. Picking the revolver up, he put it back into his belt.

Looking down at the glaring eyes of Robert Finlay, Beau said, "I should just leave and let you lie there, but my Christian upbringing won't let me."

Opening the door, he saw two farmers walking by. "Get the wagon from in front of the doc's and bring it back here," Beau requested. "I got a man in trouble."

Walking back to Finlay, he said, "I got help coming." He then took a coat from the wall hook and wiped the vomit from his face and clothing as best he could. Looking back at the stricken man, who was now lying still, he saw tears running from his eyes.

With the help of the farmers, Beau got Robert Finlay to the doctors. As they set him onto the floor inside the door, the doc looked up from the man in the chair that he was working on. "You bringing me more business?" he snapped. "You are a damn one-man tornado. And look here at the pillow. You ruined it putting it on the back of this here man."

By this time the doctor had come close enough to look at what Beau and the farmers had brought in. His eyes widened. "Damn. It's Finlay." Squatting down next to the fat man, he shook his head. "The man has had a stroke."

After helping the doctor move Robert Finley to a back room, Beau told the doc, "He was arguing with me and the next thing I knew, he was on the floor looking like this."

Leaving the doc's after the simple explanation, Beau stopped quickly at Finlay's office and got the wanted poster. Sticking it into the possible bag, he left the town and headed for his camp.

CHAPTER FOUR

With Finlay out of action, the urgency to leave was gone. It was two days before Beau's wagon train was ready to move out. The wagon that had been set on fire had been made serviceable again. The canvas only covered the front half and some of the supplies had been charred, but could still be used.

Beau got a surprise visit from the man he had protected and hauled to the doc's. He came out with the same wagon used before, pulled by six mules. It was packed with supplies and his personal gear. A canvas was stretched across the wagon bed. He asked to go with the wagon train.

"I left you at the doc's pretty broken up," Beau had told him. "How do you expect to drive the team?"

"Nothing was broken, just some deep bruises and the cut on my back," the man explained. "My name is Robin Tyler. Folks call me Rob."

"How's Finlay?" Beau had asked.

"He's in tough shape," Rob said. "If he lives, he won't be sending out any more wagons. Men from

Westport Landing are already here organizing things."

"You got a lot of supplies or gear for one man in that wagon," the mountain man had observed.

"I call it back pay," Rob replied. "It's from Finlay's warehouse. Some of it's what he promised you and your partner. It ain't right what he done to you."

Smiling, Beau said, "Welcome to the wagon train. If you need help driving, me or Jocko will give you a hand."

With Tyler's wagon they had 15 in the train. Most were using farm wagons outfitted with bows and had canvas stretched over the top. The four by twelve-foot wagons were pulled by teams of six animals. There were a dozen extra oxen that would be driven behind the wagon train.

The wagons weighed about 1,200 pounds and were loaded with about a ton of items needed for the trip or to be used once the emigrants reached Oregon. These consisted of flour, bacon, coffee, tea, sugar, lard, molasses, rice, beans, and a small amount of dried fruit. Each would also have jerky and hard bread or biscuits for quick meals.

For cooking, they carried Dutch ovens, pots and frying pans, knives, coffee grinders, coffee pots, tin plates and mugs, table ware, and a tripod to hang a cook pot over the fire. Tools were taken such as augers, hammers, shovels, hoes, double-bit axes, scythes, whetstones, froes for making shingles, mallets, broad axes for squaring logs, and metal points for plows. Specialty tools were carried by those who needed them for a trade such as a blacksmith.

Everyone one carried extra canvas for ground cloths or tents, rope, some chain, an extra wheel, a wheel jack of some kind, and leather for repairing harnesses or footwear, and a small barrel for water. Extra clothing and blankets were used to protect items during travel and then for keeping warm at night. There were axles and tongues for the wagons to share.

The occupants of each wagon were responsible for having the needed items to complete the trip. What wouldn't fit into the wagons was tied to the sides or underneath. Some had built a platform across part of the wagon box using boards nailed from one side to the other to make more storage or sitting room.

Eight mules or six oxen were used to pull a fully loaded wagon. By eliminating everything but necessary items, two people could get by with six mules or four oxen. Three wagons were owned by the Rogers clan, consisting of four men and two women. They managed to keep the weight down by sharing repair items between their wagons and each was pulled by six mules.

All the wagons using oxen had six to start the trip. The oxen had a drover walking alongside the lead team on the left side, using voice commands and a switch or rod. He held a lead rope secured to a nose ring. The mules were driven from the seat of the wagon. The ride on the wagons was bone-jarring due to lack of suspension, so most would walk alongside, climbing on only to rest.

Oxen were best suited for pulling the covered wagons. They were simplest to harness, using just a yoke for each team and trace chains to connect them together. The wagon tongue connected to the yoke ring of the team next to the wagon. The oxen could pull more weight and tended to be easier to handle than mules or horses. After a time on the trail, the teams learned to come back to their wagons in the morning.

Beau's wagon train was small compared to most, but with luck they would pick up a few more along the trail. A decision was made that each wagon would pay $10 apiece to Beau and Jocko once they reached Oregon. Rob was paid up with the supplies he'd brought.

The wagon train slowly pulled out with the shouts of the drovers, gangling of chains, and creaking of the wooden wagons. It was midday on May 2nd. There had been showers during the past couple days and the rutted trail leading out of Independence was a myriad of slippery mud. Ten of the wagons were pulled by oxen, four were pulled by mules. One of the wagons had six draft horses and they would be able to pull the wagon, but they would suffer with the plains forage. Riding horses and mules were either tied to the back of the wagons or put in with the extra stock.

In a ten-hour day, the wagon train could expect to make 15 miles, with the pace being set by the oxen. This far to the east there was little danger from any type of attacks and Beau let the wagons stretch out on the trail. Jocko rode the gray and stayed alongside the wagons for now, roving from the front to the back, watching for anyone having trouble.

They would be on the trail six days of the week. Sunday they would remain in camp and after a little rest in the morning and a church service, everyone would lubricate axles, repair harnesses, and do any other maintenance necessary. Laundry would be done and some extra food would be cooked to be eaten on the trail. Each evening and all-day Sunday the stock would be taken out to graze. They were brought within the loose circle of wagons for protection at night.

The extra oxen and two milk cows were driven

by men, women or children and followed the last wagon. Tired youngsters were often put onto the backs of the oxen. Beau and Jocko's extra horses were tied to the back of Rob's wagon. They would rotate riding the sorrel and gray, or the mustangs. Some days when Tyler's shoulder ached too much, Jocko would drive the wagon. Otto deferred the leadership to Beau and made himself useful assisting others in the wagon train and conducting the services on Sunday.

The excitement shown by occupants of every wagon for the first couple days had dampened by the second week. Boredom was a way of life on the trail and would eventually only be punctuated by the unexpected tragedies of accidents, disease, and personal conflicts. They were still traveling up the Missouri River valley and would be turning west soon to cut across to the Platte River.

The next 850 miles across the great plains would test the endurance of the folks in the wagon train. There were miles and miles of endless grass lands and a river that was said to be too thick to drink and too thin to plow. Much of the route had been grazed off by wagon trains that had proceeded them, so Beau would try and move away from the main route to better grass for the nights.

When the wagon train reached the first, more difficult, river crossing, Beau had the first challenge of his leadership. The night camp was set up on the south side. The mountain man called a meeting after supper. He and Jocko had found an acceptable place to cross.

Otto stood after Beau had finished explaining the next day's plan. "I don't think we should cross here," the old man said. "We should follow the river to the west and find a shallower place. We will have gained miles on our trip west when we reach the other side."

There was a rumbling of agreement in the group as they started to disband. Beau called them back. "I appreciate what you say, Otto," the mountain man said. "Have you ever been up this river?"

"One river or another, it makes no difference," the old man replied. "All rivers get smaller as you follow them upstream."

Feeling a little frustrated and attempting to guard his tongue, Beau replied, "I have followed this river before. It comes out of the sandstone hills to the west and only gets more and more difficult to cross as it cuts into the hills. You will end up winding through blind canyons and run up against ridges and washes that will eventually force you to retrace your steps back here to cross."

Anger showed on Otto's, and his sons', faces. Not having travelled the area in the past, they couldn't question what Beau had told them. Alvin Thompson and his wife, Tilly stopped on their way back to their wagon. "You knowing what lies ahead is why we hired you to lead us," he said. "If push comes to shove on this trip, I'll have your back."

Everyone in the wagon train had crossed scores of rivers to get to this point, but all the larger ones in the east had ferries to assist in the crossings. Beau could see the set jaws and fear in the eyes of many of the emigrants as they faced their first challenge.

Clement, or Clem, Williams and his wife Lucy had four children. One boy and three girls. He was standing by his wagon, holding the oxen lead rope as he waited to start. His wife sat on the wagon talking to the children in the back, assuring them that they'd be okay.

Jocko came back from finding the best bank to enter the river. There was a wide shallow bank to exit the water and allow for some downstream drift. "I think we're ready to go," he told Beau.

"I think I'll help the first wagon across," the mountain man said. He rode up to Clem's wagon. "I got a favor to ask you, Mr. Williams. I want to take the first wagon across. I would appreciate taking yours."

Surprised at the request, Clem replied, "I can take it across."

"I know that, but I don't have a wagon to take first and it would be a great help if you'd let me."

"Well, okay then," the man replied. "What do you want me to do?"

You can ride one of the mustangs," Beau said, smiling, "You follow behind the wagon just in case one of your young'uns can't resist and decides to take a swim."

Wide-eyed, his wife said, "Oh. They won't do that."

Giving her a grin, he replied, "I know."

Beau rode back along the train. "The oxen will be the first to cross. We will drag ropes across the river to tie to the ox and guide them across. Jocko and I will ride on each side of the teams to keep them going. Once the wagons with oxen are done, then the rest of you can drive your teams across. When the wagon in front of you gets to the shallows of the other side, the next wagon enters the river."

With the lines strung across the river, all was ready. Two men had been taken to the other side and would handle the lines, keeping tension on the ropes tied to the nose rings. It would help guide the oxen and wagon across.

The water was higher than normal from the spring rains, but the current wasn't too fast. With Beau and Jocko riding on the sides of the oxen and tapping them with the rods, the team pulled forward. The mountain man was pleased that they entered the river without hesitation. Lucy clutched to the bows of the wagon as it rocked going down the bank.

"Hang on kids," Beau called back. "We might hit some bumps in the river."

"We will," came the chorus from the back.

For a short time in the middle, the oxen and wagon were floating and the wagon swung a bit downstream. Beau and Jocko shouted commands, urging the team on as they swam. Water came up through the floor of the wagon and the children squealed, more from delight than fear. There was a jar when the wheels hit bottom again and the wagon lurched forward as the oxen found footing.

With water running from the wagon and team, Beau took a line and led the team clear of the north bank before stopping. Lucy Williams thanked him as he untied the rope to bring it back across the river for the next team. Clem leaped off the mustang and hurried over to check on his family.

"Take your wagon a little farther and then go through your gear and dry off what you can," Beau instructed as he climbed onto the sorrel and headed back for the river.

All of the wagons crossed, with only the Thompson wagon receiving damage to a wheel. It wobbled as it left the river. Alvin led the oxen to a clear area to replace it with the extra one he carried. After the last wagon was across a couple hours were spent as the families went through things to move them around to dry. The water would wash the lubricant out of the wheels and everyone would be busy tonight pulling wheels and lubricating the axles.

That evening the fire crackled in the center of the circled wagons. Everyone had buckets with a mixture of fat and tar, out as the men pulled the wheels. The women were watching the meal cook while they hung items that needed drying from the river crossing. The mood was upbeat. The crossing had been successful and decreased the fear of future rivers. There would be hundreds to cross, big and small, before they reached Oregon. Winding ones such as the Sweetwater would be crossed several times.

Beau enjoyed seeing the men and women of the train laugh as everyone came to supper. The men's hands were covered with the black tar and fat mixture used to lubricate the wheels. The brown homemade soap did little to take it off.

Some of the families combined their food to make the main meal of the day. Others preferred to make their own meal at the main fire, while a few liked cooking over their own fire. This would all change after they got out on the plains where fuel was hard to find.

Beau and Jocko tended to have meals with Rob. Jocko would bring it back from the main fire. It was simple fare of beans, rice, or something out of cornmeal. Any fresh meat was always shared with everyone in the wagon train.

Tomorrow, they would finally be heading west onto the plains. Fuel would soon be scarce, with the rare tree or brush growing along the streams and rivers. Buffalo chips or wood from abandoned wagons would be used for cook fires. Canvas would be hung under the wagons for collecting whatever was gathered.

Grass for the stock and water would not be a problem for the next two months. Soon they would be in the Plains Indian territory and would be subject to having stock stolen. They would be after horses and mules rather than oxen. Not many Indians would be looking to attack an armed wagon train, but that could not be ruled out.

Beau and Jocko carried their Hawken rifles in scabbards on their horses. Rob had an older Hawken .50 caliber that had been converted from flintlock to percussion. He also had a Colt Paterson .28 caliber. Rob took his turn rotating his position in the wagon train while Beau and Jocko rode freely and they were always on the lookout for game.

On the plains there would be buffalo, elk, mule deer, lots of pronghorn and rabbits. The wagon trains that had gone before Beau's would have driven the game farther from the trail, requiring Jocko to ride further out in search of fresh meat.

As they went west across the great plains, they could glimpse wagon trains in front of them when driving over some of the rises. Beau knew that his 15 wagons would be competing for grazing and good stopping areas near water. There was concern about cholera and other types of diseases that tended to happen where large groups camped.

During the first Sunday stop after reaching the plains, Jocko called Beau aside. "We got a group of men shadowing us."

"How many?" the mountain man asked.

"I counted six men yesterday," Jocko said. "I've been leaving just before daylight the past three mornings and caught sight of a campfire each day. At first, I thought it was others like us that were heading west, but yesterday I got closer to the men and noticed they are packing light. They all carry rifles and are tending to ride just out of our sight."

"The only thing of value that we have that they could grab quick, is our stock," Beau replied. "We are driving them a mile out to find good grazing."

Suddenly, a look of concern crossed his bearded face. "We only have four men watching the stock today, and one of them is the Williams boy."

Jocko headed for his horse, "I'll go warn them to watch out while you get some more men together."

With his Hawken across the saddle in front, his stocky friend galloped in the direction the stock had been driven. Beau ran to the circled wagon, alerting the emigrants. There were only four horses with the wagons. The rest were grazing out on the plain.

Beau saddled the sorrel, while Rob and Otto got the mustangs. Alvin joined them, riding his horse bareback. With rifles in hand they rode after Jocko. The rest of the men and women would remain with the wagons, just in case they were also a target.

The mountain man knew that the stock might not be in danger at this time, and they might be wrong about the men Jocko saw. They could just be out hunting meat, but the stock was critical and they could not take the chance. As they approached the rise that the stock was grazing behind, they heard the sound of shots!

Riding hard, they came over the rise and saw that two oxen were down and Jocko, the three men, and young Charles, were hunkered behind them. The men were returning fire at the six men working their way up a wash. The stock was scattering in fright.

Pulling their horses to a stop, Beau and his men spread out along the hill and began to fire at the men in the wash. Initially the attackers were exposed to the men on the rise and two of them were knocked down. The other four, realizing they were out-gunned, began to crawl back down the wash.

Jocko left the cover of the downed oxen and, keeping low, ran diagonally to the wash to cut them off. Swapping his rifle for Rob's Colt, Beau swung back onto the sorrel and rode hard to assist the stocky man, with one Colt Paterson in his belt and the other in his hand.

A shot came from the wash as the attackers saw him. It was fired in haste and went wide. The attackers were now up and running. Jocko stood with his Hawken and dropped one of the fleeing men. Beau pulled the sorrel up and emptied his Colt at the remaining attackers. One turned and fell, while the other two went to their knees with their hands in the air.

"We give up!" they shouted. "Don't shoot!"

Beau could hear the others coming behind him. "Shoot the son-of-a-bitches!" Otto yelled.

There was a shot that hit the dirt next to one of the attackers. Beau turned the sorrel. "Hold your damn fire!" He demanded.

The men from the wagons had no sympathy for the men who had attacked them and out here on the plains there were no lawmen. Otto glared at him with blood in his eye. "These men meant to kill our friends watching the stock, and one just a boy. They deserve no mercy."

"Vengeance is mine, sayeth the lord," Beau

reminded him. "When you were preaching this morning, did you believe what you were saying?"

"I believe an eye for an eye," Otto hissed.

"In that case, we are more than even," the mountain man replied. "We have lost two oxen, which we can eat. They have four men down, some probably dead."

While Beau wasn't winning the exchange, it did give the others a chance for their lust to kill to wane. It appeared that the only one wanting to continue was Otto, but with the mood of the crowd cooled, the old man swore under his breath and went to get the mustang.

Three of the attackers were dead, including the one Jocko had shot and the one that Beau had hit last. A wounded man had been hit twice. One round had gone through the shoulder and the other had taken part of his ear and creased his scalp. Rob and two of the other men went to find the attackers' horses. A short time later they returned, leading the animals.

The wagon train's stock had to be collected and the two downed oxen had to be butchered. Beau gave instructions to the men. "Take their horses and round up the stock. Rob, bring the wounded man back to the wagons and have someone bandage him up, then bring some shovels back so we can bury the dead. Otto, I would like you to say a few words over their graves if you would."

"The bastards will burn in hell and nothing I can say will help them," the old man snarled.

"That may be so," Beau said. "I would still like you to say some words."

"I will," Otto said, "but I ain't digging one shovel full of dirt for the . . . departed."

The Williams boy came up his eyes wide with excitement. "Can I help round up the stock? I'm a good rider."

Six of the other men had already left with the horses. Smiling at the boy, he handed the reins of the sorrel to him. "Now don't you fall off. I don't want to be explaining why you got hurt to your folks."

The stocky man came up to his friend. "We had to kill the oxen for cover," he explained. "I got there just as they were spotted in the wash. We was in the wide-open, with no cover. I dropped one ox and Hoot Johnson the other. We had no choice."

"A man's life is worth one hell of a lot more than the oxen," Beau told his friend. "Not only that, we can eat the ox. Would you and Hoot mind cutting them up?"

Jocko nodded and was soon busy skinning the oxen. By the time the three men were buried and Otto had a chance to give a fire and brimstone sermon over the graves, Jocko, with Hoot's help, had the two animals skinned, cut up and ready to bring back to the wagon train.

The stock had been rounded up and there were still several hours of daylight, so they would be kept out to graze. The uninjured prisoners had helped with the burying and were marched toward the wagons. The oxen meat was packed onto their six horses. The group came back to the cheers of the rest of the folks with the wagons.

Beau went to check on the wounded attacker. Edsel Ward had some medical experience from his time in the army and had patched the man up as best he could. "The shoulder wound went through, but the Hawken makes an awful hole. I can't say he'll make it, but I got the bleeding stopped."

"We brought back some meat from oxen that were killed," Beau told him. "Make sure your wife gets some for your supper."

Beau called a meeting after the meal was over and told the group that one additional day would be spent to give time to process the meat. While he didn't say it, he wanted the wounded man to have another day before starting the bumpy ride.

"We will be bringing our prisoners to Fort Kearny about a week from here," he told them. "There we will turn them over to the army and they can do what they think is best. The two oxen that were killed will be replaced from the extra stock."

The meat was divided between the wagons and it was cut into strips and heavily salted down to prevent spoiling. Peck Wilson, a blacksmith by trade, fashioned a set of irons using extra trace chain. The prisoners, Hal and Mick Rinker, were secured to a wagon wheel. The wounded man didn't need a chain and was left for them to attend to.

Beau realized how lucky they'd been with the attack on their stock. The attackers were after the mules and horses. But to get them, they'd have had to kill those watching. The Rinker cousins were young and appeared to have fallen in with a bad crowd. The army might very well hang them for attempted murder and stealing of stock.

Two of the emigrants had brought oxen back to replace the ones that had been shot. They were busy checking the yokes to fit the neck and shoulders of the new animals to prevent galling. Mrs. Williams had her boy close to her, letting him know that he'd not be watching the stock any more. The young boy was trying to convince his mother that the danger was over.

The injured prisoner died overnight. He had lost too much blood from the large wound made by the Hawken ball. He was buried in a shallow, unmarked grave alongside the stream while the teams were being hitched and the gear stowed. The Rinker cousins did the digging under Jocko's supervision. Otto spoke over the grave with much less fervor that the day before.

The folks were subdued as they left the camping area, with the death of the man reminding them of how fragile life is and how little could be done for someone injured on the plains. It was the Rogers clan's turn to lead the wagon train, and with their mules they began to put distance from the slower oxen.

After they were a quarter-mile ahead, Beau rode to catch up to Quinn leading the first wagon. The red-headed man pulled his team to a stop.

"I don't want you to get too far ahead," Beau warned him. "If we have trouble from Lakota, we wouldn't be able to get to you and help."

"It's them damn oxen," he complained. "We pay good money for the mules and then have to sit and wait."

"That may be so" Beau told him, "but you chose to join our wagon train and we need to stay together for safety. Remember, just yesterday the folks behind you risked their lives to make sure your mules weren't stolen."

His brother, Sean, snorted at what Beau said, but the mountain man chose to ignore it. Little could be gained by a confrontation and they needed the additional wagons with them. Turning the sorrel, Beau trotted back to the main wagon train. Glancing back, he was pleased to see the three wagons were waiting for the others to close the gap.

The wagon train was three weeks out of Independence when they reached Fort Kearny. The two prisoners had ridden or walked behind the wagon driven by Rod. While Jocko was organizing the camp, Beau took the two men to the fort.

Fort Kearny had been moved to this site when it had been determined that the original location on the Missouri River was too far off the trail. The fort covered about four acres with wooden buildings and around the perimeter there were young cottonwoods planted. The fort was well-supplied to serve the emigrants and instructed to give fair prices and to go so far as to give free supplies to those with hardships.

Beau turned the Rinkers over to the authorities at the fort. He spent some time writing out the charges against them. He was told that the cousins would be transported by an army escort back to Fort Leavenworth to be tried. Glad to be rid of the two, Beau headed back to the wagon train.

Hundreds of wagons were scattered near the fort. Men were walking to and from the commissary, some pushing wheelbarrows filled with goods, while others carried sacks over their shoulders or loaded packs on their backs. The fort had oxen for trade. Drovers with injured or tired oxen could swap for a healthy and rested bovine for little money.

The Wolsey brothers, Tom and Sam, and their wives, Bunny and Cora, had the draft horses. Tom had talked of purchasing oxen to pull the wagon and save the draft horses for working their future farms in Oregon. After just three weeks on the trail, they had become concerned at the weight loss of the horses.

Beau had let everyone know that they would be spending three days at the fort resupplying and resting the stock. At night there was music at some of the wagon camps. All were welcome to come and enjoy. Jocko had rigged their fly tarp with one side fastened to Rob's wagon. There was a small fire going with coffee water heating.

Taking a seat against the wagon wheel, Beau knocked the dust out of his coffee cup. "I kind of got to liking the cousins."

Jocko brought the pot over and filled his friend's cup. Putting the pot back onto the coals, he took a seat. "When you raise hogs for bacon, you don't name them or come butchering time it makes the killing all the harder."

"What the hell are you talking about?" Beau asked.

"We got to know another side of the boys while they were chained up." Jocko said. "Same as naming and making a pet out of your future meal. The Rinkers had every intention of killing everyone watching the stock. I believe if given a chance, they would kill again to be free."

Taking a drink of the coffee, Beau nodded. "I believe you are right." Looking out at the people coming to and from the fort, he said, "It's a damn good thing they moved the fort here. By now folks know what mistakes they made in Independence and can correct them before facing the next five months travel."

Both men were watching Tom Wolsey as he took ownership of six oxen. Outside the fort they could see three blacksmith shops. There was the ringing of their hammers working around the clock repairing wheels, fabricating parts, or repairing broken ones.

There were farriers trimming hooves and shoeing horses. Some sore-footed oxen also needed shoeing. The oxen were not able to stand on three legs, so there were rigs for tipping and securing the animals on their side. Those who didn't have the rig dug a trench and the animal would be wrestled down and trapped in the trench.

For the most part, the constant travel kept the animals hooves worn down, therefore not requiring shoeing. Beau's sorrel was unshod and he carried a rasp to keep the hooves in shape. Jocko's animals were also unshod.

Beau had noticed a group of wagons camped away from the others near a small stream. At the fort he had learned that they had a sickness. Several had died and the wagon train had been quarantined.

"I heard there was a place selling whiskey just west of the fort," Jocko said, interrupting his friend's thoughts.

"You don't say," the mountain man replied. "We just might have to go and check it out."

Rod came back from the fort to sit with them. "I ordered some things we are short of," he said as he poured the last of the coffee into his mug. "I'll use the mustangs to pick them up in the morning."

"We're going over for a drink or two tonight," Jocko told him. "You're welcome to join us."

Smiling, Rod replied, "I best stay away from that stuff. Once I start drinking, I tend to forget when to stop. I got some folks back east that don't know where I am. This here is our last chance to send out mail. I figure to write a letter tonight."

Beau and Jocko headed for the drinking establishment right after a supper made from the last of the salted beef boiled with beans. The saloon was a large tent with a plank bar supported on barrels. Boxes filled with bottles of rye were stacked against the back wall. The place was packed with customers and three bartenders were busy selling bottles or pouring drinks.

Most of the wagon trains were filled with men heading for the California gold fields. The boredom of the trail had made them look forward to some liquor. They'd push their way to the bar and purchase a bottle or two and work their way back out of the tent and then find a place to drink themselves into a stupor. The sounds and atmosphere reminded Beau of the tents at the rendezvous on the Green River.

The two men bought their bottles and then worked their way back out. There were a couple of crates alongside the tent. They tipped them on end and sat down to try the brew. Taking a swig from the bottle, Beau felt the burn of the pepper. It was apparent that the liquor had been cut with water and then doctored to add a bite.

The two men were just getting a nice glow on from the brew when the shadow of a man blocked out the warm sunshine. Grinning foolishly, Beau looked up and was about to speak when a blow to his chest from the palm of the man sent the mountain man tumbling backwards, causing the wooden crate to splinter. Scrambling to regain his feet, Beau saw a giant of a man raising Jocko over his head with the intention of throwing him.

Leaping forward, Beau tackled the man behind his knees, causing him to collapse. The man and Jocko fell on top of the mountain man, knocking the wind out of him. Like a wild animal, Jocko began to wail on the large brute. Gasping for breath, Beau struggled to get out from under the crushing weight.

The big man gave Jocko a shove, sending him rolling out of reach, and then turned to flail upon Beau. Like a cat, the stocky man was back on his feet and leaped onto the back of the brute, wrapping an arm around the man's neck, attempting to choke him. Finally free and on his knees, Beau began to throw punches, bloodying the man's nose and splitting the skin above his eye.

All of a sudden, the brute collapsed onto the ground. He had blacked out due to the choke hold Jocko had on him. It had happened so fast that Beau's last swing barely missed the end of his friend's nose.

Throwing his head back, Jocko yelled, "Watch it! I'm on your side."

Sitting back, the two men looked at the large man lying unconscious near them. They became aware of the crowd that had gathered around. They had obviously been cheering the fighters on, but Beau had not been aware of them. Laughing and pleased with the results, the onlookers headed back into the tent.

"Did I kill him?" Jocko asked.

Beau grabbed the man's hair and pulled his head up. The big brute was still breathing. "You didn't kill him," the mountain man replied. "He sure as hell wanted to put a beating on me."

Dropping the man's head face-first back into the dirt, Beau looked up as two crusty old-timers came out of the tent with a bottle of whiskey. "To the victors," one of them said, handing the brew to Jocko. "This is the first time we've seen Bull beaten."

"You know this man?" Beau asked.

"He joined our wagon train in Independence," one of the old-timers said. "Likes to start fights and has always won them. It's good to see him get his."

The other piped up, "We heard him talking about two of his friends that were turned over to the army. Must be what made him angry today." Then the man laughed, "Course, it don't take much to do that."

"When do your wagons leave?" Beau asked.

"First thing tomorrow," they told him and then the two old-timers staggered away.

Jocko and Beau headed for their camp. The effects of the peppered brew was still with them, but now it was more of a buzzing in the mountain man's head. The big bruiser must have learned that he had turned the Rinker cousins in.

CHAPTER FIVE

Beau awoke the next morning with a headache and raspy throat from the peppered brew. As he climbed out of his blankets, his body rebelled with soreness in several bruised muscles. He and Jocko had kept a watch for the big brute as they nursed the bottle given them by the old-timers. Rob had walked by them, shaking his head, refusing to sit and visit.

After getting the coffee water heating, Jocko sat next to the small fire with his head hanging. "Is the water hot yet?" the mountain man called to him.

"I don't know," Jocko groaned. "It hurts too much to raise my head to look."

Slowly the two men got their morning meal together. Robin had headed for the fort with the mustangs to pick up the supplies. Several wagon trains pulled out while the men were eating. Beau watched them as he sipped his coffee, "Good riddance to Bull."

"He was one strong son-of-a-bruiser," Jocko said. "He just walked up to you and knocked you off the crate. I tried to stop him from going after you, and he picked me up right up over his head and would have thrown me into tomorrow if you hadn't knocked him off his feet."

With a sideward grin, Beau replied, "My reward was my body hurtin' everywhere from y'all falling on top of me."

"You did break the fall pretty good," Jocko said, chuckling.

By midday both men had recovered from the day before. Rob had returned with the supplies and was busy stowing them in the wagon. Beau checked with the other wagons to make sure they were ready to leave the next morning. Otto Graf gave him a lecture about the evils of drink. The mountain man let the man have his say, then he continued his rounds of the wagons.

Another wagon had joined them. Jon and Hanna Scott. and her mother Ruth Stiles, had left a wagon train heading for California and wanted to go to Oregon. They lost the fee they'd paid the other wagon train, but with the help of her mother, offered to pay to join Beau. They were given the same deal as the others.

Jon and Hanna were a handsome couple. She had a smile that warmed the heart of anyone she spoke with. Her mother, Mrs. Stiles, was a stern woman and kept a close eye on her daughter. Beau introduced them to many of the others who would be traveling on the wagon train.

Beau headed back to his camp, pleased with the addition of another wagon. His stomach had settled, and the sun was shining. Jocko commented on Jon's wife.

"She just adds to the day," he replied. The mountain man then began to put his loose gear into the wagon in preparation for leaving in the morning. Rob's wagon was now outfitted with bows and a canvas top.

It would take about ten days to reach the point were the wagon train would cross the South Platte River. Beau planned to use the crossing that would take them to Ash Hollow. The hollow had ash trees for wood and good grazing for their stock. After they crossed the river, they would start a climb, just under two miles, that would bring them up over 200-feet to the top of the Platte River's plateau. This was the first of many climbs the wagon train would take before reaching Oregon.

Beau had spoken of this to the people of the wagon train, but what he had not expanded on was the slope from the plateau into Ash Hollow. It could not be avoided, so there was no reason to cause worry at this time.

The folks of the wagon train were up early the next morning stowing gear and getting teams ready to go. Some of the wagons had a jockey box on the front, others a seat and toe board. The box would store items needed to repair the wagon. These consisted of bolts, nails, and tools. Beau checked that all the wagons had access to a spare axle and tongues before leaving the fort. One of each was required for every three wagons, allowing them to share the weight. These were either tied under the belly of the wagon, or stored in the box. Extra spokes for the smaller front wheel and a back wheel were required for each wagon. Some of the wagons were carrying luxuries such as hope chests or other heirlooms. Once again Beau strongly encouraged the people to sell or swap them at the fort.

The mountain man walked by the wagons and

tipped his leather hat to the ladies sitting on the wagons that had seats and toe boards. He spoke briefly with the men alongside the oxen. Untying the sorrel from the back of Rob's wagon, Beau swung into the saddle and rode to the head of the wagon train. He called out "Wagons Ho!" which was then repeated from one wagon to another.

The drovers shouted commands to the oxen and the familiar sound of chains, creaking wood, and the rattle of tin pans was heard the length of the wagon train. The folks were happy to be moving again. Every step west was a step closer to their new homeland.

Some of the men moved back toward their wagon, using voice commands, once the oxen had chosen their pace behind the next wagon. The past week had been dry and the hooves of the animals kicked up plumes of dust that hung in the still air. The wagons would travel to the right or left of the trail in an attempt to avoid it. After a couple hours of the bumpy ride in the wagons, most of the folks were walking alongside.

They were just over a week from the upper crossing of the South Platte River. While the water was higher from the spring runoff, the wide, slow-moving river never got much over waist-deep at the crossings. The biggest danger was the sandy or muddy bottom, driftwood, or quicksand. Ropes across the river could be used to lead the oxen. The drovers could wade alongside their teams or ride on the lead ox for the crossing.

They reached the upper crossing of the South Platte River late in the afternoon of the eighth day out of Fort Kearny. The river was deeper and colder than anticipated. The river flowed from the high plains, where the nights were still in the low 40s. If a wagon and team got into trouble during the crossing, the drover would soon be overcome by hypothermia and would probably drown.

They camped a mile from the crossing while two other wagon trains used the crossing. Several of the men joined Beau and Jocko at the crossing to observe the other wagons. As a team of oxen were led across with a rope spanning the river, a rope for the next team was tied to the back of the wagon. It served two purposes. One would be to lead the next team across and the other to help keep the wagon in the river from being swept by the slow but relentless current.

Each of the wagons carried enough rope to use the same method. The men watched as a wagon pulled by mules entered the water just downstream. Three men rode in the wagon, one driving and the other two under the canvas top. The driver, probably a past mule skinner, sat in the front wielding a whip, snapping it loudly above the balking mules. Finally, they lunged forward into the river, the wagon rocking back and forth on the debris-strewn bottom.

About halfway across, the wagon began to lean to one side. The driver stood, shouted and began to lay the whip across the backs of the team. The mules struggled to regain their footing in the deep water, one disappearing below the surface. The wagon, as though in slow motion, continued over, spilling the driver into the frigid river.

Watching, spellbound, Beau, Jocko, and the men stared as the two men in the back of the wagon kicked and pushed at the canvas top as they tried to regain their footing and get out. All the goods in the back tumbled on top of them, trapping the men under water. The driver clung to the wagon, while the mule team broke loose, dragging the downed mule as they fought to get across the river.

Beau and Jocko leaped onto their horses and rode toward the overturned wagon. They had to ride wide around the other wagons tied together for crossing. Beau reached the man clinging to the outside of the wagon and pulled him up behind him and turned the sorrel back toward the east bank. Jocko grabbed a hand reaching out from inside the wagon, and pulled the man out, dragging him alongside the gray back to the shore. Beau dropped off the driver, rode back to the wagon and, slashing with his knife, cut the top open and saw the leg of the other man protruding out from between the boxes and bags of supplies.

Grabbing the man's boot, he pulled and could not move it. Reaching in, he pulled boxes and bags out, dropping them into the river, and then the other leg was visible. Again, he pulled and the man came loose. Beau's teeth were chattering from the cold river water. His horse was slipping and stumbling on the uneven bottom. Jocko came alongside and grabbed the man by the waistband of his pants and dragged him toward the river bank.

Hanging on to the saddle horn, Beau rode the sorrel back to the bank, where it stopped, breathing heavily. Sliding off the animal, the mountain man went to check on the last man brought from the wagon. He lay still and ghostly white on the river bank. They had been too late. Some of the men from the other wagon train had started a fire on the river bank. Beau and the other two men from the wagon huddled around it, trying to get warm.

While they sat there, riders from the other side

of the river had freed the team from the downed mule and taken them to the other side. Ropes were tied to the wagon and, using teams of oxen, it was dragged the rest of the way across the river, most of its gear and supplies dumping out into the river. After a brief stop while Beau and Jocko were trying to save the men, the crossing of the wagons continued.

Otto came up to the fire, shaking his head. "It is madness. Even death doesn't stop the wagons west."

"It's the gold," Beau said as he slowly stood. The shivering had stopped. He continued, "We have to get back to our wagons. We go across in the morning."

Talk of the death made the evening rather somber. Otto got everyone together for a prayer meeting that to a Catholic would have sounded more like last rites. The noise of wagons crossing the river continued until dark. East of Beau's wagon camp were two other camps with over 40 wagons in each. There had been three other wagon trains that had gone past the upper crossing to use another further west. Beau and Jocko's wet clothing hung from the wagon bows to dry.

While everyone was getting ready the next morning, Beau went from wagon to wagon, going over the way they'd be using lines across the river, trying to assure everyone that, with care, the dangers could be minimized. For the first time, Hanna Scott was not smiling, her eyes reflecting the fear everyone felt about the challenge in front of them.

Otto and his sons were the first of the wagon train to line up at the river. There was a fresh grave on the bank downstream. The bloated body of the mule had floated away during the night and was snagged on one of the many small islands to be picked apart by vultures, eagles, and any other animal that was willing to swim the river.

Jocko rode to an island in the center of the river with two other men towing lines. As a wagon reached the island, the lines would be moved to span from the island to the far side of the river. Those riding in the wagon were told to stay near the front or back opening. Drovers rode in the front of the wagon opening, or in the seat if the wagon had one, shouting commands to the oxen.

By midday all the wagons were across and the extra stock had been driven over. They had moved close to the incline they would be facing the next day. They'd learned that the wagon that had turned over was overloaded with goods from the fort and had been top heavy.

Beau stood outside of the circle of wagons and looked at the grassy slope they would be climbing to the plateau. He planned to talk to the folks about the other side they would be going down to Ash Hollow, after a day of traveling on the high ground. He would tell them about the spring water which was found in the hollow, and that would be a great change after drinking the muddy Platte River water.

Several fires burned around the circle of wagons. Extra fuel that had been carried was being burnt to lighten the loads of the wagons. They would find plenty of wood in Ash Hollow. Beau and Jocko were invited to join the Scotts for supper. Jon was just getting back from bringing his oxen out to graze when the two men arrived.

Hanna gave the men a quick smile as she

worked over the cook fire. There was johnnycake in the Dutch oven and a pot of thick stew made with potatoes, carrots, and some canned venison. She and her mother had taken some boxes out of the wagon and had spread linen cloth over it to serve the meal. Hanna also had hot tea with honey to drink.

Jon planned to lubricate the wagon wheels after supper and Beau offered to help. He and Jocko had already assisted Rob with his wagon. Jon and Hanna talked of their plans in Oregon. Both were excited with the prospect of building a life there and raising a family. The mother sat in a rocker without speaking. The chair was one of the few special items they carried in the wagon.

Beau got back to his camp after dark. "Jon and Hanna will make a fine addition to Oregon," he said.

Jocko said. "My Lisa will like meeting her."

Beau lay just inside the edge of the fly tarp and stared at the stars. He thought about the next two days. After a long climb to the plateau tomorrow, they would meet the next obstacle in less than twenty miles. The steep hill into Ash Hollow would test the fiber of the folks in the wagon train. They would have to lock the back wheels on the wagons and that would still not be enough to hold them back. Ropes from the top would be required to lower the wagons. Should one snap, the recoiling rope could take a person's limb off, or kill them if it hit the head or body. Once broken, the wagon would accelerate down the hill, plowing through anything or anyone in its way.

It was still dark when the men went out to bring the stock in. As the oxen slowly walked toward the wagons, most began to split off and stopped near their wagon. A few had to be chased down and led.

The mules were led to their wagons by the owners. The sounds of commands, cussing, and the smack of rods slapping the animals filled the air as the oxen were paired up for the yokes. The last to be ready were the teams of mules.

The women had a cauldron of porridge and pots of coffee ready at a central fire. The Williams had rich milk from their cows to pour over the hot cereal. As the men completed hitching the animals, they wandered over for a quick breakfast. With the formidable grade in front of them, the wagon train lined up to begin the climb to the plateau. Beau noticed that several items that wouldn't be needed on the trip had been abandoned alongside the trail to lighten the wagons.

The progress up the grade was slow. The wagons carried a short log on the back to be dropped behind the back wheels to prevent it from rolling backward in the case that the team had to stop for any reason. A ragged line of wagons worked their way up the hill, going around those that had been forced to halt ahead of them.

Jocko was helping Rob with his wagon. When the mules had to stop, the stocky man dropped the short log behind the wagon to chock the wheels. Beau walked, leading his sorrel and saw that the two men were connecting trace chains to the sawbuck pack saddles of the mustangs to help the mules pull the wagon. The mountain man looped the sorrel's reins to the back of the wagon and helped Rob line up the horses on the steep hill while Jocko connected the chains.

The Rogers were bringing up two wagons pulled by eight mules each. They would return to the bottom and bring up Sean's and Duncan's wagons. They were the first to reach the top of the plateau and headed back down, leaving four mules hitched to each of the wagons at the top. Beau was impressed with their organization. They would be very helpful once the wagon train got into the mountains.

Continuing up the hill, Beau noticed that the Scotts' wagon was in trouble. Both Hanna and her mother were behind the wagon pushing while Jon shouted encouragement to the oxen. Mrs. Stiles slipped and fell and her daughter turned to help her mother. The mountain man saw one of the oxen go to its knees. The wagon stopped and began to come back!

Dropping the reins, Beau ran up the hill, reaching the wagon. He pulled the tie that held the braking log, dropping it behind the wheels. He then put his shoulder to the back of the wagon to help stop it before it rolled over the two women. The two ladies scrambled clear, falling further down the hill. The log slid behind the wheels with the weight of the wagon due to the oxen losing the tension on the load.

Beau pushed in desperation as his feet slowly slid. If he tried to get away from the wagon it could lurch back and he would end up injured. After what seemed like an eternity, Jon had the oxen pulling again. Hanna was hurrying back up the hill to help Beau.

"Stay away!" he shouted. "Help Jon with the oxen!"

Feeling the push of the wagon lessen, Beau noticed that the log behind the wheels was holding. He slipped to his knees as he attempted to get away from the back of the wagon. He looked up and was surprised to see Ruth Stiles near him, offering her hand. Pushing himself to his feet on the hillside, he smiled. "Thanks for the offer," he said. "I'm okay now. Let's go check on the oxen."

Jon looked up as Beau came near. "The log is holding now," he said. "I'll give the animals a breather and then get them pulling again."

"We'll put a rope from the front yoke to my saddle horn to get the wagon started," Beau offered.

By midday all the wagons were at the top and they stopped for an hour while the animals were watered and the exhausted people sat and laid near the wagons. Too soon for most, Beau called them to line up and continue west. Behind them another wagon train had started up the slope and would need the area to recover.

The wagons would be about halfway across the plateau by nightfall. He instructed Otto to help set up the night's camp and keep the animals close. There would be little for them to graze on and the wagon train had to be ready to roll at sunrise. In the meantime, he and Jocko were going to ride across the plateau and get an idea of the backup at the hill into Ash Hollow.

The two men headed out across the high table. It felt good to be free of the slow pace of the wagon train. Prior wagon tracks zig-zagged across the plateau. The two branches of the river flowed on the north and south sides. Miles before they reached the west end that went down into the hollow, they could see the tops of wagons. There were over 50 wagons waiting their turn to descend.

Riding to the brink of the hill, the two men were taken by the beauty of the expanse below. The grassy hollow had thick stands of ash trees and spring-fed streams winding across the bottom. They watched as wagons were lowered backward down the hill. The back wheels were lashed so they would skid, offering some braking, and ropes tied to the tongue and held by groups of men. Some had a team tied to the rope and the drover slowly backed the team. At the top a snubbing post had been erected by prior travelers and used with the rope wrapped around it.

Beau was told it was taking from one to three hours for each wagon. As many as three were being lowered with lines at one time. He could see the results of wagons that had broken loose, in wrecked heaps dragged away from the bottom. The lowering of the wagons would continue through the night.

While they watched, a wagon being lowered by eight men got loose when one man fell, tripping others, and it began to slide sideways, striking the wagon below, the two wagons skidding to the bottom in a cloud of dust and receiving damages. Teams of oxen at the bottom quickly pulled them clear.

Having seen enough, Beau and Jocko rode back east to meet up with their wagons. The mountain man was unsure of what he was going to tell the folks, but what he knew was that they had to be informed of what lay ahead. One thing he did plan to do was talk with the Rogers men and find out if they had any suggestions.

The next day, at mid-afternoon, Beau's wagon train arrived at the hill to the hollow. A dozen wagons still remained at the top to be lowered before theirs. They had a plan. The wagon to be lowered would be pushed over the edge, its back wheels locked in place. Two ropes would be tied to the tongue and then fastened to two teams. Five men would be on each line to hold the wagon as it skidded down the hill. Two drovers would back the teams, keeping slack between them and the men.

One other thing that Quinn Rogers suggested was packing as much of the supplies and gear as possible onto the oxen and mules being brought down the hill to lighten the wagons. Beau liked the idea and had the people start transferring supplies as they arrived. Items were wrapped in extra canvas and blankets were gathered to protect the animals' backs. Leather straps and rope would be used to secure them on the animals. All the packs would have a strap under the tail to prevent the packs from shifting forward going down to the hollow.

While the people were busy making packs to be loaded onto the oxen, Beau and Jocko began to prepare the lines. They would need over twice the distance down the hill. Coils of rope were collected from the wagons and tied together. Each wagon weighed about 1,300 pounds. They would still be loaded with half their load, or 1, "They sounded like rifles,"

000 pounds. By using two lines for lowering, the strain on each was cut in half. As the ropes slid over the crest of the hill, the sand and rocks would tear at the fibers.

It was two in the morning before it was their turn to start down the hill. If they chose to wait until morning, other wagon trains would move ahead of them. Lanterns were fixed on posts going down the hill to give some feeble light. The extra stock had already been taken to the bottom with the gear and supplies. Six oxen teams were kept at the top to move wagons to the edge and to be used to hold back the descending wagons.

Rob's wagon was the first to be lowered. Oxen were used to back the wagon to the edge. Two men put the short log in place near the back wheels, lashing it using pieces of rope. With the lines fastened to the wagon tongue and stretched out to connect to the teams, they were ready to start.

The wagon rolled back a couple of feet, bringing the log up to the bottom locking the wheels. The hillside offered poor footing due to the previous wagons dragging their wheels, tearing the sod away. It left a rutted swale of dirt and rock to navigate down. Four men went down with the wagon, sometimes pushing it if it got stuck in a rut, or helping to hold it back. Five men remained at the top on each line to hold back the wagon. Soles ripped off boots or twisted ankles were a constant danger, not to mention if someone slipped under or behind the wagon.

Despite the gloves worn on their calloused hands, many would quickly be bleeding from straining on the ropes. Shouts of instruction and cussing could be heard in the night air as the men worked. When Rob's wagon reached the bottom, two men cut the back wheels loose and then four of the wives using a team of oxen took the wagon to the stream where the wagon train would make camp. The four men grabbed the rope as it was pulled up the hill for the next wagon.

While lowering Hoot Johnson's wagon, one of the ropes snapped, sending Jocko and four other men holding it onto their backs. Beau and his four men strained on the single line to hold the load. Clem Williams manning the team took the slack up, careful not to add undue tension to the line. The line that let loose had chafed and parted at the tongue pin. The men scrambled in the dark to get the rope reconnected.

After a few minutes, the wagon continued down the hillside.

Beau was very proud when he saw how the men and women worked together. Throughout the night, until mid-morning, they lowered wagons. Fresh water from the springs was sent up the hill to quench the thirst of the tired men. Those holding the lines at the top were rotated to less strenuous positions in their turn. When the last wagon reached the bottom, a cheer went up from the dust and sweat-covered men.

Aching all over, Beau started pulling a line up, readying it in a coil to be packed down to the wagons. Jocko came over, wearing his hat tilted to the front. "Is the morning sun getting in your eyes?" Beau asked his friend.

"When the line broke, I got a big knot on the back of my head when it bounced off the ground," his stocky friend told him. "Damn near knocked myself out."

Slipping and sliding down the hillside for the last time, the men and oxen from the top reached the bottom. It had been a success. Other than a few cuts, blisters, and bruises, only one man had sprained an ankle. Herb Tucker had taken a bad step while guiding one of the wagons down.

The women had herded the extra stock to a place where they could graze after unloading the packs. By the time the men reached camp, everything was unpacked and a meal of dried fruit and rice with fried side meat was ready. The topside men stopped first at the stream. Pulling their bloody gloves and sweat-stained shirts off, they plunged their hands into the clear water and splashed it on their faces and necks. Then, cupping their hands, they took long drinks of the sweet, clean water.

Peck Wilson had brandy and cigars he had planned to break into once they reached Oregon. This occasion seemed a better time and after the men finished eating, a measure of the liquor was poured into their mugs and a cigar was given to those who wanted one. Some of the women came forward with their cups, and one even accepted a cigar.

The celebration was short and within a couple of hours most were lying asleep under or alongside the wagons. The cauldron was sitting on the fire with water heating so folks who wanted to could wash up or bathe. The ladies had put up two tents, so those wanting to wash all over could have privacy.

Beau planned to stay in the hollow for two days to allow the folks and their stock to rest and partake of the clear spring water. Some of the wagons had gotten damaged skidding down the hill and Peck was busy with his hammer and tools fixing iron rims and loose wheel spokes. Edsel Ward had damage to an axle and took advantage of the trees in the hollow to rough cut a replacement. Some also made extra wagon tongues, shaping them with a draw knife. It would be hundreds of miles across the high plains before this quality of trees would be found again.

The night before leaving, Rob had invited the Scotts to have supper at his wagon. Earlier that day he'd shot a mule deer. Most of the meat had been shared with the other wagons, but he'd kept a choice piece to roast on a spit over his fire. A pot of beans and sourdough biscuits would be served with the venison.

Beau and Jocko were drinking coffee while they waited for the meal to be ready and their guests to arrive. Rob was basting the piece of venison with a secret sauce he'd learned about in Independence while working in a restaurant. The sound of laughter drew the three men's attention to the arrival of their guests. Following just behind the Scotts was her mother pulling at her shawl for protection against the cool breeze blowing in from the north.

The three men stood up quickly. "Welcome to some of the best venison you'll ever taste," Rob said.

"We are looking forward to the fresh meat," Jon said. He was carrying the rocker for his mother-in-law. Hanna helped set it upwind from the smoke for her mother.

After everyone got comfortable on makeshift seats of crates or logs, Hanna asked Beau, "How far are we from Fort Laramie?"

"The fort on the Laramie River," he said, thinking for a moment. "We are about two weeks away. You'll know when we're halfway there when you can see Chimney Rock."

"The army was to purchase the fort from the American Fur Company," she said. "My brother went with the forward company to take it over. I hope to see him when we stop there."

Slices of venison were served with the beans and hot biscuits. Everyone complimented Rob on the meat. Ruth Stiles even smiled and nodded her approval. As he chewed, Beau thought about the fort on the Laramie. The first time he'd stopped there it hadn't been much more than a fortified trading post named Fort William. When a newer fort replaced it, it was called Fort John. The white adobe walls had been used to prevent theft more than for defense.

The fort, whatever its name was, was always

called the fort on the Laramie. It was built on the south side of the Platte River next to the north-flowing Laramie River. It emptied into the North Platte River. As time went on, most just called it Fort Laramie.

The meal was finished with cups of tea and the men smoked pipes or cigars.

CHAPTER SIX

The wagon train was two days away from Chimney Rock. A shout from the folks went up as they crested a hill, realizing that they were near something that would mark the distance they'd traveled. By the evening, the landmark was plain to see but still in the distance. Little did the people realize how far away Chimney Rock still was.

After another long day's travel, the wagon train finally camped near Chimney Rock. Many were already tired of seeing the pinnacle on the endless plain. Supper was cooked in the center of the circled wagons over a buffalo chip fire. Jocko and Beau brought their plates of food back to Rob's wagon.

"I saw some Indians today," Jocko told Beau. "They were either Lakota or Arapahoe."

"Did they have women and children with them?" the mountain man asked.

"No," the stock friend said. "They looked like a hunting party. Mostly young braves, maybe a dozen of them."

"Did they see you?" Beau asked.

"They did," Jocko replied. "They came out of a swale all of a sudden-like. Scared me out of ten years of my life."

Feeling a tightness in his stomach, Beau asked, "How were they armed?"

"I saw a few muskets," Jocko said. "Most had bows or lances."

"Did they ride toward you or chase you?"

"No, they didn't," his friend replied. "They just sat there looking at me for a minute. I think they were just as surprised as I was. I had one shot in the Hawken and the wagon train was a couple miles behind me. I knew the gray could outrun them, but didn't want to bring them here. While I was debating what to do, they just turned and rode away."

Beau knew that the braves would be out this time of year looking for meat for their camps, but after the long winter of inactivity, some might be tempted to go after some of the wagon train's riding stock. Since leaving Ash Hollow the oxen had been kept close to the wagons at night and the mules and horses were kept within the circle.

"Until we get to Fort Laramie, you best stay within sight of the wagons," Beau recommended.

A meeting was held with the emigrants of the wagon train, letting them know that extra caution would be required. They were told not to string out along the trail, and to travel in groups with loaded rifles when moving away from the wagons.

The mountain man had heard accounts of attacks while watering stock, collecting fuel, or hunting for meat. Most often the deaths were a result of resistance to stealing the horses or mules. Other prizes were the weapons carried by the emigrants. Scalps were taken as personal trophies by the braves.

It was three nights later when some mules were stolen after they wandered outside the circle of wagons. It shook up the people as they realized that they were probably being watched in the dark by braves just waiting for an opportunity to steal something. Many of the folks would go out from the wagons to relieve themselves at night. A new rule of doing one's business within the wagons was adopted.

Fear of an attack increased the night before reaching the fort when an ox was killed by an arrow. No doubt it had been one of the braves testing the effectiveness of his bow on the large animal. It was still warm when they discovered the animal, so some time had been taken to butcher it. Clem Williams had to fit the yoke to one of the spare oxen trailing the wagons.

Beau felt relief when the fort came into sight across the Laramie River. The people in the wagon train were under constant stress of being attacked at any moment from an unseen enemy. As they approached the river, they could see several teepees standing outside the walls of the fort. Indian braves and their families sat around the teepees, watching the wagons approach. Everyone on the wagon train stared back, wondering if they were some of the braves who had been harassing them.

Jocko rode out to check the river crossing. It was only three feet at the deepest point, so the wagon teams could be led across by the drovers. Without stopping, the first wagon entered the water, Hoot Johnson leading the oxen. Water dripped off the animals and the wagon as Hoot led the team out of the river.

Ironically, as the folks crossed the river, it was like a door slammed with the danger behind them and safety in front. After two days of tense faces and little conversation, the people suddenly smiled and began to talk. They camped near a small stream just to the west of the fort. A column of soldiers riding in from the plain stopped to welcome them and were quickly told about the losses they'd experienced.

Hanna came up to the captain leading them and asked if he knew her brother David Stiles. The captain gave her a big smile and confirmed that her brother was assigned to the fort. He was out supervising a working party collecting firewood and should be back toward dark. He then asked to see the wagon train leader. He was directed to Beau.

The captain rode over to Rob's wagon where Beau was pulling the saddle off the sorrel. Looking up, Beau asked, "Can I help you?"

"I was told that you were in charge here," the captain said. "You'll have to come to the fort and make a report for our major. He'll want to know what tribes attacked you and of anyone that was wounded or killed."

"As soon as I get everyone set here, I'll be by," Beau promised.

It was late afternoon when the mountain man arrived at the major's office. He walked into the white adobe building and looked at a young private sitting behind a small desk. "I am Beau Levesque, the leader of the wagons that just came in."

"You the ones that were attacked?" the private asked, leaning back in his chair.

"Well, you might say that," Beau replied. "It

was more about stock that was attacked."

A look of disgust crossed the private's face. "So, you weren't attacked?"

"We were dogged by Arapahoe or Lakota for several days looking for opportunities to steal and kill if necessary," Beau replied through tight jaws. "Where do I write the report?"

A half-hour later, the mountain man left the major's office having only met with the captain again. He was unsure if he'd gotten any satisfaction in submitting the report. He saw a column of soldiers with a wagon heaped with wood coming in. A sharp-looking second lieutenant was leading them. Beau took the reins of the sorrel and walked toward the soldiers.

"You wouldn't be David Stiles?" he asked.

Calling the column to a halt, the second lieutenant replied, "I am. Is there something I can do for you?"

"No, Lieutenant," Beau answered. "I can do something for you. Your sister and mother are in the wagon train I just brought in. We're near the stream west of here."

He saw the face of the lieutenant light up and he smiled a smile Beau had often seen on his sister's face. "Tell her I'll be out as soon as I get this detail squared away."

"I will do that," the mountain man said as he swung up onto the sorrel.

Beau rode back to the wagons, to let Hanna know that he'd seen her brother. They would be spending only four nights at the fort, so she wouldn't have much time to visit with him. When he reached the camp, a group of men met him, led by Otto Graf.

"Is the army going to help us?" the old man asked.

Beau swung down from the horse. He turned to face the men. "I spoke with the captain we met coming in," Beau told them. "He had me write down what happened."

"What did the major say?" Otto demanded.

"I did not see the major," the mountain man replied. "He had more important things to do."

The old man' s face turned red, "What the hell do you mean, more important!"

Not wanting to deal with the blustering old man, Beau addressed the other men. "The army can't go running across the plains on a report of stolen stock. Right now, there are only two companies. Another is coming in the next week or so and in August, the 6th Infantry will be here. Once that happens, they might have the manpower to send patrols up and down the trail."

Very upset, Otto stomped off, muttering, "I should have gone to the fort myself."

Alvin Thompson remained with several of the others. "Did the captain have any suggestions?" he asked.

Rubbing his hand over his mouth and beard, Beau looked after Otto for a moment before looking back. "What he suggested was exactly what we've been doing. Keep the stock close and if possible the mules and horses within the wagon circle. Stay alert, keep the wagons close on the trail, and keep our rifles loaded."

Peck Wilson looked satisfied. "You got us doing the right things."

"He did mention one other warning," Beau said. "The captain cautioned me of going off at half-cock. Shooting at shadows or going after a group of braves just for riding by could provoke an attack."

Most in the group were satisfied and left nodding in agreement as they headed back to their wagons. The mountain man hoped that he could eventually make Otto and his sons understand. He turned to lead the sorrel back to his wagon when he saw Jon and Hanna walking towards him.

"Did you see David at the fort?" Hanna called to him.

Smiling at her, he replied, "Yes I did. He has a couple things to do and he'll be coming over."

"Good!" she squealed, beaming from ear to ear. "Jon, get a fire going and I'll make him supper."

"You might want to wait," Jon said. "Your brother might have plans for us at the fort."

Giggling and talking with her husband in anticipation, the two headed back to their wagon. A flash of loneliness went through Beau. There had been a woman when he had first come west into the mountains. They had gotten close and he had hoped to marry her. He could picture walking and talking with Ana and making plans together.

He got back to the wagon and Jocko was getting their cook fire ready. "We need a meal out tonight," Beau said.

"Chow at the fort?" the stocky man asked. "I got a couple rabbits while you were at the fort. I think they'll taste better than what they're cooking there."

"I know a place outside the fort that serves a fine meal and has beer or rye to wash it down," Beau said, "and the rye won't be doctored with pepper."

Looking over at the two rabbits, Jocko said, "Maybe the Wolseys would like these for supper."

It was early evening when the two men rode out of the camp on the mustangs. "Last time I was here they were serving mashed potatoes," the mountain man said.

"I can't remember the last time I ate taters mashed," Jocko said, rubbing his belly.

The front of the Buffalo Hide Saloon was lit with shiny brass lanterns. They tied the mustangs to a post with metal rings. It had been a long time since Beau had eaten off china plates. He caught sight of the owner, Louie, working behind the bar. He had first met the grizzled, white-haired man while he still owned a trading post. After the walls of Fort Williams had been torn down, he'd sold the inventory to a trapper looking to open a place near Boulder Creek.

"It is good to see you again, Beau," the owner said. "Lucy has a nice ham tonight."

"Does she have mashed potatoes?" Jocko asked.

"Yes, she does," Louie replied. "She also has a nice mess of greens."

"We'll start with a shot of rye," the mountain man said.

For an hour the two men talked with the owner about the good old days. Louie served the finest rye and brewed a tasty beer that would be enjoyed with their meal. Lucy came by and told them they'd best have a seat before the kitchen closed.

She served it family style with thick slices of ham, a bowl heaped with potatoes, another with greens, and fresh-baked bread. A bowl of sweet cream butter sat near the bread. Jocko dug into the mashed potatoes, putting a large heap onto his plate. Lucy had made a tasty gravy with the ham drippings and this he poured over his potatoes. Seconds were eaten by both and the food was washed down with mugs of beer. Just as they thought they couldn't eat another bite, pieces of apple pie came out with a pot of strong, black coffee.

With the meal finished, Louie came over with brandy and cigars. The bright lamps on the chandeliers had been turned down and the other customers had left. Beau asked Louie what he had heard about trouble with Indians.

"The Lakota are upset with what the army has been doing. They say the army is expanding the fort without talking to them first. The Arapahoe and Cheyenne have been mostly quiet. Further west the Crow have been in scrapes with some of the other tribes, but seem to leave the wagon trains alone," the owner told them. "I'd watch your horses. They are a prize for any of the tribes."

With a nice glow on and full stomachs, the two men left the Buffalo Hide Saloon and rode back to their camp. It was late and the cook fires had burnt down to coals. Duncan and Sean Rogers were sitting near their wagon, finishing off a bottle. Feeling sociable, Beau was tempted to go over for a drink, but as he slid off the mustang the ground moved and he decided it would be hard enough just pulling the gear off the horse.

The next day, Beau learned that Hanna's visit with her brother had gone well and their family had been invited to dine at the fort this evening. The mountain man could hear Hanna talking excitedly with her mother.

After making rounds of the wagons, Beau returned to find Jocko emptying Rob's wagon. "Did you lose something?" he kidded.

"There are buffalo west of the fort and I plan to shoot a couple and make some jerky while we're here," Jocko told his friend.

"I'll come with you," Beau offered. "I need to do something to work off last night's meal."

Rob promised to have the drying rack ready when they got back. Riding the sorrel, Beau followed the wagon being drawn by the two mustangs. They traveled in a southwesterly direction, having to get away from the trail. They pulled up on a rise about three miles out. Several dark clumps were slowly moving across the plain.

"Let's cut up the valley and we should come out near the buffalo," Jocko suggested.

"We will only shoot two. Agreed?" Beau confirmed with his friend.

"Agreed," Jocko said. "The meat from two will be all the team can pull."

Their intention was to skin and debone two of the buffalo. They would take the tongue and hump back for their evening meal. As they reached the end of the valley, they could see several buffalo grazing less than 100 paces away.

The two men checked their Hawken rifles and stepped away from the wagon. "On three," Jocko said.

The Hawken gunfire shattered the quiet of the plain. Two of the wooly beasts went to their sides and kicked their last. The other buffalo continued to move away, grazing as though nothing had happened. After reloading the rifles, they were ready to start. For the next two hours, the two men worked feverishly, skinning and cutting the meat from the carcasses. One of the hides was laid hair side down in the back of the wagon, and as they cut the meat and fat free it was tossed onto it for transport back to camp.

After they finished, the second hide was laid over the meat to keep dust and flies off. With the meat ready to transport, they wiped their knives and hands on the grass to clean them as much as possible. The two mustangs leaned into the harnesses as they slowly turned the wagon around to head back to the fort.

Jocko slapped the reins on the horses' rumps, shouting encouragement. Suddenly, the right horse stumbled, followed by the sound of a rifle shot. "What the hell . . ." Jocko said as he leaped from the wagon, wood splintered from the seat where he had just been sitting. As Beau threw himself off the horse, he heard the sound of something hitting the hides on the wagon. Their reaction was followed by the sounds of rifle shots. Reaching up and grabbing his rifle, Jocko ducked under the wagon. Beau was already there, holding his Hawken.

The sorrel ran a distance away, startled by the shots. The two men clutched their rifles, trying to figure out where the shooting had come from. "I think we're being shot at from two sides!" Beau shouted.

"They sounded like rifles," Jocko replied. "Who the hell would be shooting at us?"

"Some Indians have rifles," the mountain man told him. "Maybe they're after the meat."

"That doesn't make any sense," the stocky man said. "If they had rifles, they could shoot all the buffalo they want."

Again, there was a shot. It hit the dirt right next to Beau's leg. It had come from the boulders on the rise to the right. "They are in the rocks on both sides of the valley," Beau said. "I think they shot the mustang to stop the wagon."

Suddenly, Beau saw something appear from behind one of the boulders. He lined the Hawken sights on the dark form and fired. Smoke appeared near the rock just as he pulled the trigger. He felt a searing pain across the back of his leg. He had been hit.

The two men crawled forward between the front wheels. The downed mustang offered Jocko protection as he searched the boulders on the left. Beau could feel the blood running down the side of his leg. He clenched his teeth against the pain.

Then, Jocko fired. "I got the bastard!" he hissed.

The sun was burning down into the valley as the two men, pinned under their wagon and their throats dry, searched for a target. Just above them, on the wagon, was a canteen. After an hour, with only the sound of buzzing flies, Beau said, "I think they've gone."

"How do we find out?" Jocko asked, his eyes watering from straining to spot another target.

To the right of Beau there was a small cluster of rocks. "I'm going to run for the rocks over there," he replied. "If I make it, I'll work my way to the top."

Without waiting for agreement from his friend, Beau rolled free of the wagon and attempted to leap to his feet. The wounded leg wouldn't hold him and down onto his side he went. The mountain man held his breath, expecting a shot at any second as he tried to pull himself back under the wagon.

Without thinking, Jocko came out to his friend's assistance. He pulled Beau to the back of the wagon. The two men sat, realizing that they hadn't drawn fire. Jocko looked at his friend's bloody pants. "When did you get hit?"

"A while back," Beau said, trying to move the leg to cut the pants. Groaning at the burning pain, he slit the pants and exposed the gash on the back of his leg.

As Jocko ripped some strips from the bottom of his shirt, he scolded his friend, "You should have told me. I could have stopped the bleeding sooner."

"And you could have got your head shot off," Beau replied.

Keeping low and muttering, Jocko fashioned a bandage on the leg.

"They have to be gone," Beau said. "We've been moving around and the ones on the right had plenty of time to shoot. You said you got the one on the left."

"I'm going up there," Jocko said. Without waiting for a reply, crouching low, he ran to the cluster of rocks and then began to work his way up. Beau watched as his friend reached the top. He disappeared and the mountain man sat waiting, heart pounding, hoping he wouldn't hear a shot.

Then there was a shout. Peeking out from behind the wagon, Beau saw Jocko standing near the boulders, waving. The mountain man stood, testing the wounded leg. He was able to put some weight on it. He saw the sorrel and called to it. The horse looked up and, with head stretched out, walked toward him expecting a treat.

Supporting himself with his rifle, Beau met the horse and managed to get into the saddle. He rode to the top of the rise and headed for the boulders. Jocko was crouching next to a wounded man. Beau recognized him. It was Mick Rinker!

Jocko came over to the sorrel. "Before he passed out he said Bull helped them escape from the army. He wanted to kill you and convinced them to help him before heading for California. They've been staying ahead of us since Fort Kearny, just waiting for an opportunity to ambush you. You hit Mick and I'm sure I killed Hal on the other side. Bull ran out on them."

Jocko went to check on Mick. Shaking his head, he came back. "He's dead."

Anger flashed through the mountain man. "Let's get the meat back to the wagon train and then we can come back and bury them," Beau said.

After his friend got Mick's horse and rifle, they rode to the other side. Hal had a bullet hole through the upper center of his chest. "It was his shot that barely missed me when I jumped off the wagon," Jocko said. "When he showed himself from the rocks for the next shot, I didn't miss."

"They both have army saddles," Beau noted.

"Yah," his friend acknowledged. "They were carrying .54 caliber Model 1841 army rifles also."

With the horses and rifles, they rode back into the valley. Once back at the wagon, Jocko began to pull the harness off the downed mustang. "I won this one. It was a damn good horse."

Beau sat on the sorrel, watching, feeling helpless, his leg throbbing. His friend tied some rope to the back legs of the mustang and handed it to the mountain man. Beau took a couple wraps around the saddle horn and then dragged the dead horse clear of the wagon.

Choosing the Rinker's dun because it best

matched his mustang, Jocko put on the harness. The dun danced around, trying to kick or bite Jocko as the harness was secured. Taking it in stride, the stocky man ducked and dodged. He said, "This one ain't pulled a lot of wagons."

After a little encouragement, Jocko finally had the dun pulling with his mustang and the wagon slowly rolled toward their camp. A crowd gathered around them when they reached the wagon train. Beck and Ludwig assisted Beau off the sorrel and helped him limp to Edsel's wagons. The bullet had cut a furrow along the back of the mountain man's right leg, just below the knee. Once Mr. Ward cleaned the wound and bandaged it, Beau pulled his bloodied pants back on.

"You'll need to be careful until it scabs over good," Edsel said. "It ain't deep, but it will keep your attention."

"I got to go after Bull," the mountain man told him. "When I first got to the mountains, I had someone chasing me and a friend I was with. It damn near got me killed. It ain't happening again. I am going to track that son-of-a-bitch down and put him in the ground."

"That could take some time," Edsel said. "We need you here to lead the wagon train. Though I don't like to mention it, the outcome could be him killing you."

"Well, I figure, he'll keep trying no matter what I do," Beau replied. "While I'm gone, Jocko can lead the wagon train. He knows the trail as good as me." Then, trying to make a joke, he said, "Figure it this way. If I don't come back, you all save the $10 you'd have had to pay me."

Snorting, Edsel said, "You're a damn fool to go after the man." Then, looking Beau in the eye, he said, "I just hope the hell I get to pay you the $10."

Limping back to his camp, Beau was pleased to see that everyone had pitched in making the buffalo meat into jerky. It would save on the cost of supplies. Jocko had his gray saddled, ready to go and bury the Rinkers. Concern crossed his face when he saw Beau grab his saddlebags and start putting stuff into them.

"How the hell long do you figure it will take to bury them boys?" he asked.

"I'm going after Bull," Beau said, without stopping what he was doing.

"We got this here wagon train to take west," Jocko reminded him.

Settling the bags behind the saddle, Beau turned to his friend. "I'll need you to lead these folks until I get back." He then took his blanket roll and tied it onto the sorrel.

"Did you forget how things went the last time we met the bastard?" Jocko asked. "There were two of us and he damn near kicked our butts."

"It won't be a fight of strength, Jocko," Beau said. "I am going to find him and kill him. It won't be with a shot in the back, either. I want the son-of-a-bitch to see it coming."

"Are you sure killing him will be worth it?" the stocky man asked, trying to reason with his friend. "We'll be in Oregon and will never see him again. You saw how he ran after we shot the Rinker boys."

Beau hung his canteen onto the saddle horn. "It's also for them boys. That's why he needs killing. They had good in them and with a little guidance they would have been fine men to have in the west. Bull led them the wrong way to satisfy his own interests. It's his fault they are dead."

"What do I tell these folks?" Jocko asked. "How long do I say you'll be gone?"

"Tell them I don't expect to be gone too long, but you best figure you might be taking them the rest of the way to Oregon," Beau admitted. "After a week or so on the trail, they'll be looking up to you and won't hardly remember me."

Jocko tied a shovel on the gray, swung into the saddle and rode out with his friend. "You want to draw Bull away from the rest of us, don't you? You figure he'll keep coming and maybe kill some innocent folks."

"I didn't say there wasn't more than one reason for the man to be dead," the mountain man said.

When they reached the valley, a cluster of buzzards were already sitting around the buffalo remains. It would take a few days before animals would be drawn to the rotting meat of the mustang.

The stocky man dismounted and grab Hal by the back of his collar and his pants, tossing him over the saddle of the gray. "I only want to dig one hole for these two."

He looked up at Beau. "You may as well get started hunting Bull. I can get these two under the sod. I'll get the horses and rifles back to the army."

"I plan to meet you at Independence Rock at the latest," Beau said. "We'll chip our names into the granite, so folks will never forget us."

It was the third week of June and they were two weeks from Independence Rock. It was said that a wagon train had to pass the rock by the 4th of July to make it through the mountains before snow. Beau's wagon train was in good shape time-wise, and barring any big delays should make the mountains before snow blocked the passes.

CHAPTER SEVEN

Bull's tracks were easily found. They were cut deep into the sod as he'd galloped away from the fight. He and the Rinker cousins had gotten into position while Beau and Jocko were butchering the buffalo. Their plan had been to fire three shots at the same time. Two were aiming at him and Jocko and the third was to shoot the wagon horse to stop its movement. It had been luck that the one aiming at the horse had fired too soon.

The early shot had given him and Jocko just enough time to react and get out of the line of fire. Beau was sure that the last thing Bull had been expecting was to have both of the cousins hit by return fire. The tracks led south, away from the North Platte River. The mountain man had to trust that Bull was a coward unless he had the advantage. Because of that, he wouldn't stop to ambush anyone following him. He'd keep running until he was sure he was a safe distance away.

Beau expected that he'd ride to the south until

panic subsided and then turn to the west to get near the trail. Mick had been hit hard and Bull might have thought he was already dead, or would be shortly. He had probably figured that nobody would find out he was with them. The Rinker cousins had had blanket rolls and food for a few days on their horses. The mountain man guessed that Bull carried about the same. He would have to join one of the wagon trains for food and safety. He might even have friends with one of the trains.

The mountain man decided that he would need to overtake one or two of the wagon trains to find the big man. He could be riding into danger coming into a wagon train that Bull joined. If Beau was spotted first, the big man would hide and then attack when Beau didn't see him coming.

He cut back toward the trail, wanting to hit it well back of the nearest wagon train. The wagon train that would have left this morning would only be 15 miles west. His sorrel could carry him 40 miles in a day, so Beau could overtake up to three trains in one day. It was getting dark when the mountain man spotted a large circle of wagons. They were below a rise to the south of the trail. He could see drovers bringing their oxen to the river for water.

Turning the sorrel toward the river, he slowly rode toward the drovers. A thin man with a bushy moustache looked up at Beau. The mountain man noticed him reach to his waist belt.

"Good evening," Beau called out. "I'm with the wagon train back at the fort. Just checking out the trail while the folks catch some rest."

Showing his hands, Beau swung down from his horse. Two other men with oxen stood behind their animals just in case they needed cover. "It's kind of strange you'd be this far out checking on the trail," the mustachioed man said.

Beau's Hawken was in the scabbard, and his knife and Colt were in his broad belt. Dropping the sorrel's reins, he held his hands wide and walked closer. "I have a special reason for being away from my people. I am hoping you can help me."

Standing well away from the horse, he told them, "I'm looking for a big man, goes by the name Bull."

"This big man," the man said, "Is he a friend of yours?"

"I can't say he is," the mountain man replied.

"He spent two days with our wagons," the man replied. "He killed a man. Most say it was a fair fight, but he was one hell of a lot bigger than the man he killed. We run him and the two men riding with him off of our wagon train."

"I wish you'd have let the two young men stay," Beau said. "The three of them tried to ambush me and my scout. The boys are dead and I'm looking for Bull."

A man watering another team spoke up, "Supper's on the fire. You are welcome to join us. The man Bull killed was my friend."

The wagon train was heading for California and had over 50 wagons. Most were occupied by men on their way to the gold fields. A few of the wagons had a wife along, and even fewer with any children. The men he met were bachelors, and the fare they offered for supper was simple. It was beans with sliced side meat floating in them. The coffee was good. Bull and the Rinkers had joined the wagon train just this side of Chimney Rock. The fight had been a day before they'd reached Fort Laramie. They had been told that the Rinkers had just gotten out of the army and had gotten their gear as part of mustering-out pay.

The man with the bushy moustache was named Carlo. He told Beau that the big man would ride the backtrail each day, claiming to be hunting. He never brought in any meat for the cook pot. Beau figured that he had been watching for their wagon train. The small number of wagons would make it stand out from a distance.

Thanking the men for the meal, Beau told them, after checking around a little, he'd be back and sleep near the river. He let them know this because he didn't want to surprise any of them coming back in the night and end up being shot at as an intruder. Beau wanted to ride around some high ground looking for any fires.

Riding away in the dark, he rode up the rise behind the wagon train. The sky was clear and filled with stars. The moon would be coming up in a few hours and would be near full. Riding in a westerly direction, Beau held to the top of the hills and ridges to watch for any fires. He stayed south of the trail, hoping to see any camp out on the plain. The mountain man caught sight of a butte to the west. Beau figured that he was at five or more miles from the wagon train he'd shared the meal with. He continued toward the butte and tied the sorrel to some brush at its base. The moon was orange and large on the horizon.

Climbing through the rocks, Beau gained the high point on the butte. He estimated that he could see ten miles from his vantage point. He was able to catch the flicker of three fires. Two were farther south on the plain and the other was east toward the river, in line with the moon's reflecting ribbon on the water. A chill went through Beau, realizing that one of them might be Bull.

Tomorrow, he would catch up with the next wagon train and continue his inquiries. The big man might have to come in for food. Beau also realized that Bull might also stay on the plain and watch for campfires at night. He could be wondering if he was being chased for the ambush.

Climbing down from the butte, Beau stripped the gear off the sorrel. He had ridden too far west to go back to the wagon train. He rolled out his blankets at the rocky base and lay thinking about his next move. He dozed off to the sounds of wolves calling to each other as they were getting set to take down an unsuspecting buffalo calf or other prey.

Sunrise found the mountain man lying on top of the butte, scanning the plain for any movement. He could see dozens of buffalo grazing or rolling and creating clouds of dust as they attempted to rid themselves of parasites. His heart pounded as he spotted six or so braves heading for the trail. Beau guessed that they were Lakota. He estimated they were about two miles away. They dismounted on the lee side of a rise so they could observe any wagons passing without being noticed. Beau felt safe, sure that they were unaware of him on top of the butte.

To the east he saw a lone wagon slowly working its way along the trail. It had probably been the fire he'd seen toward the river. It was being pulled by six mules, with the driver on the wagon and three other men walking. Beau looked back toward the braves. They continued to lie motionless on the hillside as the wagon continued to roll west toward the rise.

Suddenly, the mountain man caught sight of movement out of the corner of his eye. Blinking, he squinted as he looked to the southwest. It was a single rider. If the rider continued in the same direction, he would pass near the Lakota. Lying flat, watching, Beau realized that the lone rider could be Bull. With the distance, and with heat waves rising from the plain, it was impossible to know.

Again, he glanced toward the wagon. It was now about a quarter-mile from the rise. The braves remained motionless, making them hard for him to pick them out on the hillside even though he knew they were there. Looking back to the plain, the lone rider had disappeared from sight. He had most likely ridden into a dip.

There was motion on the rise, which brought Beau's attention back. The braves were moving to their horses. The mountain man hoped that they'd become bored with watching the trail and had decided to move away. They rode along the base of the rise, keeping below the crest. Beau held his breath as he watched. They were closing in on the wagon!

The ridge was out of hearing distance for shouting or firing a shot to alert the wagon. Keeping low, Beau worked his way across the top and climbed back down to the sorrel. It stood picketed on the grass without its saddle. The mountain man looked to the east. He could no longer see the wagon or the braves. He also remembered that there was the lone rider who might be Bull. The first thought that flashed through his mind was to take the Hawken and ride bareback as fast as he could to assist the wagon.

The mountain man swore as he set the Hawken down and hurriedly put the blanket and saddle on the sorrel. Bareback with one shot in his rifle and four in his Colt would be an act of stupidity, an act that would no doubt get him killed. Within a couple of minutes, he was in the saddle, his possible bag slung over his shoulder, riding hard toward the trail. His blanket roll and saddlebags were left lying next to his cold campfire.

Less than a mile away and beyond the rise, Beau heard the muffled sound of shots and the shrill cries of the braves as they attacked the wagon. The mountain man intended to make the rise above the braves and fire with the Hawken as fast as he could load it, to try and break the attack off the wagon. He would save the Colt in case the braves came at him and use it for cover fire as he tried to outrun the Lakota with the sorrel.

Beau rode up the rise, reaching its crest just to the west of the wagon. Leaping off the horse, he witnessed the horror as the braves cut and slashed at the downed men. The mules had been cut loose of the harnesses and were being driven past him by three braves. Ignoring those driving the mules, Beau's attention was on those near the men. He knelt to steady himself and raised the Hawken, fighting to control his heavy breathing. He fired at one of the braves leaning over a downed man. The Lakota twisted and fell forward.

Surprised by the shot, and unsure of who was shooting, the Lakota, including the wounded brave, headed for their horses. Beau poured powder down the rifle barrel and then took a ball wrapped with a greased patch. It slipped from his fingers as the Lakota rode past him toward the west.

Angry at his clumsiness, Beau dropped the rifle and pulled the Colt, emptying it at the Lakota. If he had hit any of them, it didn't slow the Lakota as they rode west and over the rise. Looking at the empty revolver and useless Hawken, he growled, "You damn fool. What are you going to do now if they come back? Throw the revolver at them!" There was the sound of a rifle being cocked.

"You could," a voice behind him said, "or you might want to beat them with that empty Hawken."

Spinning around, Beau stared into the cold eyes of Bull! The big man raised his rifle to his shoulder. "I saw the Lakota attacking the men. I was waiting for them to finish having their fun. I figure there might be something I need in the wagon. Then, like a gift from above, here you come up out of the valley, right to me."

Bull's lips curled into a cruel smile as he pulled the trigger. He flinched, anticipating the recoil, but the only sound was the hammer falling on a bad cap. Beau saw and heard nothing as he threw himself to his right, desperately attempting to dodge the lead from the rifle. Rolling in the dust, the mountain man couldn't be sure if he'd been hit or not. Some years back he'd been told by an old soldier that you don't hear the shot when you're hit.

A little disoriented, Beau came back to his feet, still sure that he'd been hit somewhere and expecting to feel pain and weakness at any moment. He saw Bull trying to put a fresh cap into the rifle. Realization that the rifle had misfired dawned on Beau and the survival instinct set in as he leaped forward, putting his shoulder into the big man's middle.

The two men went to the ground, Bull's rifle falling to the side. They rolled over and over in the dirt, Beau clinging to the big man, pinning one of his arms, hanging on for dear life, knowing that if Bull was able to get loose and get him in a bear hug, the big man would squeeze the life out of him.

All of a sudden, the two men rolled over a ridge and went head over heels to the bottom, the impact breaking them apart. Beau scrambled away and was back on his feet, facing Bull. They each pulled their knives and began to move in a circle. The mountain man could see the sorrel standing, reins dragging the ground. For a split-second, he thought of trying to get to the horse and ride away before Bull could close in on him.

As though anticipating the move, Bull put himself between the mountain man and the sorrel. Beau could hear the cries and pleading for help from the wounded men with the wagon. "I know you want to hurt me, Bull," the mountain man said. "We should be helping the folks with the wagon. We may be able to save some of their lives."

"You listen to them good," Bull said. "Soon you will be lying in the dirt, crying the same as they are. It will be music to me."

Watching the heartless man in front of him, Beau had expected that he had no sympathy for the injured. The mountain man was attempting to delay the attack until he and Bull moved back to level ground. Right now, the big man was on higher ground and had the advantage of quickly closing and the size of the behemoth could crush and kill Beau from the impact.

"You are a miserable bastard, Bull," Beau said.

"I can't figure what I did to keep you coming at me. It sure as hell wasn't the Rinkers. You ran like a coward as soon as they were down."

The mountain man watched anger swell inside the man in front of him. Bull suddenly threw his knife, sending it flipping end over end, barely missing the side of the mountain man's head as he charged in. It was evident that the big man was not a knife thrower, but had hoped to bruise or injure Beau just before attacking.

Bull charged, expecting to end the battle with the surprise move and his brute strength. Unable to dodge out of the way, Beau thrust up with his knife as the big man wrapped his arms around his middle and began to try and crush the life out of Beau. Unable to breathe and with his arm and the knife pinned between their bodies, Beau attempted to stomp on the big man feet or trip him. Pain shot through his body as a cloud of darkness engulfed Beau as he fell.

* * *

Something wet was hitting him. Beau opened his eyes. Large drops of rain struck his face and eyes, forcing him to blink as he fought to see. It was dark and the only sound around him was the patter of rain. The mountain man tried to move, but he could not. He was trapped under some heavy mound. Thoughts raced through his mind. *Was he dead? Could he be paralyzed?*

Quickly turning his head to one side, he attempted to roll over. He could not! Panic began to set in. He could be partially buried. The rain might have washed the dirt off his face. Along the trail, Beau had seen more than one body in a shallow grave partially exposed by scavengers or the weather.

He moved his legs. They were free. Slowly, Beau was able go gather his thoughts, recalling the fight with Bull. Moving his head forward, his chin felt the damp woolen shirt of the big man partially on top of him. Using his legs, Beau tried to arch his back to push himself free. Pain shot up and down his spine, forcing him to collapse back down.

In the darkness Beau finally determined that Bull's arms were still wrapped around him and the big man's body was pinning him down. Pushing with his left leg, the mountain man was finally able to roll the two of them over. Bull fell to the side, pulling Beau's right arm with him. Jerking it free, the mountain man realized that his knife was glued to his hand by dried blood. His other arm and hand were numb from being pinned behind his back.

Free from the weight, Beau managed to move away, pushing the man's other arm off him. Sitting in the darkness, with his back spasming, the mountain man put together what had happened. When Bull had attacked him, he'd thrust up with his knife seconds before the big man had wrapped his arms around him. Bull would have squeezed in desperation as his life's blood flowed from the wound.

Beau must have passed out before Bull collapsed, dead, on top of him. It had been morning when the fight had happened, so they had lain like corpses throughout the day. The mountain man sat with his head hanging, the rain beating down on him. Every time he tried to move, spasms would return to his back. Feeling was coming back to his arm and hand. He closed his eyes and listened to the night. The horses were grazing not far off. No sounds were coming from the direction of the wagon.

Slowly, Beau rolled over onto his side, lying in the rain, pain shooting through his body. He wondered what damage Bull might have done to his back. Suddenly, Beau opened his eyes. The rain had stopped and the eastern sky was beginning to get light. He must have passed out again. Beau was cold and began to shiver. His woolen shirt and pants were soaked and the ground side of his clothing and bearded-face were covered with mud.

Pushing himself upright, Beau sat looking at the wagon. While he was cold, his back no longer spasmed. He ran his fingers through his beard, removing dirt. The air smelled fresh. He looked over at Bull. He lay twisted in a heap next to the mountain man. Getting to his knees, Beau pushed himself to his feet with the help of the ridge they'd tumbled down.

The rifles and the Colt lay on the muddy ground where they'd fallen. The sorrel stood looking at him, bobbing its head and snorting. "I'm glad to see you too," Beau replied. Bulls had been riding a bay and it had worked its way up the rise, grazing.

Leading the sorrel with two rifles stuck into its scabbard and the Colt back in his belt, Beau walked down to the wagon, avoiding looking at the bodies of its occupants. There was tinder and some wood in the tarp tied under the wagon. With shaking hands, the mountain man got a fire going. He looked inside the wagon, found a coffee pot and, digging through some packs, found coffee. Filling the pot from the barrel tied to the side of the wagon, he set it near the flames to heat.

He then went to get the bay, each step an

effort. The grass along the trail had been chewed down, exposing the dirt below, but a short distance away on the plain it was green and fresh from the rain. By the time he had both horses tied to the wagon and their saddles pulled off, the water was hot. He put some ground coffee into the pot. The smell of the boiling coffee went a long way, perking Beau up.

The mountain man chewed on some hard bread he'd found in their packs and drank coffee, while staring at the big man. In Bull's mind, his sheer size had given him permission to abuse those smaller. The world would not miss what Bull had brought to it. Taking the last sip of his coffee, Beau knew that it was time to deal with the four men who had been with the wagon.

Toward the front of the wagon, the driver lay with an arrow in his side and back. He had been scalped and slashed. Looking up, Beau saw the other three men. They had made a dash for the brush along the river for protection. The two closest to him had been scalped. One had been shot, the other struck with arrows. They had also been slashed with knives.

He walked toward the fourth man, lying on his back with his head turned toward the wagon. The brave had been over him when Beau had taken the shot with the Hawken. The man still had his hair. "At least they didn't get a trophy off you," he said.

Beau knelt to close the man's eyes. As he reached, the man blinked. Jerking back in surprise, the mountain man almost fell over. "Help me," the man whispered.

Leaning back over the man, his hands shaking from the shock of finding one alive, Beau answered, "I'll do what I can."

Looking in the direction the man was staring, the mountain man could see the coffee pot. Guilt ran through him. For the last hour the wounded man had watched him dig through their packs and then sit drinking coffee while he lay unable to move.

A quick survey of the injuries revealed that the man had been hit several times with musket fire. One ball had gone through his side and another had entered his back and come out just below the collar bone. He had a crease alongside his skull that could have been caused by an arrow. Everything around them was mud from the overnight rain. Beau ran back to the wagon and found a pot. Filling it with water, he put it on the fire.

He returned to the man carrying a tarp and a canteen. Holding the wounded man's head up with one hand, he helped him drink some water. Coughing and choking the man attempted to drink. Then Beau spread the tarp out near him and carefully moved him onto it, enduring the moans of the injured man.

For the next hour, the mountain man worked on the wounded man. He removed the rain and blood-soaked clothes and washed the wounds. He tore a shirt he found into strips and bound the wounds as best he could. Then, covering the man with blankets found in the wagon, he promised to make some hot broth for him to drink.

All the while Beau worked on him, the man's unblinking gray eyes stared at the mountain man. Beau couldn't tell if they were looking at him with appreciation for the help, or disappointment for not coming right over and checking on him. With that in mind, he went over to the other three men and made sure they weren't lying there wounded. One showed evidence that he'd tried to crawl away after being attacked. The other two had not moved from the place they'd fallen. All three were dead.

After feeding the wounded man broth made with jerky, Beau went back to the three men. He went through their pockets, placing the contents into separate piles in the wagon. He then found a shovel and dug the graves, burying the men. He wanted to keep the blankets for the wounded man, so he just placed items of clothing over the dead men's faces before shoveling the dirt over them.

After taking a moment to say words over the graves, Beau went back and concentrated on the wounded man, feeding him hot broth several times. The man continued to stare at Beau, having only muttered the couple words when he'd been found.

Sitting next to the man and chewing on a piece of jerky while drinking the last of the coffee, Beau told him, "I have to ride over to my camp and get my gear. I'll only be gone maybe a half-hour."

He went and got his saddle and as he put it onto the sorrel, he looked over at the man. "I'll be right back," he promised again. The man just stared, giving no indication that he understood.

Riding by Bull's body, he said, "I am in no hurry to take care of your sorry bones."

The butte stood out on the plain in the bright sunshine. It looked much closer than he recalled when thinking back to the desperate ride he'd made to assist the wagon the day before. He sat on the horse, looking across grass-covered plain for any sign of movement before riding away from the rise.

The camp was as he left it, other than everything being dampened by the rain. He had worn his clothing dry trying to help the wounded man. Being away from the carnage and the freshness of the air out on the plain helped to lift Beau's disposition a bit. Knowing Bull was dead had removed the burden he'd been carrying since the ambush.

As he rode back he thought about the three men he'd buried. One had had a money belt with some letters and a fair amount of cash. The others had had a clasp knife used for whittling, some coins, pieces of flint, and a few personal odds and ends.

All of the weapons they'd been carrying had been taken. Beau was unsure of what else might be in the wagon. He figured he'd already caused the wounded man enough concern without getting back into the wagon and digging around. He rode over the rise, the horror of the previous day washing back over him, altering his mood. The first thing he did was check on the wounded man. He half-expected to find him dead from the wounds and blood loss. His eyes were closed, but the shallow breathing told Beau he was unconscious, or sleeping.

The mountain man knew he didn't have the knowledge to take care of the man's wounds. He had to find a way to get him back to the fort. After getting a fire started near the man, he put water on to heat. Beau then went to look over the harnesses lying in front of the wagon. Between the six cut harnesses, he was able to put two good ones together. Bringing them back to the fire, he looked over at the man. His eyes were open again.

"After I make you some more broth, I'll hitch the two horses to the wagon and pull it over by us," Beau told him. "I got to get you to the doc at the fort. I am going to empty the wagon and make you a bed as best I can, then we'll be ready. If there is anything that you want me to keep in the wagon, just tell me."

The last request was more to encourage the man to speak. For the horses to pull the wagon, it would have to be almost empty. The two horses took to the harnesses without a problem. Once hooked to the wagon, Beau led them near the fire. By this time, it was late afternoon. He would start with the wounded man at first light tomorrow.

After feeding the man more broth and taking care of the horses, Beau looked at the dark bulk of Bull lying near the ridge. "If it weren't that you'd stink the whole area up, I'd let you lie there and rot," he called.

Looking back at the wounded man, Beau smiled. "I don't much like that man up there. If it weren't for him, I'd have been able to help you yesterday. I should have come check on you first thing this morning, but I was kinda in rough shape from meeting with the bastard up there."

The man lay staring at the mountain man. Beau hoped he understood. Taking a shovel, he walked up to the big man. He was bloated and hardly recognizable. Bull's shirt was cut and bloodied where the knife had entered. Beau cut the strap from the possible bag and set it aside. Looking at the ridge they'd fallen down, Beau decided it was a good enough grave.

Grasping Bull's feet, he dragged him to the bottom of the ridge and then caved dirt over the body until it was covered. While Beau had said words over the graves of the other three men he'd buried today, he found it difficult to say any words over Bull's resting place. Finally, he bowed his head and prayed for the wounded man.

That night he made a pot of coffee and offered some to the wounded man. Beau could feel the gray eyes following his every move. The man's blood-stained clothing lay in a damp pile near the fire. After going through the pockets and taking out the few personal items, Beau tossed the garments beyond the fire. There had been a watch in the pants pocket. The mountain man took his time going over it, hoping to find initials or a name inscribed on the case. There was nothing.

Beau went to the man and placed the watch into his hand, closing the fingers around it. "I figured this might be important to you. I got to take some stuff out of the wagon now." There was no indication that the man understood him.

To lighten the wagon, he removed the spare wheel and spare tongue. He also removed boxes with pans and tools for mining in California, extra pots and the Dutch oven. The water barrel was half-empty so he left it tied to the side of the wagon. He also kept some of the food supplies, using the bags to make up the bed for his wounded passenger. He would add his gear and Bull's in the morning before leaving.

There was a small wooden box in the wagon with papers, a small cross on a chain, and some money. It probably belonged to one of the men. Beau sat where the man couldn't see him as he went through the papers. He found one with a contract from a wagon train with the names of four men: Walter Hask, Everette Hask, William Johns, and Albert Goodin. The man with the money belt had letters addressed to William Johns, so that left three possibilities for the wounded man.

Beau wished that he had looked at the men

he'd buried more closely. Maybe two of them would have stood out as brothers. Thinking back about the mud and blood-covered faces after being scalped convinced him that it would have been impossible. The wounded man was sleeping when he came back to the fire.

That night, when Beau lay in his blankets near the fire, he was awakened several times by the cries from the wounded man. Twice the mountain man got up and checked on him. Whether it was pain or bad dreams, Beau didn't know. The man's face was warm in the cool night air. If the wounds became infected, he'd never make it to the fort.

After a restless night worrying about his patient, Beau got up and put the harnesses onto the horses and hitched them to the wagon. He had water for coffee and broth heating near the flames. After a breakfast of hard bread and coffee for himself, he gave the wounded man some broth and then a little coffee. He then changed the bandages. The wounds were surrounded by angry-looking bruises. None had a bad smell to them. The gray eyes had tears in them as Beau lifted him into the wagon.

While getting him comfortable, the mountain man asked, "Is your name Walter, Everette, or Albert?" Watching close to see if there was any reaction, Beau saw none.

"I prayed over your friends' graves," the mountain man said. "I buried them good and deep."

The sorrel and bay stepped out lively as the wagon headed east toward Fort Laramie. With the lightened load, and being pulled by horses, he should be able to double the distance of a wagon pulled by oxen and make the fort by nightfall.

Beau regretted each jarring bump of the wagon. The man's face was pale and his gray eyes stared at the canvas top of the wagon. While driving the wagon, he wondered about the lone wagon on the trail. Had they been impatient to get underway and had left their wagon train, or had there been a problem that had left them behind?

In the distance Beau saw a line of wagons coming in his direction. The scout raised his arm to stop the wagons a good distance from Beau's. "Stop where you are," he called to the mountain man.

"I got a man here that needs a doctor," Beau called back. "Their wagon might have come from your train."

"There are no wagons missing from us," the scout replied. "I imagine you do need a doctor. You brung the sickness to our wagons."

"Sickness?" the mountain man asked. "Who's got the sickness?"

"Your man there, and probably yourself," he replied.

Frustrated, Beau told him, "I know nothing about any sickness. The man with me was attacked and wounded by the Lakota. If I brought sickness to your wagons, I'd be dead now. You might have something, but it ain't from me."

The scout rode closer, still keeping a safe distance. "You come and ate at our fire and then went away telling us you'd be back. Some of our folks were sick the next day. When you didn't come folks figured you up and died of the sickness."

"Did Carlos or any of the others that ate with me get sick?" Beau asked.

"No, no they didn't." the scout said. "We got

to be careful."

"Do you have any kind of a doctor with the wagons?" the mountain man asked.

"No, we don't" the man said.

"Then I'll be riding wide around your wagons to make sure the wounded man don't catch your sickness," Beau replied sarcastically.

Slapping the reins on the rumps of the horses, he drove them to the south side of the wagon train. Three hours later, he passed the wagons with sick folks left behind by the wagon train. They stared out at him with haunted looks on their faces. By tomorrow they could all very well be dead.

He stopped near a babbling brook to rest the horses and check on the wounded man. He was either sleeping, or unconscious, and felt warm to the touch. Beau made a small fire and warmed some water from the brook. He pulled some wild onions and other greens to simmer in the brew. Then, straining the hot liquid in a mug, he climbed into the wagon.

A gentle prod awoke the man. Supporting him as best he could, Beau got him to drink most of the broth. Using a piece of rag and some cool water from the brook, he bathed the wounded man's face. His face was still pale, with dark rings around his eyes, but the eyes were gray and clear as he watched his caregiver.

With the horses watered and rested, Beau continued toward the fort, picking at the onions and greens in the pot for his meal. It was dark when the fires and lanterns of the wagon trains camped outside of fort appeared. The mountain man had half-expected to meet his wagons on the trail. Something must have delayed their departure.

On the last check, the man in his wagon was

more dead than alive. The only thing that showed any life were his gray eyes. Beau kept a constant conversation going with the man as the wagon bumped along the rutted trail. He couldn't be sure that it helped the wounded man, but it helped Beau endure the uncomfortable plank seat he was sitting on.

The trail ran closer to the fort than Beau's wagon train, so he drove the wagon directly into the fort. A sleepy private was on guard near the gate. "I got a man here that was wounded by the Lakota," the mountain man said, his voice harsher than he meant it to be.

"The Lakota?" the guard said, coming to the wagon.

Trying to keep his voice less agitated, Beau said, "Yes, the Lakota. He needs to see the doc right now."

The private called to another soldier to guide the wagon to the doctor. Beau climbed down from the wagon, his back and bottom aching. Leading the wagon, he followed the soldier to a long, narrow adobe building that served as the hospital.

A white-haired man wearing only pants over his long johns came out, carrying a lantern. "Where's the wounded man?" he asked.

"In the wagon," Beau said. "He was hit three places and looks awful bad."

The doc climbed up and held the lantern over the wounded man. "This here man's dead," he replied.

"Are his eyes open?" the mountain man asked.

"They are," the doctor replied.

"If they're looking at you, he's still alive," Beau told him.

Climbing down, the doc sent the soldier after

help to carry the man into the hospital. Suddenly, the weight of the wounded man was off Beau's shoulders. He stood and watched them carry the man on a stretcher into the adobe building.

"Stick around," the doc told him. "We'll need some information."

The private came out after helping carry the stretcher. "My name's Sherm," he said, introducing himself. "We got some coffee on the stove in the mess hall. Can I get you some?"

"That would be great, Sherm. I'm Beau," he said, leaning on the wagon wheel.

In a couple of minutes the soldier came back with a mug of steaming black coffee and a big piece of corn bread. "If anyone askes, you don't know where the corn bread came from. Someone left the officers' mess door open."

"The secret is good with me," Beau replied. "Can someone get a message to a wagon train outside the fort?"

"I'm off watch in an hour," Sherm said. "I could go for you, but they might be sleeping."

"I lead the 15 wagons near the stream to the west. I'm with the wagon furthest to the east. Jocko and Rob should be sleeping there. Let them know that I'm at the hospital with a wounded man. They should be planning to leave in the morning."

The soldier smiled and headed back toward his post. The corn bread was still a little warm and tasted like heaven. The coffee, then again, had been made a while back and one could have stood a spoon in it. The mountain man did not mind. He was two days eating hard bread as a main course.

Licking the last of the warm corn bread from

his fingers, Beau went to tend to the horses. There was a water trough in front of the next building. He unhitched the team from the wagon and led them to the trough. While they drank at one end, the mountain man washed the dried mud out of his beard and hair on the other. It helped the burning of his eyes from staring out on the plains with the wind in his face.

Beau was bringing the horses back to the wagon when he saw the doctor just inside the hospital door. "How is the man doing?" he asked. The doc just waved him away and disappeared within the building again.

Tying the horses to the wagon wheel, Beau climbed into the wagon and lay on the blankets and bags, his Hawken next to him and his head on his saddle. He intended to watch for the doctor to come back, but within minutes was fast asleep. A shout and pounding on the side of the wagon brought him upright and wide awake. It was Jocko.

For the next hour the two sat on the hospital step while Beau brought his friend up to date. Jocko was pleased to learn that Bull was dead. He was somewhat concerned to hear about the Lakota attacking the wagon. Every time there was movement inside the hospital, they would stop and watch for the doctor, without success.

Finally, Beau asked, "Why are you still at the fort?"

"It's my fault," Jocko replied. "Otto was wanting to leave this morning, but I convinced everyone to give you a day or two more." The stocky man chuckled. "Otto agreed to another day, but no more."

"I got to do some checking around the fort

tomorrow and I'm sure the captain will want to know about the attack," Beau said. "If they're so intent on leaving, I can catch up in a day."

"After I tell them about the Lakota and the wagons with the sickness, they'll be willing to give you another day," Jocko assured him.

The stars told Beau that it was only a couple of hours before daylight when the tired doctor came out of the hospital. His face did not look happy and the mountain man expected him to say that the unknown wounded man had died.

The doctor pulled a clay pipe from his pocket and lit it with a short stick near the lantern. After taking a couple of deep puffs, he looked at Beau. "You friend is in bad shape. If it weren't for his eyes, you'd bet he was dead. He hardly moves when he breathes. You did a good job cleaning the wounds you found. There was another on his calf. He lost a lot of blood and may not pull through. You kept liquids going down him and as long as infections don't take over he just might make it. One other thing: The watch in his hand. Did you put it there? I couldn't pry it out of his fingers."

Smiling for a moment, Beau said, "I put it there. He spoke only once when I found him," Beau told the doc. "He asked for help. He lay for almost a day before I got to him. He got rained on and everything." A wave of guilt swept over the mountain man again, remembering how he'd eaten before checking on the four men.

"Not being able to move may have saved him," the doc said. "It allowed the wounds to stop bleeding."

Those words didn't make Beau feel much better. The two men started to stand when the doctor asked, "What's your friend's name?"

"Jocko?" Beau asked, pointing at his stocky friend.

"No," the doc said. "The one that you brought in."

"I wish I could tell you, Doc. I found him and brought him in, but the closest I can guess is three names. Walter or Everett Hask. Or it's Albert Goodin," Beau said. "Other than staring at me, he didn't say."

Shaking his head, the doctor replied, "His not reacting could be from the blood loss or whatever hit his scalp. Things may not be connected very good in his head."

"I'll be by in the morning," Beau said. "The wagon is his and the horses are mine." With that, he and Jocko got the horses and headed for the camp.

Beau's blanket roll was musty, so he just spread a tarp on the ground, set his saddle on one end and was soon asleep. The sun was up when he awoke and he was covered with a blanket. Jocko was frying side meat and had the coffee on.

"About time you awoke," his friend kidded. "I was about to check if you had slipped to the other side."

While they were eating the meal, Otto and his sons came over. "Why aren't we getting ready to leave?"

Beau was tired and in no mood to talk to the old man. Jocko got up quickly and took them aside and explained the need of another day and about the attack on a wagon, of sickness, and whatever else made staying sound like a good plan.

Otto did not look happy but he agreed, not liking

the part about a wagon being attacked. Jocko gave him assurances that the wagons would leave the first thing tomorrow. Scowling, the old man turned to leave and then stopped. "Glad to see your back safely," he said and then headed for his wagon.

CHAPTER EIGHT

It was late morning when Beau stopped to check on the wounded man. The doc was not there, but an orderly brought the mountain man to see the patient. He lay in the bed on clean sheets, with bandages showing a slight seepage of blood. Beau touched the hand holding the watch.

Smiling at the man, he said, "I see you still have the watch. The doc is a good man and will take care of you. I have to take the wagons I'm leading to Oregon. We leave in the morning. Your important things are in your wagon. Your mules were taken by the Lakota. You and your friends had a bit of money and I will leave that with the folks at the major's office. I'll get something in writing and bring it back to you."

Beau stopped talking for a minute. He didn't know if the man understood him or not, but hoped that some of the words gave him a little comfort. The wounded man looked at him, unblinking.

"I'll be in Oregon in the Willamette valley if you ever get that way. Just ask around for Beau

Levesque, someone should know me."

He left the hospital with a feeling of helplessness. The captain was expecting him. Beau told the story of the attack one more time. He placed the wounded man's money onto the desk and asked for a receipt, promising to bring it to the man.

The captain counted up the money and wrote out the receipt. Handing it to Beau, he said, "By the way, we'll be sending some men out with your train. We want to look over the attack site."

"We'll be leaving at daylight," the mountain man said. As he was getting ready to go, the captain asked him to wait a second.

Out of a wooden box of old paper he brought out the wanted poster. Beau sat stone-faced looking at the man. "We were given a lot of old documents and posters when the army took the fort over," the captain said. "I was responsible for going over all the old stuff and saving what might be important."

Looking at the poster on he and Elijah, Beau asked, "I take it you think the poster is important?"

"This?" the captain asked. "Not to the army, but I thought you might like it for old memories, or starting a fire."

He then handed it to Beau, and said, "You've done a good thing for the man you brought in. Some would have taken the money and left him to die. In fact, you spoke about a man named Bull and the Rinker boys. They would strike the last blow and take everything the man had."

Beau looked the captain in the eye and said, "Bull won't be a problem anymore."

The man stood up and smiled. "It had been good talking to you, Mr. Levesque. I'll write up the report on the attack."

Stepping out of the captain's office, the mountain man folded the poster and headed toward the hospital. The wagon had been removed from the front. The day felt good. Above, the sky was blue, with cottony clouds. A breeze brought in the fresh smells of the plains grasses and wild flowers. Beau was anxious to be back on the trail.

After dropping the receipt off and talking one more time with the wounded man, Beau was done at the fort. He had gotten the sorrel some grain to build up its strength and now, because of Bull, had a pack horse and a second rifle. It was an older, converted Hawken rifle, but would be helpful should the wagon train get into a scrap. As he rode, he took out the ten year-old wanted poster and ripped it into small pieces. Chuckling he thought, *How many of these did that bastard Angus spread around the west?*

Jon and Hanna were walking to the common fire and saw him coming. She smiled and waved, "We heard you were back."

"I am back," Beau said. "Come tomorrow we continue to Oregon."

"David convinced the major into letting a detail ride with us for a while when we leave," she said. "I think they want to see where the attack was." Her face clouded a bit at the mention of an attack.

"We can use the company," the mountain man said, not mentioning that he knew this already. "I'm glad you had a few extra days to see your brother."

"He talked of coming to Oregon after he gets out of the army," Jon said.

"I hope he does," Beau replied. "I've got to make rounds to let everyone know what time we're leaving."

Edsel insisted on checking Beau's wounded leg. It had scabbed over and the calf was severely bruised, but appeared to be healing okay. By the time he got back to his camp, Beau felt drained. Everything about the past couple days had taken its toll. After a quick supper, he crawled into his blankets and was soon asleep.

* * *

The good weather held as the wagons rolled out of Fort Laramie. The next chance to purchase staples would be at the Mormon Ferry. With the dry conditions came the dust from the trail. When possible, the drovers would choose to travel away from the ruts of the trail, to avoid breathing plumes raised by those ahead. Beau couldn't prevent them, but would have preferred a more organized line for defense purposes. The soldiers rode along the south side of the wagons, keeping them between their column and the river.

Late the first day out of Fort Laramie, the trail went over granite outcrops or ridges. Some of them had been chiseled to make going over them less difficult, others had been worn down by the repeated contact with the iron rims of the wagon wheels.

The June grass was tall and mature. Clouds to the west gave the promise of some rain ahead. Beau was hopeful that it would come to help maintain forage for the animals. Soon the lack of rain and the summer heat would turn the green sea of grass to golden brown.

There were still a few hours of daylight when Beau had the wagon train make camp. A full day's travel would have taken them to the area with the wagons that had the sickness. Beau had let Second Lieutenant Stiles know about the wagons with sickness. The lieutenant agreed that there was little that could be done with them and it was wise to stay clear of their camp.

The soldiers set up away from the wagons, with their two-man tents set up to allow them to get into action quickly if attacked. Once the guards were set up and necessary order were given, David came over to the wagons and joined Hanna and her family for supper.

It was still dark when Beau awoke to the sound of the soldiers breaking camp. The Wolsey families were already up and had coffee ready at the fire in the center of the wagons. The mountain man compared the folks in the wagon train to the soldiers as they awoke and prepared to leave. He smiled, realizing that while it took the wagon train a bit longer, they were as well-organized as the soldiers. And that was without someone barking orders.

It was late morning when the tops of the three wagons near the river came into view. The soldiers rode out ahead to determine what help they could provide. Beau stopped their wagons, awaiting some word from the lieutenant.

Looking forward to a break with many walking on new boots purchased at the fort, the people sat in the shade of their wagons, resting their feet. Several carried food that was planned for a light midday meal. While still a bit early, it was broken out, everyone assuming that this stop would be considered the break. Jocko and the mountain man met David as he rode back with information.

The strained look on the lieutenant's face told them that it was not good news. "Two of the wagons had four men with them. They are all dead," he informed them. "The third wagon had a family. The man died of the sickness, but the woman and two children didn't get sick."

Seeing smoke billowing up ahead of them, Beau asked, "Are they burning everything?"

"Everything but the woman's wagon. The husband's brother was in one of the other two wagons. He stayed behind to try and help," David said. "He wouldn't let his family near the others. When the husband got sick he made them keep away. They sat helpless, watching as he grew weaker and died. That was just an hour before we got here."

"Are you going to take them back to the fort?" Beau asked.

Looking back toward the wagons, the lieutenant replied, "If you're willing, they want to go on with you."

The mountain man felt a chill go through him. The sickness they had had was cholera and why folks got it wasn't well understood. The only thing in common with the breakouts was that it showed up in places with groups of people living together. Many suspected that it had something to do with the water, or was in the dirt.

"I can't be sure the folks with me would allow them to join us," Beau replied. "People are fearful of what they had."

"The woman said her husband sold everything to make this trip. What's carried in their wagon is all the family has. She says there is nothing to go back to," Lieutenant Stiles told him. "I told them you were going to Oregon, not California. It made no difference to her. She claims she can't go back and asked me to beg you to let her go."

Beau stood, his mind racing, saying nothing. Hanna's brother shrugged his shoulders, "I can't make you take them. We still have bodies to bury. I'll be back when we're done and you can let me know."

Several people from the wagon train surrounded their leader to find out what the lieutenant had said. He turned to Otto and his sons. "Would you bring the rest over? We have a decision to make."

Once the folks arrived, Beau climbed on his sorrel so he could address them all. "I have a question to ask you. Depending on your answer, I will ride over to Lieutenant Stiles and let him know. There is a woman with two children in one of the wagons that wants to join us. Her husband died of the sickness trying to help a brother in the other wagons. When he fell ill, he wouldn't let his family come close to him as he died. The woman and children did not get sick."

There was a rumbling of dissent in the crowd. Beau held his hand up for silence. "I will not make you folks take them, but I want you to at least consider it. There are things we can do to keep them away from everyone until we feel sure they aren't getting sick."

It did not sound good for the widowed woman and her children and then Otto came forward. Turning to the crowd, he began to talk of Jesus going among the lepers and others in the Bible that had helped the sick. For the next half-hour, he gave the sermon of his life and when finished, he asked, "Who among you will step forward and help this woman and her children?"

The crowd was no longer speaking against taking the woman, but they all stood fixed, looking to someone else to step forward. From within the people, a man pushed through the crowd. Aarno Hanson was a short, white-haired, man with a tobacco-stained beard. Behind him was his son, Kimi, a raw-boned young man with unruly, sandy hair. They were both dressed in worn and patched clothing.

"I will drive her wagon, Kimi here can drive ours," Mr. Hanson said. "We will follow behind the extra stock until everyone is satisfied they won't get sick."

Beau was surprised to see Aarno stepping out and even more so to hear him speak. The Hansons were very private and tended to keep to their selves. Beau hadn't heard him say but a few words since leaving Independence. "I appreciate your offer, Mr. Hanson. I will let the lieutenant know."

Aarno accompanied Beau to see the lieutenant. Two of the wagons had been reduced to charred wood and iron. The third stood away from the others with six oxen hitched to it. The soldiers were just finishing the burials. The dead had been buried in a single, large grave.

Lieutenant Stiles saw them walking and rode to meet them. "What should I tell, Mrs. Burns?" he asked.

"We will take them," Beau replied. "Aarno Hanson here will help her with the wagon. They will have to remain away from the rest of the people until everyone is convinced they aren't carrying the sickness."

David looked down at the short, disheveled man. "You are doing a good thing for her."

Uncomfortable with the compliment, Aarno just grunted. Beau noticed something about the wagon. "They have no water barrel," he pointed out to the sergeant.

"It was burnt," Lieutenant Stiles replied. "That and his clothing, blankets, and personal things. We tried to get rid of everything he might have touched."

"I can share water from my wagon," Aarno said.

"Yes, that would be good," the lieutenant agreed. "The woman's name is Helena Burns. Her children are Theo and Lilith."

"Are they ready to go?" Beau asked.

"In a bit we'll be saying a few words over the grave," David told him. "I'll let her know she'll be going with you."

He rode back to his men. It appeared that they were finished with the burial. Aarno nervously wiped his hands on his pants. "I best get over and check her oxen. Would you have Kimi bring our wagon to the back when you get started?"

Without waiting for an answer, he hurried to the woman's oxen. Her two small children were playing near the wagon. Mrs. Burns was sitting on the ground next to the wagon with her back to Beau, watching the soldiers finishing up at the grave.

This would make 16 in the wagon train. As the mountain man walked back to the others, he figured they had another six hours of daylight. He remembered a stream this side of the attack that would be a good spot to spend the night. Beau was pleased to find that Jocko had the wagons ready to roll.

As the wagon train approached, the soldiers mounted and rode out ahead. Aarno stood holding the lead rope of the oxen. The children were in the wagon and Mrs. Burns still stood near the grave, wiping her eyes with a hanky.

Some of the wagons pulled away from the trail to give themselves more space from the carnage that had befallen the three wagons. At the end of the wagon train, Kimi waved to his father and the old man led the widow's wagon to the back. Riding over to make sure they got in line with the other wagons, Beau got his first good look at the widow. She was a handsome woman, but the time on the trail and the loss of her husband showed on her face.

That night the Hansons parked the two wagons away from the rest. Helena was making a meal over a small fire. Beau sat near Rob's wagon with a plate of cornbread and beans. He hoped that the fear of the woman carrying the sickness would leave the folks of the wagon train soon so they could join the community and security of the other wagons.

The next day the wagons reached the area of the attack. The soldiers rode out ahead and spread out over a rise along the trail. Beau and Jocko rode at the front of the wagons with their Hawkens across the saddle in front of them. The mountain man noticed that the mining gear and other items that had been left from the wagon had been picked over and scattered by passing wagon trains.

Beau pulled up near the ridge where he'd buried Bull. Some wild animal had already started digging into the dirt, attracted to the rotting smell of the big man's body. While it would have been a good place to take a midday rest, the area had bad memories for the mountain man and he continued to lead the wagons past.

The soldiers rode out of sight beyond the rise, following any sign left by the Lakota. Just knowing they were around was a comfort for Beau and the folks with the wagons. An hour past the attack area, they stopped for a rest near a creek flowing into the North Platte.

He saw the soldiers led by Lieutenant Stiles coming down the other side of the creek. Turning the sorrel, he trotted over to meet them. "We'll be leaving you here," David told him. "The Lakota rode south of here and we're going to make a sweep in that direction before heading back to the fort."

"We'll be here another hour," Beau told him. "I'm sure Hanna would like to see you before you go."

The lieutenant barked a couple of orders, having the men stand down for a midday rest, before joining the mountain man and riding back to his sister's wagon. While it was considered a midday rest, the men and women were kept busy watering stock, fixing something to eat, and filling water barrels.

All too soon, it was time for the wagon train to continue west. After a tearful goodbye from Hanna, David gave his sister a hug and then rode away with the column of soldiers. Beau stood, watching them leave. Anxious to be moving, the sorrel nudged him with its nose. As the soldiers disappeared beyond the ridge, the mountain man suddenly felt alone, despite being surrounded by the folks with the wagon train.

It would be another six hours before Beau would halt the wagons for the night. The security they'd felt with the soldiers around was gone and everyone traveled with the rifles close at hand. Beau rode to the back, giving support to the Hansons and Mrs. Burns.

The sun was low on the western horizon when Jocko found a creek to camp on. The wagons set up a defendable circle and the horses and mules were kept close while the oxen were allowed to graze a short distance from the camp.

Beau rode to make sure the Hansons and Mrs. Burns were okay. They had stopped downstream closer to the river. Kimi was being playfully pestered by the young children as he checked the wagons over and watered the oxen.

Helena had a pot of coffee going and some hard bread out for a simple meal. She looked up at Beau as he rode up. "I want to thank you again for letting me join the wagons," she said. "If needed, I can handle the oxen. I don't want to be a burden on you."

"Please, don't consider yourself a burden," he told her. "When we reach the Mormon ferry you can join the rotation with the rest of the wagons."

Tipping his hat, Beau rode back to the other wagons. The iron wheel rim on one of the wagons had been loosened by the granite ridges and the wheel had to be switched out. Peck Wilson would be busy tonight repairing it. That night, Beau slept light, bothered by the memories of the wagon that was attacked. He knew that his wagons were better prepared to defend themselves, but the scene of the scalped and mutilated bodies kept flashing through his mind.

The next morning, clouds in the west moved over the wagon train and wind-blown rain began to fall. With his hat pulled down to protect his eyes, Beau led them away from the creek. They were a week from the Mormon ferry. The wagon train had been steadily climbing in elevation since Fort Laramie. It was a subtle incline but they would go from 4,000 feet to 7,500 feet by the time they reached the South Pass.

By the time the wagons stopped for the night,

the rain had become just a drizzle. The trail had turned into slick mud, causing wagons to slide to the side when crossing slopes. The boots of those trudging along with the wagons became heavy with damp dirt.

They were now traveling on the more arid plains, with shorter grass made up of blue grama and buffalo grass. They were seeing more dark patches of sage brush and tumble weed. There were also areas covered with boulders left behind by the runoff of past glaciers. Despite the mud, Beau was thankful for the rain.

The fires that night were small and smoky from the moisture. At Beau's request, Rob had his wagon parked between the circled wagons and the two driven by the Hansons. Marauding Indians often targeted wagons that strayed from the others, or fell behind. Beau and Jocko sat under a fly tarp with drops of water running off the edge, discussing the trail to the ferry and on to Independence Rock.

Jocko estimated that they were two weeks from Independence Rock, allowing two days to cross the North Platte River at the Mormon ferry. That would put them at the rock almost a week after the 4th of July. Up until Fort Laramie, the wagon train had been well on track to reach the rock just before the 4th, but the weather, and Bull, had cost them days.

"We will be crossing the Sweetwater River about eight or nine times before we reach the Wind River range," Beau said.

"Most are easy crossings, except for a few in the middle, so not much time will be lost," Jocko replied.

"After we leave the Platte we have some dry stretches until we reach the Sweetwater," the mountain man said.

"Also some bad springs that can make man or beast sick," Jocko pointed out.

For a while the two men sat staring out into the gray drizzle falling onto the plain. Rob came under the tarp with a pot of soup made with greens and venison. "We'll be scratching for things to make a fire with if this damn rain don't stop."

Chuckling, Beau said, "A little water on buffalo chips and you got manure. Good for the garden, but not for cooking."

The next morning, they awoke to a gloomy day with low clouds, but it wasn't raining. The arid soil had absorbed the water and quickly dried. Most everyone ate a cold meal rather than trying to search out fuel dry enough to burn. Jocko left before the wagons were ready, hoping to find some game for tonight's cookpot.

Three hours into the day's travel the wagon train was stopped by a large herd of buffalo coming to the North Platte River for water. Jocko was cut off by the buffalo somewhere beyond the herd. Sean and Quinn Rogers walked to the front of the wagons and shot two of the buffalo. Several from the herd surrounded the downed wooly beasts, preventing the men from starting to butcher them.

It was just past midday when the wind direction changed and suddenly the buffalo became restless with their noses in the air snorting. Soon, several were running to the southwest, away from the river. Those with the wagon train had no idea what smell was brought in by the wind, but they were thankful as the trail ahead was again open.

The Rogers drove their wagons to the two buffalo they'd shot and began to skin them and cut out the best pieces. Much of the edible meat was left behind as the wagon train moved on. Four miles later they caught up with Jocko, who had a large buffalo cow skinned and cut up.

Beau rode up to his friend. "I sure hope we can find cooking fuel tonight. With your buffalo and the two that the Rogers shot, we got a hell of a lot of meat to deal with."

CHAPTER NINE

It was the 1st of July when the wagon train camped near the Red Buttes. The buttes were brightly colored in the early morning sun rising above the river basin. The folks in the wagons were up early preparing to get underway. It was another day's drive to get to the Mormon Ferry. Before the ferry, the mountain men and trappers had only horses or mules and they would swim them across at the Red Buttes.

Beau had the extra oxen, horses, mules, and milk cows remain at the Red Buttes crossing. He also had the wagons reduce their teams to four, so more animals could be waiting on the far side once the wagons were ferried across.

This stock would swim over at this crossing and then be driven down the north side of the river to the site of the ferries. Once all the wagons were across, the stock used to pull the wagons to the ferry crossing would be driven back to Red Butte to swim the North Platte River.

The ferries were built from two large canoes,

each with planks spanned across them, creating a platform for the wagons or gear. The ferries were pushed with poles and paddled during the transit. The price of the ferry crossing changed depending on the condition of the river and the demand. Right now, they were charging $2.50 per wagon.

Beau stayed with the wagons while Jocko led those bringing the stock across. Those going to the ferry looked back at the animals swimming the river as their wagons moved away from the Red Buttes. The men astride their horses shouted and yelled, encouraging the animals with lariats, and rods used by drovers of the oxen. The cold river water splashed and churned, soaking the animals and riders.

Jon's and Hanna's wagon was in the lead as they pulled up to the crossing. The Mormons were running two ferries. There were wagons from a wagon train ahead of them, waiting their turn to go across. The young Mormon men worked hard, rolling the wagons onto the rafts and then pushing and paddling them across. Men from the wagons would come back to help with the next to go.

Hanna smiled at Beau as he rode up to their wagon. "It's been two months since we left," she said. "Getting away from this river will feel good."

"We'll have some hills and dry country to cross on the other side," Beau replied, "But, I agree. It will be good to ride away from it."

"What time do you think we'll be crossing?" Jon asked.

"They'll be shutting down after the rest of the wagons ahead of us are across," the mountain man said. "We'll be the first ones in the morning."

There was a small trading post run by the

Mormons where folks could replace items they had depleted. Mrs. Burns would be replacing her water barrel here. The Mormons also had firewood for sale brought in from the hills to the north. It was priced reasonably and several of the wagons purchased enough to have a private fire to enjoy.

About a mile back on the trail, they had passed a shanty that had a crude sign with "Whiskey" written on it. Once the wagons were parked and the stock taken care of, several men rode back to purchase some while the women started the meal. Beau had sent one of the men with a couple of dollars to bring him some.

A short time after they had arrived at the ferry, Beau saw Jocko with their stock on the other side. The stocky friend rode to the river bank and held up two bottles. Evidently there was another shanty on the other side. The sun was low in the western sky as Beau took a seat on a nail keg and watched the ferries. He marveled at how much nicer riding the ferry was as opposed to floating the wagons across with the team struggling as they swam in front.

The slow-moving water was cold coming out of the foothills. The currents they'd seen a month ago were gone. Had the river water been higher, the ferry crossing would have cost more. A couple of men who had helped drive the stock down came back over on the last ferry to help get their wagons ready for tomorrow's crossing. Beau spoke with one of the Mormon boys about starting times and how they wanted the wagons staged.

With the two ferries running, the Mormons could take 40 to 50 wagons across each day working from dawn to dusk. Beau felt good about their timing. He had been warned that there could be a two-day backup at the ferry. They had reached the ferry with only a few wagons ahead of them. Then a young Mormon told him they would be first up for crossing in the morning. He also let Beau know that Jocko would be spending the night on the other side with some of the people who had helped him when he was injured.

Along with Jocko were Hoot's brothers Web and Slim, as well as Beck and Ludwig Graf, remaining on the other side to watch the stock. Beau and Rob made themselves fried side meat and hard bread for their supper. Hanna's and Jon's wagon was to the left of them. The Hansons and Helena Burns had been given permission to join the other wagons and were to the right of Rob's wagon. Beau had decided that enough time had lapsed, and if she or the children were going to get sick it would have already happened.

After the meal was over, Beau called a meeting to let the folks know what order they would be going across. Time would be needed on the other side to rest the stock and lubricate wheels, check harnesses, and fill the water barrels. The mountain man told them to have the stock and themselves well-watered, warning them about the alkaline ground that they would be crossing, with springs that would make them ill if they drank from them.

With the meeting over, everyone wandered back toward their wagons. Tilly Thompson walked beside Beau. "I have a dessert made with dried apples in the Dutch oven," she told the mountain man. "You and Rob are welcome to help us eat it this evening."

Smiling at her, he replied, "You won't have to ask me twice. I do need to check on the stock first."

Alvin Thompson was sitting near the fire,

smoking a short-stemmed pipe, when the two men came carrying their tin plates. Looking up, Alvin said, "We'll be serving after the coffee is done."

Tilly was kneeling near the fire, making the coffee. She had just moved the Dutch oven off the fire and took the cover off, filling the air with aromas of its sweet contents. It was a type of cobbler that bubbled through a flaky crust.

Alvin got up and reached into the back of the wagon. "I got a little something that will make the coffee as special as the cobbler," he told them. He was holding a bottle of brandy.

She looked up at him, pretending to frown. "Special?" Tilly questioned. "That will ruin a fine cobbler and the coffee served with it."

"We'll put the brandy in the second cup of coffee then," Alvin said, grinning at her.

Soon everyone was sitting with fresh coffee and a plate of dessert. Beau slowly ate his warm cobbler, savoring every bite. Tilly smiled, watching the men eat, and talked about riding the ferry across with their wagon.

After the dessert was done, Rob went back to the wagon to ready everything for going across on the ferry. Beau remained talking with Alvin and smoking a short cigar and enjoying a second cup of coffee.

Alvin took a sip of the brandy-laced coffee. "Not as good as the cobbler, but its not bad." He then turned to Beau. "How far have we gone since Missouri?"

Beau tasted his coffee before answering. It was good brandy. "We are just over 800 miles from Independence, Missouri. We have about 1,200 miles left to go."

The mountain man continued to answer questions about the trail ahead until he finished his coffee. Beau then excused himself and headed back to his camp.

Jon and Hanna were busy arranging things in their wagon when Beau got back to camp. He took a bottle of whiskey from his gear and walked over. Seeing him, Jon got his mug and held it out for a measure.

The two men sat near the fire, sipping the liquor and listening to the sounds of the camp. Hanna was in the wagon, making up the bed and humming a gospel tune. "She is looking forward to crossing tomorrow," Jon said.

"It marks the next leg of our trip," Beau replied. "Then come the mountains."

Looking at his boots, Jon noted, "I best get another pair of boots when we reach Fort Bridger. These and my extra pair will just about get me there."

"That will be a month of walking," Beau told him. "A lot of it is over rocky ground. One of the Mormons on the other side is a fair cobbler. You may want to have him resole one of the pairs."

Hanna came over after getting things ready. "You had better let the fire die out," she suggested. "We are the first wagon across and they'll be starting at first light."

"I hate to say you are right," the mountain man agreed. "The nights are short this time of the year, but I sure hate to bring this evening to an end."

Gulping the last of the whiskey from his mug, Beau went back to his camp. He looked at the bottle of whiskey and thought about taking another drink. Shaking his head, he mumbled, "You got lots to do tomorrow. You best save the bottle for another time."

As he lay down in his blankets, he thought about the men and their wives on the wagon train, how they did for each other and benefited by it. He hoped that he would meet such a woman when he settled in Oregon.

* * *

Those who overslept the next morning awoke to the shouts and sounds of wagons being loaded onto the rafts. Jon's and Hanna's wagon went onto the first ferry. Mrs. Stiles hung on to the rear wheel for dear life as the raft moved away from the landing. Hanna stood at the back of the wagon, smiling and waving at everyone. Her husband Jon was helping push the raft with one of the poles, his extra boots hanging around his neck by the laces.

The Wolsey wagon was being rolled onto the second raft. Sam Wolsey stayed behind to help drive the stock. All four wheels were secured with ropes and chocked with blocks of wood. The tongue was supported on a forked pole, keeping it out of the water and available to be grabbed on the far side to help roll the wagon off. Teams of oxen were waiting on the other side to pull the wagon to a camping area.

The remaining wagons were being positioned into two lines, awaiting the return of the raft. Each wagon with its supplies weighed a ton and a half. Six men would roll it onto the ferry after the oxen had been unhitched. The Williams wagon got a little extra help from their four children pushing for all they were worth at the back of the wagon.

Each transit back and forth across the river for

the ferry took from 30 to 45 minutes. With two ferries it would take about five hours to get all the wagons across. They would then have to drive the stock back and forth from the Red Butte crossing. If they pushed the extra stock, the 20-mile round trip could be completed by supper time. It would be an exhausting day, but the wagon train would be across the North Platte River and, after a day's rest, be ready to start the trek to the Sweetwater River.

It was just before midday when the last two wagons were rolled onto the ferries. There was a stack of yokes, ropes, and chain that still needed to be taken across. A collection was taken to have one of the ferries take the items and the extra men across. Jon had come back, wanting to help with driving the stock to the upper crossing. Including Beau and Jon, there would be five other men, Art Rogers, Quinn Rogers, Hoot Johnson, Sam Wolsey, and Alvin Thompson, to drive the oxen, mules, and a few extra horses. One of the men going back on the ferry had an open bottle and passed it around to the men driving the stock. The mood was quite festive.

Just before Aarno Hanson's wagon was rolled onto the ferry, he had told Beau that Kimi was going to be married to Helena by Otto as soon as they got to the other side. He had told the mountain man to make sure he got back with the stock in time for some cake the other ladies were going to bake.

Short courtships on the trail were not an unusual thing. The frontier had few women compared to men, so a woman didn't stay single long. Beau felt good about the two getting together. He had watched Kimi with her children and how the two of them had sat near their fire talking. Kimi had made her laugh again, and in turn she had made the two Hanson men's lives more comfortable with patched, clean clothing and good cooking.

Beau was riding Bull's bay, letting the sorrel join the rest of the unburdened animals. Jon was riding Peck Wilson's piebald. He was a skilled rider and looked natural on the black and white horse. The Rogers were riding mules, Sam had a buckskin, and the other two men had mustangs. The oxen looked up from grazing as the men surrounded them.

With the warm feeling from whiskey in his stomach, Beau took the drag. He sent Hoot to take the lead. The others were on the flanks. As planned, they pushed the animals at a pace much faster than when hooked to a wagon. The 20 miles up and down would normally take a day and a half with the wagon train. They intended to do it in eight hours, maybe ten. There was cake and more good whiskey to be had at the end of the drive.

A cloud of dust surrounded Beau as he pushed some of the stubborn oxen. Sam came back to help him. They had neckerchiefs covering their faces. A long wagon train came toward them, so Hoot turned the stock out onto the plain to give them room. There was a tiredness in the new people. They walked slow and stared at the ground. In a couple of hours, they'd be at the ferry and their spirits would pick up.

The brick red buttes rose in the distance. They had made good time, only to be disappointed by seeing the stock from the wagon train they'd passed being driven across the river. Beau would have to keep his stock back to prevent the two herds from mingling. Otherwise hours would be wasted trying to separate them on the other side.

The men dug into their saddle bags for jerky or biscuits to eat while they waited. Quinn pulled out a bottle of whiskey and Beau asked that he wait until they were done. "Just one drink, and I'll put it away," the man promised. Art Rogers and Hoot Johnson also took a quick drink, and then the bottle was put back into the saddle bag.

The mountain man was relieved to see the stock that had crossed the river were moved away quickly, allowing them to start across. On the other side a man had a team of horses hitched to a wagon. He had boxes next to the wagon with bottles of whiskey for sale. No doubt he was competing with the other shanty's and was trying to catch thirsty customers first.

The water was cold and over six-feet deep in the middle, so the animals would be swimming for a short time. The current would push them downstream a little but it was not as bad as during the spring thaw. Once their horses start swimming, the men would cling to the backs or slide off the horses, and hang on to the saddle horn. The trick would be getting back onto the horse once its hooves contacted the bottom again.

Sam took the lead with Jon and Alvin on the right flank of the animals. The Rogers took the left flank while Hoot and Beau were at the back, shouting encouragement and slapping the stragglers with their lariats. The plunging stock entering the river splashed the men. Suddenly, the bottom fell out and the animals were swimming.

Beau was at the left rear and Hoot to the right as they slid from their saddles, continuing to shout as best they could as choking water splashed over their faces. All of a sudden, Hoot was shouting and trying to get his horse to swim to the right. Beau pulled himself up to try and see over the heads of the oxen. Panic went through him. The cattle had drifted down surrounding the piebald. He could not see Jon!

The mountain man was helpless, clinging to the bay as Hoot and Alvin swung their ropes and yelled, trying to part the oxen so they could get to the piebald. Then the animals touched bottom, turning the water into a froth as they lunged forward to reach the other side. Beau was back in the saddle and spurring the horse through the water, desperately trying to get to the right side.

The piebald continued to the far side with the rest of the stock. Beau stopped the bay, searching the river for any sign of Jon. Hoot was further downstream with Alvin. Suddenly, his rope shot out, looping over something that looked like a log root. Snugging the noose, he pulled the object to the shallower water and reached down. It was Jon!

Pulling the man over the front of his saddle, he kicked the flanks of the horse as it headed for the shore. Beau reached the bank at the same time and jumped from the bay, almost falling as his feet slipped in his water-filled boots. Hoot handed Jon down to the mountain man and Beau gently lay him onto the ground. Jon's head rolled back and forth.

There was a severe bruise on the man's temple and Jon lay there with his head twisted in an unnatural position. Staring wide-eyed, Alvin said, "His neck is broken." Then, dropping to his knees, he held his hands over his face and repeated, "Oh my God. Oh my God."

The Rogers and Sam got the animals bunched together and then rode back to see how Jon was. "He's dead," Beau replied, unable to say anymore.

With a look of shock Art asked, "Dead?"

Hoot stood up. "He must have been bumped by one of the oxen and lost his grip. He went under water into the hooves of the swimming animals. His . . . his neck is broken."

Beau's mind was racing. It was hard to think, but he knew that he had to make some decisions. Looking up, he saw that the man with the wagon had come over. "I need to borrow your wagon."

Stepping back, the man said, "I got to have it to carry my goods."

Anger swept over Beau. "I am taking the wagon. This man's wife is at the ferry and I am bringing him to her. I don't give a good God damn about your stuff. My friend here is dead."

Complaining, the man said whimpering, "This whiskey is all I got and if I lose it and the wagon, I'll die out here myself. You can't just take a man's wagon."

Pointing at the bay, Beau told him, trying to control his anger, "That's my horse. I'll leave it here with you. I have a sorrel with the stock and that's yours also if your wagon or your horses are hurt."

As he spoke, Beau began to unload the rest of the whiskey boxes and the man's gear from the wagon. Both of the Rogers helped him, then Hoot and Alvin carried Jon's body to the wagon. The wagon owner stood back, watching.

As Beau climbed into the wagon seat, the man asked timidly, "Will you leave the sorrel here also?"

The mountain man looked at Hoot. "Cut the sorrel out for him. Then head this drive up and bring the stock to the ferry." He then said to the man,

"You'll have your wagon and team back by morning and I'll be expecting to find my horses here."

Beau brought the team to a gallop for the first few minutes and then slowed them to a trot. The wagon was bumping and bouncing on the rutted road. Jon's body rocked from side to side in the wagon box. The mountain man had one and only one thought. Bring him to Hanna as quickly as possible. An hour after leaving the crossing, he passed the stock that had crossed before them. The riders waved to Beau, but he was focused on driving the wagon and did not notice.

Several times the mountain man slowed the team to a walk for a breather. If he drove the horses too hard, they would collapse, leaving him stranded. Slowly, the full realization of Jon's death sunk in as he rode in the wagon. Tears began to run down his cheeks. He prayed for Jon and Hanna. He prayed for strength to get through what lay ahead. Beau was unaware of the wet clothing that chafed his skin.

About a mile from the ferry, Beau stopped the wagon. He wiped his nose with his sleeve, blinking the tears out of his eyes. Then, climbing into the back of the wagon, he did his best to arrange Jon's stiffening body, closing his unseeing eyes before getting back into the wagon seat. It had been two hours since he'd left the crossing. The team was lathered and Beau kept them to a walk for the last mile to let them cool down.

While he had been hurrying to let Hanna know, he dreaded the pain it would bring to her. As the horses walked, his heart was pounding. Beau had no idea of what he was going to say. He just prayed that he didn't choke up.

As the crossing came into view he could see the

Mormons busy bringing wagons across. Everyone was busy pushing and pulling wagons, hitching teams and calling to friends as they worked, or barking orders at the oxen.

He could see his wagon train just beyond the ferry. The wedding of Kimi and Helena had been held and everyone was gathered in the center of the wagons celebrating the union. Herb Tucker was playing fiddles with his brother and a few people were dancing. Most of the men had mugs that probably held measures of whiskey.

Beau felt like he was in Hell, trapped in the misery of what he was bringing to the wagons. He prayed that he would awake and it would have been a bad dream. But there was no waking from this dream. The ache of his body from the punishing drive, and pain in his heart, was all too real.

He stopped the wagon just outside the camp and stiffly climbed down. As if in a trance, he walked toward the celebration. Hanna saw him coming and broke into a smile. She walked toward him saying, "Back so soon. Goodness, you are a mess."

Then she saw his face. Concerned she asked, "What's wrong?" When he hesitated to speak her voice rose in fear, "What's wrong, Beau?"

"It's Jon," he said. "I'm sorry . . . I'm . . ."

She ran at him and grabbed his shirt, her voice getting shrill, "What happened?"

"He's dead, Hanna. I'm so sorry, he's dead . . ." his voice trailed off.

She began to wilt and he grabbed her to stop her from falling. "It happened crossing the river." The others had gathered around, listening in shock.

Suddenly, she looked up and pushed Beau

away. "Where is he?" she screamed. "Where is he?"

"In the wagon," he whispered. "I'm so sorry."

Hanna did not hear the apology as she pulled away and ran to the wagon. Beau turned and watched as she climbed up into the box. There was the sound of her dress ripping as it caught on the box. She gasped as she looked at the dust covered body of her husband. Throwing herself on him, she wailed in grief.

The mountain man stood fixed as her mother rushed by, followed by several other women who moments before had been celebrating a wedding. He became aware that someone was standing beside him. It was Jocko. "What happened, Beau?"

While Beau told his friend about the accident, Hanna leaned over her husband, her tears splashing on his face as she attempted to wipe the dust away with her dress. Mrs. Stiles had climbed into the wagon and knelt with her hands on her daughter's shoulders.

Otto and his sons had grabbed a shutter that was leaning against a small cabin that the Mormon men stayed in. They went to the wagon to get the body. It took a great deal of coaxing by her mother to get Hanna to move away from her husband so they could take him. While this was happening, all the others began to help.

Aarno and Kimi helped Edsel and Rob clear the long table that had been borrowed for the celebration and moved it next to the Scott's wagon. Web and Slim had a troop tent. With the help of Peck Wilson, they quickly started erecting it to put the table and body into. Jocko had gone to take care of the team Beau had driven in. The mountain man knew that he should be doing more but couldn't see where he could help.

As Otto's sons carried Jon on the shutter, Beau could see that flies had already begun to collect around his eyes, nose, and mouth. Otto walked beside the shutter and tried to shoo them away. Slim and Peck were still pounding in the guy lines for the tent when the table was put inside and Jon's body was placed onto it. Mrs. Stiles and the new bride, Helena, had supported Hanna as they'd followed the body to the tent.

Edsel Ward asked to have a moment with the body before others came in. Someone had brought Mrs. Stile's rocker over and Hanna was sitting in it, leaning forward with her head in her hands weeping. Beth and Cora knelt near her. Molly, Ava, and Mary waited with water and cloths for Mr. Ward to finish. They then went in to clean the body as best they could.

Beau was near the tent and as those who were helping finished they approached him with questions about the river crossing. When the ladies were finished in the tent, Hanna and her mother went inside. The sounds of her sobs tore at the very insides of the mountain man. Right now, he would have gladly traded places on that table to have prevented her pain.

Rob and Jocko finished with what they were doing and walked up to Beau. "You look like hell," the stocky man told his friend. "Let's go back to the wagon and get you cleaned up. There is nothing you can do here right now."

Unable to give a reason why he shouldn't go, Beau followed them to Robs' wagon. Rob placed a bucket of water onto the tail gate and the mountain man slowly began to wash the road dust off as he blinked the persistent tears from his eyes. Jocko got a fire going and put on some water for coffee while Rob got a curry brush and went to take care of the team that had pulled the wagon from the crossing.

The mountain man finally stripped down to nothing and put on clean, dry clothing. He was chafed raw in several places from driving the wagon in wet, woolen clothing. Tossing out the dirty wash water, he placed the bucket back onto the tailgate and went to join Jocko and Rob at the fire. They handed him a steaming cup and Beau sat down gingerly on a rock.

"I saw the dust of the stock about a mile away," Rob said.

"That would be for the wagons coming across now," Beau replied, his voice flat. "Our stock should be about an hour behind them." The coffee was hot but he tasted nothing.

"Jon's death was not your fault," Jocko told his friend.

"Whose was it, then?" Beau challenged him. "I put him on the downstream side of the oxen. I should have kept him with me at the back."

"So you could protect him?" his stocky friend asked.

"He wouldn't be dead now," the mountain man hissed.

"No, he wouldn't be," Jocko replied, "but more than likely one of the other men would be. Would that make you feel better?"

Beau wanted to snap back at his friend. Hell, he wanted to do more than that. He wanted to hit him for all he was worth for what he had asked. Fighting these urges, he asked, "Why would anyone have to die?"

"That," Jocko said, "you'll have to take up with the Lord."

Rob broke in to change the subject. "I assume we have to take the wagon back to the crossing."

Smiling for the first time as he thought of the man he'd taken it from, Beau replied, "We do have to take it back. There's a whiskey seller that has my sorrel and bay for trade if we don't get them back."

Jocko grinned, pleased to see the change in his friend. "A whiskey seller. Hell, he'll be long gone and selling your good horses before we can get back to him."

"Well, he'd have to leave most of his whiskey behind so we could pick it up and stay drunk all the way over the mountains," Beau replied.

Getting serious, Rob offered, "I'll take the wagon back and get your horses."

"No, I should go," the mountain man said, secretly wanting to get away from the misery that he'd brought to the camp.

"They need you here," Jocko said. "I'll grab my saddle and Rob and I will go get the horses. People will be paying their respects to Hanna and eventually they will be back to finishing the cake and having a drink or two. They're your people, you got to be with them."

With their coffee finished, Rob and Jocko went to return the wagon. Beau walked back toward the tent. Otto met him. "The Mormons had some coffins, so come morning we can bury Jon right."

"That's good," Beau said. Nodding, he repeated, "That's good."

"When do we leave?" the old man asked.

The mountain man hadn't even considered that point yet. His first thought was, a day or two, but then he realized it had to be sooner. "Tomorrow after the funeral," Beau replied. "Maybe you could give a sermon to help the folks and then as soon as the animals are hitched we can go."

Puffing up a little at the request, Otto said, "I'd be proud to do so. Maybe some hymns too."

Agreeing, Beau moved past him toward the tent. Several were in line to file past the body. They stepped back to allow the wagon train leader to go first. "No, please, you go ahead," he said.

Edsel motioned him over. "I looked Jon over pretty good. There were several broken bones. If he hadn't gotten the one that broke his neck, he'd have never been able to go on with us."

"At least he would have been alive," Beau replied.

"Maybe not for long." Edsel said. "I didn't cut him open to see, but one of the broken ribs might have punctured the lung. His spleen might have been damaged too and he would have ended up bleeding inside."

He was quiet for a moment, then added, "The broken neck may have been the most merciful thing for him."

Although Beau couldn't fully agree with Mr. Ward, he thanked him and went to get back in line. Blankets had been spread out for the wedding meal, and as the people left the tent they went over to eat a bit and discuss what had happened. Several of the men moved away from the ladies to have a drink while smoking or chewing tobacco.

Finally, it was Beau's turn to go into the tent. Hanna and her mother were seated on chairs someone had brought over. Jon's body was dust-free and protected by some cheese cloth to keep the flies off.

He was lying on a blanket and there was a small pillow under his head. The bruised side was away from the viewers. Beau noticed that he had the newly soled boots on. The ladies had done a good job. He looked at rest lying on the table.

Standing near the body, Beau bowed his head and prayed for Jon's soul and for his own forgiveness for letting the tragedy happen. This was not the first friend he'd lost, but it was the first time that he had to look at the pain on another's face. Even the pain he'd seen on Helena's face was not personal. He had felt something for her, but it wasn't the ache deep inside.

A soft voice said, "Beau." It was Mrs. Stiles.

Turning away from Jon, he looked at her. "Yes, what is it?"

"I have to leave for a minute," she said. "Can you stay with Hanna?"

For a second the mountain man looked at her, not quite expecting or comprehending what she had asked. "I have to go outside. Can you sit with Hanna while I'm gone?" she repeated.

"Of course," he said. "I'll stay with her."

The elderly lady went out of the tent and the mountain man took her chair, sitting more to the edge. Alone with her, Beau felt he had to explain. "I am sorry, Hanna. It is my fault this happened. I should have kept Jon at the back with me. I hope you will be able to forgive me someday."

"Forgive you?" He was surprised at how clear and gentle her voice was. "There is nothing to forgive. Jon was his own man, doing what was expected of him. He wouldn't have wanted you to hover over him trying to protect him."

For a while they sat in silence, Beau trying to

think of the right things to say. "I should have done more. I could have sent him back on the ferry."

"Do you think he would've gone?" she asked. "I ache inside, but I am proud of him. That pride will live on long after the pain has dulled."

Again, there was silence. Feeling uncomfortable, Beau began to look at the flap, waiting for her mother. "She had to go pee."

Turning back to Hanna he asked, "She had to what?"

"Go pee. We have been sitting here for the longest time and mother kept hoping Helena would come back so she could go out," the girl explained.

"Oh," was all Beau could say, feeling a bit embarrassed.

"We are going back to Fort Laramie," Hanna told him.

"You don't have to," the mountain man said. "Oregon was your dream and there are many on the wagon train that will help you. I can put you at the front and lead your oxen many of the days."

"It was Jon's dream and I wanted what he wanted," she said. "Mother never wanted to go west, but had to if she wanted to be with me."

Sitting next to her, Beau wanted to blurt out, *I want you to go so I can be with you,* but he sat realizing that tomorrow she would stay and he would go on to Oregon.

"You were a good friend to Jon and I," she said. "Even mother liked you. I will miss seeing you riding ahead on your horse leading us west."

You don't have to miss seeing me, he thought, but said, "You and Jon meant a lot to me . . ."

The flap being pulled back by her mother

interrupted Beau. She was carrying a lantern. He quickly stood up to give her back her chair. As she passed him, he caught the whiff of whiskey. No doubt to settle her nerves.

"The wagon train will be pulling out after the funeral tomorrow," Beau told them. "Again, you are welcome to come with us, but I understand you wanting to go back and be with David."

Stepping out, he saw the men having a drink. Striding toward them he thought, *I don't understand. I just don't.*

Aarno handed him a mug with a measure of whiskey and a cigar. "The first is to celebrate my son's wedding. Your next one will be in memory of our good friend, Jon."

Beau raised the mug, "Here, here!"

Otto came over carrying a mug. "The men came in with the stock. Beck and Ludwig went out to relieve them."

Looking back at the shadows cast by the lamp in the tent, Beau said, "They are going back to Fort Laramie."

"Helena told us," Otto replied. "After her brother gets out of the army, they'll probably go back east."

"Back east. Even farther," Beau murmured.

"What?" the old man asked.

"Nothing," the mountain man replied, "nothing at all. After a drink to Jon's memory, I have to go check on the stock."

"Most everyone is here," Otto said. "You might want to let them know what the plans are for tomorrow."

At the moment, the last thing Beau wanted was

to be the center of attention, but Otto was right. After swallowing the last of his whiskey, he took a deep drag on the cigar. *I may as well get it over with,* he thought.

The people on the wagon train seem pleased to hear they would be moving out sometime before midday. Once again, he reminded them to fill all barrels and water their stock before hitching them. Things would be dry until they reached the Sweetwater.

CHAPTER TEN

Several of the folks on the wagon train woke up with headaches the next morning. Jon was buried in a small Mormon graveyard and Otto gave a fine, uplifting sermon. Tears were shed by many as the coffin was lowered into the ground. Mrs. Stiles and her daughter stayed by the grave while two men filled it. The rest had left to water stock and ready the wagons.

Beau had wanted to stay with them longer, but there was much to do before pulling out. Jocko and Rob had gotten back with his horses after midnight and had a short night's sleep. By 10:30 the wagons were ready to roll.

Jocko led the wagon train from the ferry camp while Beau rode over to say goodbye to Hanna and her mother. "I hope when you see your brother, he changes your mind and convinces you to continue to Oregon," he told them. "I will be in the Willamette Valley and will welcome seeing you."

Hanna's eyes were red from crying at the funeral, but she managed a smile. "I would like to extend the same invitation should you return to Fort Laramie, having not found what you are looking for in Oregon," she told him.

For a moment, Beau caught his breath. Was she asking him to come back? Truth was, she was probably just being polite with the offer. Maybe it was guilt over the thoughts he had had last night before drifting off to sleep. Mrs. Stiles walked up to his horse and extended her hand. "I want to thank you for everything you did for my daughter and her husband. We will all long remember you."

Holding her gloved hand for a moment, Beau smiled down at her. "Meeting you folks has been my pleasure. When I get to Independence Rock, I'll carve your names for all to see as they pass."

Not trusting himself to get down from the sorrel, Beau removed his hat and nodded. "Hanna, Ruth, until we meet again." Turning the horse, he rode after the wagons, wishing he had said more.

* * *

The wagons rolled through loose sand, making the start tiring. After a couple of miles they started a gradual climb with hardpan. They began to see what looked like snow on the arid ground. Gusts of wind blew the alkali dust, which stung their eyes. As they climbed, they saw large bluffs and ravines, which were a refreshing change from the long trek along the unchanging North Platte River Basin.

By mid-afternoon they were traveling in an area that was void of any good forage for the animals. All around them was sage and greasewood. They entered a gap that was fairly level. The sides rose with jutting rocks.

Beau had traveled the area many times. He now rode paying little attention to the terrain, but rather thinking about Jon and Hanna, and her decision to go back to Fort Laramie. Beau had enjoyed the company of Jon and Hanna. He'd never thought beyond their friendship. Yet, already last night, he'd been thinking about her traveling to Oregon without Jon, and how he might be of help. With Jon's death, things had changed. Before she'd told him about going back to the fort, he had dared to think that a relationship between the two of them could have developed after a proper amount of time for grieving.

As he rode back and forth along the wagons, those walking would call to him with problems or pointing out some interesting landmark. It brought Beau's thoughts to the tasks at hand. Once through the gap they started down a rough, rock-strewn part of the trail. They passed a spring-fed pond that was avoided after noticing a white crust surrounding the edge. When the descent became steeper, some locked their back wheels to help control the speed. Those with working brakes had someone ride in the wagon pulling back on the handle.

At the bottom of the rocky slope there was a mineral pond, again with the crusting. The thirsty animals were led wide of it. Beau had warned the folks that even a small drink could make them or the animals violently sick.

Just beyond the slope the wagon train made dry camp. There was little grazing for the animals and they had to be carefully watched to prevent them from straying toward the glimmering pond.

After unhooking the oxen, the men swabbed

the oxen's nostrils with a damp cloth to remove the white alkaline dust from them. The use of water was kept to a minimum when making the evening meal. All the cooking liquid was saved and drank. Any water used for cleaning pots was to be given to the animals rather than being poured out. Everyone was cautioned about drinking whiskey. There was not enough water to quench the thirst of those who partook.

The mountain man needed to keep busy to prevent thinking about Hanna. He stayed with those watching the stock, making sure they didn't go near the mineral springs. The spiny greasewood had succulent leaves and some flowers. The cattle pulled at them for forage. Even with these, they were risking illness if the animals ate too much, but the amount of plants was not plentiful, therefore assuring that they couldn't be over-eaten.

With the stock bedded down a safe distance from the pond, Beau walked back toward the wagons, leading the sorrel. Jocko was boiling bland beans over a sage fire. "In another half-hour they'll be tender enough to eat," he promised.

Sitting on the ground next to his friend, the mountain man said, "I have a problem."

"We all do," the stocky man replied. "There ain't enough water in this hellhole."

"Mine ain't the water," Beau told his friend. "Guilt is what I am dealing with."

Jocko paused from stirring the beans. Sitting back, his head down, he gave his friend a sideward look. Tersely he said, "It ain't your fault that Jon died."

"It ain't about Jon dying, either," Beau replied. "It is how I felt about Hanna after he died. I once told you about a girl named Ana that I'd met in the Mexican

Territory. I think I was in love with her. She chose to follow her father south into Mexico and, being a gringo, I couldn't go. It hurt leaving her. Hell, I stayed drunk for a good, long time."

"I do know about love and being apart," Jocko said, thinking about Lisa. "I miss her but it don't hurt because I know I am going back to her."

"Well, think about if you couldn't go back," Beau told him. "Then you would feel the hurt."

All of a sudden, a look of concern crossed Jocko's face. "You didn't ask a newly grieving widow to marry you and come with you to Oregon?"

Smiling, the mountain man replied, "I did not. But while it ain't right with Hanna, I guess I feel the same about both of them."

"Well, it ain't lusting after another man's wife, so you aren't breaking any rules in the good book," Jocko said. "And it ain't wrong to admire a beautiful woman, and Jon's wife was all of that. Right now, I recommend you get your mind right and concentrate on getting these folks to Oregon. Soon, her grieving time will pass and if you got to drag your tail back east after her, then the time will be right."

Rob came back from taking his turn, watching the stock. "Those beans done yet? I was about to start chewing on greasewood flowers."

Beau was glad for the interruption. Talking about feelings wasn't something the mountain men and buffalo hunters tended to do. If it hadn't been for the guilt of having feelings for Jon's wife so soon, Beau would have taken the rest of it to the grave. Jocko was a common sense kind of man and his advice helped with the guilt, but did little for the feeling of loss from leaving Hanna behind.

The next morning, Beau made a check of the water barrels on each wagon, cautioning those he found had used more than necessary. They had a full day's travel to the next possible water at Willow Springs. Several wagon trains had left ahead of them and though there might be water, it was unlikely that they would find much grass for the stock. Clem Williams had a Mormon travel guide that called the springs an oasis with lush grass and groves of willow trees. A cold, clear spring ran through it, which would quench the thirst of all travelers and their stock.

The lowing of the thirsty oxen awoke the weary travelers before daylight. A simple meal was made over sage brush fires and eaten. The stale water from the Platte in their barrels was made palatable when brewed into coffee. Soap was not used to clean up, not wanting to make any of the water undrinkable. By daylight the wagon train was moving.

Beau took the lead, riding the bay. A great deal of effort was required by those driving the extra stock to prevent them from breaking for the mineral pond. In the past the trappers and mountain men had found this part of the trip to be easy. It consisted of one day's travel on horseback and then a comfortable stay at Willow Springs. With all the wagons that had gone before, he couldn't be sure of what he'd find.

The chill of the morning was gone and the sun beat down on the slow-moving wagon train. Most walked with neckerchiefs over their faces to protect them from the dust. They entered a valley with a hogsback on each side. The guide called it Rock Avenue. A row of rocks to one side was called the devil's backbone. The rough, gravel base was tough on the animal's hooves and tore at the soles of the people's shoes and boots.

For the past ten miles there had been scores of dead oxen next to the trail. The wagon trains couldn't take the time necessary to salvage any of the meat. The sun was getting low in the western sky when the wagon train finally reached Willow Springs. A year ago Beau had spent a week resting and enjoying the pleasant valley. He was shocked at what he found as the wagons pulled near.

Most of the willow trees were gone. The clear-running spring and stream had been churned to mud by the stock. There was little grass for the animals. This paradise had turned to a hell. The oxen pulled and bellowed as they smelled the wet mud ahead.

Beau shouted, "Keep the animals away from the spring!"

It was all the drovers could do to prevent a stampede. "Take buckets of water from the barrels, and rags to wet their mouths. Keep them hitched to the wagons," he ordered.

Riding down the line of wagons, he instructed them to get all the shovels they had and join him on the hill near the spring. Leaving his bay tied to Rob's wagon, Beau led the men, women, and children who could be spared from holding the oxen to the spring.

"We have to dig it out to get the water flowing," he told them. "Some of you work on clearing mud from the stream bed. The rest can dig at the spring."

For the next hour the people dug and sweated as they removed the sticky mud from the spring and stream. Slowly, water began to collect in the hole dug near the top of the hill. They continued to expand the depression. Soon the muddy water was knee-deep.

Those digging couldn't help but scoop handfuls to drink. Though muddy, it was not alkaline.

Suddenly, the water flowing into their depression began to increase. The clear, cold water quickly mixed with the dirty water. Finally, it spilled over the edge and flowed down the streambed. Beau sent those digging after buckets. "We'll give each animal a bucket of water before unhooking them from the wagons."

Beau knew it wouldn't be enough to quench their thirst, but it might prevent them from rushing the stream. Below, in the stream bed, they had fashioned a dam to collect water in another pool. Once filled they would lead the animals and allow them to drink again.

As the sun went down, the air quickly cooled, causing many of the sweat-covered people to shiver from the change. Beau filled a bucket and walked down to water the bay. As he watched the folks of the wagon train working together, he thought of the way they had reacted when he'd brought in Jon's body. With very little instruction, they all pitched in doing what needed to be done. They worked as one, a family, or maybe a village for the good of all. He felt a great deal of pride being with these people.

It was long after dark when all the animals were watered and the task of refilling the water barrels began. A large fire using sage brush and greasewood was started. Several Dutch ovens were used to make biscuits or corn bread. The caldron was filled with items shared from the various larders of the wagon owners to make a hearty stew.

The spring was now clear. Many people took the opportunity to bathe and wash clothes. Beau decided that they would spend another day at the spring before taking the next leg of the journey. Less than two miles away was Prospect Hill. The wagons would require double teaming to be pulled up the 400-foot, mile-long rise. While the mountain man dreaded the climb, the reward of what the folks would see at the top would help them forget the pain.

It was Sunday and the sun was up when Beau awoke. He had only gotten a few hours sleep, staying awake until the last folks had bedded down. A chilly morning breeze was coming from deeper inside the valley.

A shout from near the spring caught his attention. One of Sam Wolsey's oxen had wandered back to the spring overnight and had drank so much water that now it stood shaking, its stomach extended by the large quantity swallowed. Beau called to Sam, assuring him that the ox should be okay after the water had a chance to work its way through.

He took a walk along the grazed-off ground toward what used to be a grove of willows. The putrid smell of decaying meat carried on the breeze. Spread across the valley floor were the carcasses of dozens of oxen. Some had been partially butchered, most had not.

Stumps marked spots that only a year ago had been groves of willows. What had once been green, lush hills covered with grass had now been grazed to dirt. He saw a man camping near one of the remaining trees.

Noticing the mountain man, he called to Beau, "I got no water down here. My horses are down below, chewing on whatever they can find."

"We got the spring flowing again," the mountain man told him. "You are welcome to lead them up and water them."

"Give me a hand," the old-timer said. "Lets go fetch 'em. By the way, my name's Doolittle. Folks call me Doo."

As they walked to get the animals, the mountain man said, "I'm Beau Levesque. I heard about you at the rendezvous. You brung in some of the best beaver pelts."

"All you got to do is find the good ones, and then you catch 'em," Doo said. "I shore do miss the days of trapping and rendezvous."

"We all do," Beau said. "They were some good times."

Seeing the wagons as they led the animals toward the spring, the old-timer asked, "Your wagons going to California?"

"No. We're headed for Oregon," he said. "A farm will give you back what you put into it. A bank of gravel in a stream owes you nothing."

Looking around, Doo shook his head. "I was through here a month ago and it was green and most of the willows were still standing. The stream was flowing clear and sweet. Now look at it."

"It's a shame what a few hundred wagons in a month can do to a place."

"Once the gold runs out in California," Doo said, "the wagons will stop and then the spring and grass will come back. But I'm a feared the trees are gone for good."

Doo watered his horses in the lower part of the spring and filled his canteens in the upper part. Then he and Beau joined several others for leftover stew and biscuits from the night before. Clothes were hanging all over the wagons, drying. Some had strung ropes between their wagons to make more room for clothing. Despite the condition of the valley the mood was good. They had water.

The axles were pulled and lubricated. The stock was watered again, and repairs were made as needed. Beau brushed his horses and fed them the last of the grain he had gotten at Fort Laramie. One of the oxen was unable to get up due to an injury to one of its back legs. Jocko and Hoot killed and butchered it. Blackened skillets were pulled out and the meat was fried for both midday and supper. Some of the remaining meat was salted down to be used later. Doo left at noon, heading back east. He took the tongue and liver with him.

After supper, Beau and Jocko rode down the trail to Prospect Hill, planning for tomorrow's climb. They would use double teams, rotating them so each ox would only make two trips up the hill. When they rode back, they saw another wagon train a couple of miles away with thirsty animals, heading for the spring. Beau estimated that it had over 50 wagons. It would be an unstoppable wave.

"Let's get the wagons hitched and move to Prospect Hill," he called to the folks.

Several let their stock have one last drink from the stream before putting on the yokes. All the water barrels were filled with clean, clear water. The move would only be to the foot of the hill and would take less than an hour. As their wagons pulled out, men from the other wagon train were unhooking their oxen and hurrying them toward the water. With regret, Beau realized that the spring would be stomped to mud before dark.

The campsite below Prospect Hill was rocky,

arid, and unwelcoming. The stock could wander, chewing on the sparse grass or greasewood leaves. Some of them had bloody scratches on their noses from the thorns. Those watching them had to make sure that none wandered away, back toward the spring. Beau held a meeting before everyone turned in.

"The ridge going up the hill is only wide enough for one wagon in some spots," he informed them. "If a team can't continue pulling, all those below would be forced to stop. If the oxen tried to move to one side or the other, a tongue could snap, letting the wagon head back down the hill. I doubt dropping the log would help."

Peck Wilson spoke up. "Talk is that we will be using double teams to go up Prospect."

"That is correct, Peck," Beau replied. "The hill in front of you doesn't look that steep, but it is a mile-long pull. We'll double up with the team from another wagon in front of yours. We have enough teams so at least four wagons can be on the hill at one time."

Then he addressed the Rogers. "You'll have to rig your harnesses to pull with another team of mules. I would recommend leading them up the hill rather than driving them."

"What time do you want us to be ready?" Edsel asked.

"I would like to start before daylight. Maybe two hours before," the mountain man replied. "The stock will need a rest at the top and we can have breakfast then. Now, let's get some sleep."

The ridge ahead of them was covered with sage brush, some grass, and greasewood. Rocks were scattered across the ridge. Once at the top, there would be enough for the cattle to eat. The sandy soil of the hill was rutted by prior wagons, creating a swale, making travel even more difficult.

The wagons had been left in a line rather than trying to make a circle on the sage and rock-strewn area at the bottom of Prospect Hill. After a few hours of sleep, the folks on the wagon train were up and getting the teams hitched. Alvin Thompson's was the first wagon ready, so Beau sent it on its way. Alvin was leading the dozen oxen hitched to his wagon while his wife Tilly followed, ready to release the chocking log if the wagon was forced to stop.

They had 11 extra oxen that would be used for the pull up the hill, but those at the top still had to be driven back down because they did not have extra yokes. Just over a half -hour after the first wagon started, the fourth wagon followed up the hill. It was an exhausting and hard pull. A man walking by himself would find his legs fatigued before reaching the top.

Peck Wilson had some extra chain and assisted the Rogers with rigging their harnesses. The dozen mules in front of Quinn wagon were impressive. It reminded Beau of the freight wagon teams used to bring supplies to Fort Laramie. He was ready, and the fifth wagon started up the hill. His wife Molly sat on the wagon, holding the reins for the first six mules while Quinn led from the front. Beau smiled as Molly shouted at the mules to start and snapped the whip above them. She could match any muleskinner.

Helena's wagon wasn't rigged with a log at the back to drop as a wheel chock. Aarno went up sixth and was to bring the one from his wagon back down with the oxen. Jocko rode to the top with the first wagon to help with the unhitching and organizing the wagons at the top. Beau planned to stay down and help drive the extra stock up the hill after all the wagons reached the top.

As the Williams wagon went up the hill, Lucy and their son Charles led two cows. Once they reached the top the animals would have to be milked. Folks walking alongside the wagons would stop and rest, sitting as they watched the wagons slowly trudge by. It was late morning when the last wagon headed up the hill. Beau, Hoot, and Ludwig followed with the extra stock. The animals were trail broke and stayed within the ruts as they climbed Prospect Hill.

The promise of a view written up in the guide books did not disappoint. At the summit, the folks were able to see over 20 miles. The could see all the way to the Sweetwater River range. To the west there were mountain ranges, some still covered with snow. Beau pointed out Independence Rock visible on the horizon 25 miles away. It was definitely a grand prospect of what they would soon be traveling through.

While the oxen and mules were readied to for the day's travel, the women worked on breakfast. Pots of porridge cooked over the sage brush fire sent steam into the still, cool air. The milk from Mrs. Williams' cows was added to the breakfast cereal. Honey was mixed in to sweeten the porridge.

Once the wagons and teams were ready, everyone sat down to enjoy a hearty breakfast before starting out. Beau decided that the creamy, sweet porridge was more a dessert than a meal. As the people finished eating, they lay back where ever they were and rested. After giving everyone a half-hour, it was time to get started.

The wagon train would have one night without

water and then they would reach the Sweetwater River, near Independence Rock. Forage would help the stock's thirst tonight. Endless ruts stretched out in front of the wagon train, continuing out of sight as the ground slowly fell in front of them. Jocko had ridden out ahead of the wagons to do some hunting. Pronghorn and mule deer were plentiful on the plain this time of year. With luck he might even run across an elk, although they had mostly gone into the valleys and high meadows of the foot hills and mountains.

Beau continued to see the carcasses of oxen that didn't survive long after the pull up Prospect Hill. They had lost some oxen on the trail, but due to some luck and proper management of their burden, Beau had kept the losses to a minimum. Tomorrow they would pass Saleratus Lake, with its layers of white crust at it banks. This was useful as a leavening for baking.

Jocko was waiting for them at a good camping area with adequate forage for the stock. He had shot two pronghorn and was busy skinning them when the wagons pulled up. Traveling through the sandy soil had taken much out of the animals and the people. Everyone moved slowly as they unhitched the exhausted animals, standing with their heads hanging.

The pronghorn's sage-flavored meat was roasted over a fire on a spit put together by Peck. After the meal was finished, conversation quickly died as the people headed for their blankets. Beau sat up alone in the darkness. Tomorrow was the 10th of July. His wagon train would be at the halfway point. They were only a few days late and, barring early winter storms in the mountains, they would be fine.

CHAPTER ELEVEN

A cheer went up from the wagon train as they approached Independence Rock. There were several other trains already near the rock. The Sweetwater was a short distance away. After finding a suitable camping area, the stock was unhitched and driven down to the river for water. There was little wood in the area, and much of the sage and greasewood had been used in earlier fires.

A half-dozen wagons that had been scavenged for useable parts were scattered around the area. Some of the boards had been ripped off to use in fires. All had one or more wheels missing. Several people were climbing onto the rock with hammers, chisels, or short axes, chipping their names into the surface. Once done, many would fill the grooves with wheel tar to make them stand out.

With plenty of water available and the need to unwind, several men pulled out bottles of whiskey that evening. Tobacco was shared and some sat on a blanket playing cards. Kimi and Helena, followed by their children, headed for the 128-foot-high piece of granite to put their names into stone. Beau remembered the promise he'd made to Hanna. Come morning, he'd borrow a hammer and chisel from Peck and add their names.

Common lore was that Independence Rock was named because it was the date wagon trains had to reach it in order get safely over the Rocky Mountains before winter. Beau and many of the mountain men had heard other stories. Jedediah Smith was said to have stored his winter's catch near the large, domed rock on July 4, 1824, after finding the Sweetwater and Platte Rivers too rough. He had named it before heading out to Missouri to get pack animals. Others believed it was named by William Sublette in 1830 after his party had spent the 4th of July at the rock while carrying supplies to the rendezvous.

That night, the mountain man and Jocko joined in the festivities, drinking whiskey and telling stories. The children and several of the men gathered around Beau, listening about his life in the mountains. He talked of some of the grand ranges they would see as the wagon train traveled west. After several embellished tales of trapping in the mountains, Jocko took over with stories of buffalo hunting on the plains.

After midnight, Beau went to sleep, feeling no pain. His dreams were of Hanna and then became confused with Ana down in Mexico. When he awoke the next morning, his head pounded and his stomach was upset. Worst of all, he felt a loneliness from the dreams.

After several cups of coffee and only a bite or two of breakfast, Beau met with Peck and got the tools for engraving the names. Walking around to the back side of the rock, he climbed to the top. After sitting for a while to enjoy the view and catch his breath, he then scooted down the front side as far as he dared.

First, he carefully chiseled Hanna's name into the granite, running his fingers in the grooves after finishing each letter. He then frowned. He wasn't sure how Jon had spelt his name. Was it John or Jon? He chose the latter because it required less letters. This he cut into the stone, feeling pangs of loss as he thought of the two of them together. Remembering her mother in the promise, he quickly chiseled Ruth's name. Beau was sweating under the burning sun as he sat performing his task and was anxious to finish. He wanted to add his name near them, but felt it wouldn't be right. Years ago, he'd carved his own name in another area of the rock along with Ana's.

For two more days the wagon train rested at Independence Rock. The women were busy baking using the saleratus they'd collected at Saleratus Lake. It worked very much like baking soda. Each day Jocko rode out to hunt and brought back meat for the wagons. He'd taken young Charles with him and they'd brought down a small mule deer.

Several of the folks made the five-mile trek from Independence Rock to Devil's Gate and carved their names onto that stone also. They washed a few clothes, and swam, or bathed, in the Sweetwater River while the clothes were drying on low bushes. They caught sight of bighorn sheep climbing in the cliffs. Returning in the evening, they talked excitedly about the gorge the river had cut through the granite.

Jocko was sitting with the mountain man, skinning his day's kill. "Beau, you should tell them how the gorge came to be."

Several of the adults and children gathered around, asking for a story. Beau grinned, remembering when he'd first heard the story. "Back years ago, there was a beautiful valley and a clear pool of water near the cliffs. There was no cut in the granite to let the pool flow away. The Indians in the area wanted to graze their horses on its lush grass and pick the sweet berries that grew there."

"Why couldn't they?" Charles asked.

"Well," Beau continued, "the valley was the home of a great beast with large tusks. It was protective of the valley and wouldn't allow anyone in. One day the Indians decided to try and kill the beast. They snuck near the valley, hiding behind brush and boulders. As one, they notched arrows in their bows and fired them into the large beast."

"That should have killed it," one of the younger Williams girls said.

"No, Hazel, it didn't," Beau replied. "It just made the large beast angry. Again, they fired into the tough hide of the animal. Suddenly, it raised its large tusks, roaring in anger and it slashed at the granite wall, cutting a large gash in it, allowing the beast to escape. What remained is the gorge we see today."

"Is that true?" young Charles asked.

Smiling, the mountain man looked at the young man. "Probably not, but can you imagine how big the beast would have been to cut a gouge in the 300-foot rock?"

Everyone wandered away, taking some of the meat from Jocko's kill. They laughed and talked of the tusked beast. Beau had smelled the women's baking all afternoon and was soon enjoying venison steaks fried in a blackened skillet with fresh-raised biscuits on the side. With his hunger satisfied and still plenty of daylight left, Beau decided to wash his clothes that had gotten soiled crossing the North Platte River.

Walking down to the river, he scrubbed in homemade soap while rubbing his clothes on a large stone. Once rung out, he draped them over some bushes. While his clothes dried, he sat on the bank of the Sweetwater, fishing. He caught a couple of cutthroat trout and was looking forward to having them for tomorrow's breakfast.

Helena had come down and was nearby with her laundry. Beau figured that if he caught a few extra, he'd give them to her. "I want to thank you again for letting me come with the wagon train," she said as she rubbed the clothing on a washboard.

"You have thanked me enough. You and your family have been a good addition to the wagon train," he told her.

"Mr. Burns wasn't the father of my children," she told him. "I married him because he promised to take me away from St. Louis."

Half listening while thinking about catching another fish, he asked, "Did their father die in St. Louis?"

She scrubbed the shirt on the board, appearing to be thinking quite hard. After rinsing it and wringing out the water, she said, "I'm going to tell you something and I would appreciate if you kept it to yourself."

"You're not going to tell me that your wanted or something?" Beau asked, kidding her.

Helena laughed. "No. I'm not wanted. At least not by the law."

She had Beau's attention, he not having

expected that answer. "What is it that you want to tell me?"

"I can't tell you who their fathers are because I don't know," she said. "I worked in one of the houses down near the water. Being pretty, I was a favorite in the house, which wasn't an advantage. Twice I got pregnant and had two wonderful children. The man who ran the house said he'd met someone that would take care of them for me. I knew he'd never do anything that didn't make him some money."

Feeling uncomfortable, Beau interrupted, "You don't have to tell me this."

"Yes, I do," she insisted. She had finished washing and set the wet clothing aside. "I couldn't let him sell my children. I think he thought they got in the way of me working more hours. I couldn't just leave, because I owed him money. I'd fell behind when having the children. One night, Mr. Burns came in and I spent time with him. He said he was going to California. I asked if he'd like to take me with him. To my surprise he said yes. The day the wagon train was leaving, I snuck out with the children and left."

"I still don't think I needed to know this. Does Kimi know?" he asked.

"He does. When he asked me to marry him, I told him before saying yes." Tears filled her eyes. "He's a good man. Too good for me."

"When you come out west," Beau told her, "folks don't care what you did back in the east. You are judged by what they see you do out here."

"I tell you this because one of the men with the wagons had been in the house. I didn't stay with him, but I did have a drink at the same table as him," she explained. "He may not remember me, but if he did, I wanted you to know ahead of time."

"Do you want to tell me who he is?" Beau asked, not really wanting to know.

"Sean Rogers," she replied. "He has seen me around, but has never indicated that he remembered me."

Wanting to get back to catching fish, he said, "Then let's assume he hasn't recognized you and it should not be a problem. I will not be telling anyone else what you have told me."

Picking up her wet clothing, Helena thanked him and headed back to the wagons to hang them to dry. Beau looked at her walking away. He then blushed, thinking, *I can see why she was a favorite.*

That night, during rounds, Beau told the folks they'd be leaving the day after tomorrow. He wanted to be on the trail ahead of some of the bigger wagon trains. After a couple days of rest the stock would be ready, and along the Sweetwater River the grazing would be better. Beau arrived back at Rob's wagon to find Jocko sitting under the fly tarp and a pot of coffee over a small fire.

"Our boy is sleeping," Jocko told his friend. "Fill your mug. I got a bottle here to give it a bite if you want."

"I'll have the coffee, but I best stay away from the whiskey," Beau replied.

"I'm going to ride down toward the narrows in the morning and see how backed up the crossings are," the stocky man said.

"If we take the route around the narrows, we will be pulling wagons through a day of deep sand," Beau pointed out.

"There could be a couple days' backup in the

narrows," Jocko warned. "We would skip four of the Sweetwater crossings by going around."

Taking a sip of his coffee, Beau said, "Could be we'll kill some of our oxen in the sand, but we might get ahead of a couple of the wagon trains." Giving his mug a long stare, the mountain man said, "Pass me that bottle."

Jocko was gone by daylight, riding his gray. The Sweetwater River wound back and forth, requiring wagon trains taking that route to cross it nine times. The granite cliffs closed in at the second crossing, which had a narrow cut in the bank to enter the water. The river was about 100 feet wide. The animals were forced to swim in the middle. The third and fourth crossings required the wagons to travel along a narrow trail at the edge of the river, and were only a few miles apart. If a wagon had problems, all the rest were stuck until the troubled wagon was able to move again. The waiting wagons could easily stretch out a mile.

The stocky man found a backup of over a hundred wagons. Tying the gray to some low brush, he climbed to the top of the steep, granite cliff. To the east he could see Devil's Gate, which the Sweetwater River ran through. Along that part of the river, it was not passable with wagons, so they entered the river downstream after the gate.

Looking to the west along the narrows, Jocko saw countless wagons, with some standing in the chilly water of the river. Along the trail there were several dead oxen carcasses and some mules. One wagon owner was busy putting wooden blocks between his axles and the wagon box to raise it for the river crossing. The line of standing wagons could be seen down the narrows, disappearing around the bend, hidden by the granite gorge.

As Jocko climbed back down the cliff, a gust of wind from the west brought the smell of rotting carcasses. It reminded the stocky man of the smell that the buffalo hunter lived with on the plain. Riding out of the narrows, Jocko saw another wagon train coming toward the first crossing. He decided that he'd recommend Beau take the sandy bypass. Only four miles of the bypass had the deep sand, and after that the trail was firm but had no water. They should be able to get to the river again near the fifth crossing.

Taking advantage of the extra day before leaving, Peck had the men help him make blocks to raise the wagon boxes. They wouldn't be used on every crossing, but by having them ready, it would save time if the water was deeper. From the broken wagons that had been abandoned, Peck had the men pull the axles and broken tongues to make blocks. The blocks would be secured with a length of chain using bolts to draw them tight. After use they would then be saved in case of a need at later crossings.

Beau had seen the wagon train with over 40 wagons leave. He regretted taking the extra day for rest. Another group of wagons ahead of them in the narrows would just cause more delay. He waved when he saw Jocko trotting toward him. His stocky friend pulled up and swung down from the gray.

"We best stay away from the narrows and use the alternate route," he said.

"The heavy sand could kill some of our oxen," Beau cautioned him.

"Being in the back up in the narrows will kill more and add a couple days," Jocko explained. "Some of the wagons are packed so close that the horns of the lead ox are digging into the wagon ahead. Worse yet, nothing was moving when I was down there."

"We'll have to find ways to lighten the wagons," the mountain man said. "We'll be a day on the dry alternate route. The animals can be watered crossing the Sweetwater getting to the other route. We should reach the river again by dark."

Then he instructed Jocko, "Have everyone empty their water barrels, keeping only what they'll need for the day."

"The couple hundred pounds of water off each of the wagons will help," Jocko said, "but many still carry things they don't need on the trip. They can get rid of them here and maybe save an animal. If they wait, we know they'll have to get rid of them in the mountains."

The mountain man looked at the people busy near their wagons. "Most folks have items they're taking to Oregon to help remind them of the homes they left behind, or of family members that have passed," Beau observed. "It is time to let some of them go. I'll see what I can do."

The two men headed out to talk with the people. Beau couldn't fully appreciate what he was asking the emigrants to do. He had fled Arkansas with only the clothes on his back, his rifle and possible bag, and a poke sack with food and cooking items. He did have his father's felt hat and coat. The coat had been threadbare and was too small for him. This he'd given to Elijah Weber, the young slave running with him. The hat had been lost on the trail. What he'd been carrying had been needed to hunt, cook, keep warm, or cover his head. Even now he had little of value except the horses and weapons. These also had no ties. Well, maybe the sorrel. He'd gotten it from Ana's father.

By the time supper was finished, each of the wagons had been lightened by 300 - 400 pounds. Stacks of china, extra pots, a couple of hope chests, duplicate tools, a bed headboard, and other furniture, and many other items that would have made life more comfortable in Oregon, but wouldn't be needed for the trip.

Beau had also instructed each of the wagons to make up a 100-pound pack of food supplies or other things to be put onto the extra oxen and mules. By doing these things, the total weight carried by the wagons would be reduced by a quarter or more in some cases. This should help save a few animals. As Beau walked back to his camp he noticed Mrs. Williams putting some of her china into the pack for the ox. He had seen enough sad faces today and ignored what she was doing.

The mountain man led the wagons away from camp before the sun was up. As they headed for the Sweetwater, Beau looked back and could see the sun coming up behind Independence Rock. They had made their first goal. He caught sight of movement near the stacks of items left behind. Folks were scavenging for anything good in the piles. As they traveled over the mountains, Beau knew that his wagon train would pass many such discarded items. Folks were best off to turn their heads and pass them by.

Reaching the river, Jocko and Beau sat on their horses. The mountain man pointed to the west. "Once across the river we can use the Split Rock to guide us."

Nodding, his stocky friend replied, "It's about two days' travel. It'll keep us from wandering out of our way until we get back to the Sweetwater."

Split Rock was a notch in a distant mountain range that had the appearance of a gun sight cut into the top of the granite. The mountain rose almost 1,000 feet above the plain and was located on the north side of the Sweetwater River. It was in line with the river and the South Pass. By using it as their guide, it kept them going directly toward their objective, still a week's travel away.

They crossed the Sweetwater and were soon almost up to their wagon hubs in the loose sand. As the drovers led the oxen, others with them walked alongside the animals with rods slapping the animals, shouting to keep them pulling. The feet of the people walking were sinking ankle-deep into the sand and all were soon fatigued and aching as it felt like for every two steps forward, they slipped a step back. Beau was fearful to let the wagons stop for a rest. If they sank any deeper, the axles would be pushing sand and once stopped the sand set around the wheels, making starting again difficult.

Halfway through the stretch of sand, one of the oxen hitched next to the Thompson wagon collapsed without warning. Beau rode to the team and Alvin was kneeling near the ox. "The damn thing is dead," he said.

Swinging down from the sorrel, Beau helped him get the yoke off. He then looped his rope around its neck. Taking a few turns around his saddle horn, he had the horse pull the carcass away from the trail. Taking the rope off, he looked at the gaunt body of the ox. The animals weren't getting enough forage. Beau knew he would have to find an area for them to graze before facing the challenge of crossing the mountain.

He also hoped Fort Bridger or Fort Hall would have oxen that they would be willing to swap for the trail-worn animals, and charge just a few extra dollars for the fresh ones.

Another ox had been brought up to take the downed animal's place. Its pack was put onto Beau's bay. They lost three more oxen before leaving the sand. Travel became easier once out of the sand, but it would be another four miles to the Sweetwater. The mountain man had them keep the wagons at a slower pace. What would have normally taken two hours took almost four. Both the people and the oxen were exhausted by the time they arrived.

While they had probably saved two days taking the alternate route, it had taken an expensive toll of energy and stock. Each new obstacle was faced with animals that had less to give. Beau knew what they had to do. Near the Green River there was abundant grass and water. They would have to stay there a week to rest and gain strength.

Right now, they were at the fifth crossing. It would be 16 dry miles until they reached the next. Beau had everyone fill their barrels and put the packs back into their wagons. The wagons then moved to a spot Jocko had found to camp, everyone looking forward to a night of rest.

While Beau's wagon train was camped on high ground just beyond the fifth crossing, wagons that had gone through the narrows came out. The folk looked disheveled and disheartened. Some wagons had blocks under the box, others had broken boards or ripped covers. Several of the oxen had open wounds from being struck or gored. The mountain man spoke with one of the drovers and had to listen to the horrors of the trip through the narrows. They had left Independence Rock two days ago.

Feeling good knowing that they'd gained a day by taking the alternate route, Beau went to check on the wagons and their stock. They were down to seven extra oxen and two mules. Lucy and her son Charles were milking the cows. With the poor grazing and days with little water, the amount of milk was down. Mrs. Williams worried that the hard conditions would cause the cows to go dry.

Heading back to Rob's wagon, he found Jocko skinning two pronghorns. "Water might be a problem," he said, "but with all the pronghorn I can keep our folks in fresh meat."

Beau talked to Jocko about spending a week near the Green River to let the animals graze. His friend agreed that the area had good grass and their stock and the people needed a break. It would be two weeks before they reached the Green River, which put them at the end of July. They would be using the Lombard Ferry to cross, but would have to camp well north to find grass.

The next day, Beau rode in front of the wagon train. Jocko was ranging out, looking for signs of danger and hunting for fresh meat. Standing next to his horse, giving it a breather, he spotted a small herd of buffalo well to the south of the river. Several Lakota were riding toward the animals. Jocko watched as their horses suddenly broke into a gallop and they charged the buffalo with bows drawn or muskets to their shoulders. The buffalo broke and ran over a hill with one falling, mortally wounded, before it reached the crest. The braves continued after the animals, disappearing from sight. Jocko led his gray into a swale before mounting and riding to the west. The buffalo should keep the Lakota busy, but he didn't want to alert them by any shooting he did.

Beau led the wagons toward the sixth crossing of the Sweetwater River. After traveling through a soggy area on the south side of the river, he had the wagons stop on a grassy slope. Riding along the wagons, the mountain man instructed them to unhitch the oxen and let them graze, but leave the pairs in their yoke.

Clem Williams came over to Beau. "Is this it?" he asked. "Is this where the ice is?"

The man had read about the Ice Slough in the guide book. Beau pointed to the soggy area they'd driven through. "See all those spots where folks have been digging? Get you shovels, an ax, and a pail," the mountain man told him. "About a foot down you hit clear, sweet ice."

The others had listened to Beau and hurried to get tools to harvest some ice. Soon the mossy mass had eager diggers all across it. Alvin Thompson was the first to reach ice and as he chipped the first clear piece free, Tilly cheered as she picked it up and pressed the frozen shard to her lips.

Beau smiled as he watched the folks, happy as children reaching into a peppermint stick jar. Hoot came back with a bucket filled with ice. "Hey, Beau," he called. "Come over to my wagon."

The mountain man followed him. Hoot reached into his wagon and brought out two mugs and a bottle. Putting ice into the mugs, he poured the liquor over it. Handing the drink to Beau, they clicked the mugs together and took a sip of the ice-cold whiskey. It flowed down the mountain man's throat as smooth as silk.

"It sure as hell takes the bite out of the stuff," Beau replied.

"In the east, some folks put mint leaves and sugar in with the whiskey," Hoot said after taking a big drink. "It makes a fine combination."

The two men sipped the chilled whiskey as they watched the others filling their buckets with chips of ice. Young Charles helped his sisters and Helena's children chiseled pieces to suck on. Hazel complained that the ice hurt her teeth.

An hour later everyone was back at their wagons. All the water barrels had been topped off with the clear, sweet ice. Using a knife, Mary Ward shaved ice into mugs and poured a little maple syrup over it, making sweet treats for the children. Several of the adults lined up with their mugs and helped with the shaving of ice.

Kimi sat near his wagon drinking some ice-cold water. Beau squatted near him, watching the crowd around the shaved ice. "Too bad we couldn't have ice wherever we stopped. My pa and I used to cut ice off the lake in Wisconsin. We would pack it in wood chips or sawdust and it would last most of the summer."

Beau could picture the raw-boned man hefting blocks of ice and carrying them to the ice house. "Once we leave the Sweetwater," the mountain man told him, "we'll travel for miles over dry areas until we get to the Snake River."

"But today we have ice-cold water," Kimi said, raising his cup to Beau.

With the remaining ice in the barrels and a few chunks wrapped in peat moss, the teams were hitched to the wagons and they pulled away from the Ice

Slough with everyone smiling and invigorated at such a find. They traveled the next nine miles to the sixth crossing before they camped. Jocko was waiting for them.

Beau rode over to his friend and swung down from the sorrel. "No luck hunting today?" he asked, noticing that Jocko had no game near him.

"I could have shot a mule deer," he answered, "but I had just left some Lakota hunting buffalo. The shot could have been heard by them."

"Lakota," the mountain man said. "It was them that attacked the wagon near Fort Laramie."

"They were a ways off and might have been Arapahoe or Crow," Jocko said. "Whatever they were, they're hunting this area."

"We best stay alert," Beau said. "I'll call a meeting tonight." Then he smiled at his friend. "You might want to see Mrs. Ward. I think she had some ice wrapped in peat for you."

Grinning, Jocko said, "You stopped at the slough."

That night the mountain man put a little damper on the mood that had been generated by finding the ice. They became serious when he warned them about the Indians. "I want you all to keep your rifles loaded and close at hand. These Arapahoe, or whatever they might have been, were hunting for meat. But they wouldn't hesitate to go after a horse or mule."

The next morning the wagons pulled out with rifles cleaned and loaded, within easy reach. The extra stock was driven alongside the wagons, rather than behind. Many who normally walked rode on the wagons, giving them a higher point to watch for danger.

Two days later the wagon train reached the ninth crossing. The area leading to the river was marshy, with deep ruts cut into the mud. Peck had assisted raising all the wagon boxes using the blocks. The extra six inches would keep the river water just below the box, keeping the gear and supplies inside dry. Once again Beau had them use ropes stretched across the river to lead the swimming teams, with each wagon trailing another rope for the next wagon.

The last wagon crossed by midday. Normally the mountain man would have rested the animals after the crossing, but there were additional wagon trains close behind them and he wanted to get a head start for the South Pass. They would be climbing Rocky Ridge, which rose several hundred feet in two miles. The trail up the slope was littered with rocks. After the misery of climbing the ridge, they would have a less difficult, but continuous, climb for 10 additional miles to the South Pass.

There was a buzz of excitement as the folks talked of going over the Continental Divide near the South Pass. From then on, the rivers and streams would be flowing west or northwest, emptying into the Snake River, which would join the Columbia and eventually reach the Pacific Ocean. The only barrier between the wagon train and the Snake River was crossing the Green River, and that would be by ferry.

Beau had the wagon train push on to the crest of the South Pass before setting up camp. They were five days from the Green River. The mountain man had them bypass a stream flowing down from the southern slope. Previous wagon trains had grazed off the grass and left nothing but stubble and dust. He knew of another place that might offer better grazing for the oxen.

One thing in their favor was they had managed to gain distance from the closest wagons following them, but Beau also knew that by being alone they would have to worry more about being targeted by Indians looking for a quick hit.

The mountain man had both his and Bull's Hawkens, and kept them loaded. He slept with one under the edge of his blanket. He also kept the Colt loaded and under his saddle at night and in his belt when riding. During the rounds he made sure everyone was ready to defend the wagons should they be attacked.

The next morning, Beau was woken roughly. It was Alvin Thompson, who had been watching the animals. "We got Indians sitting a half-mile away!" he hissed.

Beau swung his legs out from under the blankets and grabbed his boots. "Wake everyone up and have them get ready in case of an attack," he said, "but nobody shoots unless I give the order."

The animals outside the wagon circle were between the Indians and the wagons. Beau moved to that end and stood by the oxen. Looking over the animals, he noticed the women and children with the braves. That was a good sign. They wouldn't attack and put their families at risk. He estimated that there were 40 to 50 in the group.

Then he saw one of the braves step out from the others. The brave held up a hand. Beau stepped out around the animals and held his hand up in reply. "Get back in," Otto whispered at him. "It could be a trick."

All of a sudden, a smile broke out on the

mountain man's face. He called out, "Is that you, Elijah?"

"How are you, Beau?" the brave called back.

Turning to the folks in the wagons, he said, "These are Flathead and the man is my friend, Elijah Horst."

The sound of rifles being put on half-cock echoed behind Beau. Several of the Flathead joined Elijah and walked toward the wagon train. Beau trotted out to meet him.

Eli was now a Flathead chief. He was dressed in buckskin britches and moccasins. He wore no shirt to cover his muscular upper body. His hair was shaved up the sides of his head and there were eagle feathers and beads braided into his hair at the back. Others on his council, along with his family, approached the mountain man. His wife Saka'am, with two young girls, walked just behind him. Hides were then spread out on the grass and everyone sat down to visit.

"I have been receiving reports on your progress for the past week," Eli told him. "I wanted to thank you for the meat you brought us last winter."

"We have shared for years, my friend," Beau replied. "I was honored to bring you the meat."

"We are heading out onto the plains to hunt for buffalo," Eli said. "We could use lead and powder."

"I can help you with that," the mountain man told his friend. "Are there any dangers on the trails through the mountains that you can warn us about?"

"The Bannocks and Shoshone have been attacking along the Snake River," Eli warned him "You will need to sleep light until you get to Oregon."

Not seeing a rifle with Eli, Beau asked, "Do

you still have the flintlock Hawken?"

"I got it, but I need a man like we used to work for to fix it," Elijah replied.

"Your talking about Peter Bauer," the mountain man said.

"Yes, I am," Eli replied. "He had the tools to fix most anything that shoots."

"Let's go talk to Peck Wilson," Beau suggested.

He and Elijah went over to see the resident smithy. Peck was skeptical when Beau asked him about fixing the Flathead chief's rifle. Taking the mountain man aside, he asked, "We gonna be fixing it so he can shoot emigrants?"

"I can assure you that Eli here won't be sighting in on any folks with wagons unless they shoot at him first," Beau promised. "He needs it fixed to hunt buffalo."

"Well, bring it over," Peck said, "but don't tell anyone who I'm fixing it for."

Leaving Peck, Beau and Eli walked around the circled wagons so the mountain man could introduce him. The fact that he was black did not go without notice. While everyone was polite, several did not come forward to speak with Elijah.

Suddenly, there were excited voices from the braves outside of the wagons. Beau and Elijah hurried back to find out was the commotion was about. A large elk was moving across the slope just over a quarter-mile away. One of the braves held up his bow and spoke to Eli. He was going to go after the elk.

Beau leaned toward the chief. "Ask him to wait. I'll get Jocko and his Hawken."

While Eli spoke to his braves, Beau went to find Jocko. His stocky friend was brushing the gray.

"We got an elk down the slope a way," the mountain man said. "I think you could bring it down with your rifle."

Reaching for his Hawken, Jocko replied, "That depends on what a way means."

The walked outside of the wagons and looked down the slope. The elk was walking away from them. "I might be able to hit it in the butt, but I doubt it would be a killing shot at this distance," his friend said.

"You just get yourself ready," Beau replied.

Jocko cocked the Hawken and checked the percussion cap. He then raised the rifle and pulled the set trigger. "Now what?" he asked.

Putting his fingers to his lips, Beau let out a piercing whistle. The elk jumped a couple steps and then turned broadside to see what made the sound. The Hawken beside him fired, sending a lethal ball at the animal. With the shot echoing off the cliffs on each side of the pass, the elk stumbled for a moment and then began to run full speed down the slope.

"You hit it . . ." Beau said, but before he could finish his sentence, the elk collapsed, sliding in the grass. Smiling, the mountain man added, "Nice shot. You killed it."

Eli said something to his braves and they ran for their horses and were soon galloping toward the downed elk. "They will bring it back here for the women to cut up. We will feast on the meat."

"If it is okay," Beau said, "I'd like my friend Jocko to cut some parts for those in the wagon train that may not want to join us out here."

"I understand," Eli said. "The people you are with and my people come from different places. If they were all mountain men as you are, we would all eat at the same fire."

Beau had Jocko cut meat for the wagon train, taking care to leave the hide intact. The Flatheads would want to scrape and tan it. While he was working, several of the braves came over and touched Jocko on the shoulder. Feeling a bit uncomfortable, Jocko whispered, "Why are they doing that?"

"You should be proud that they touch you," the mountain man said. "That was a great shot, showing you have strong medicine. They touch you to take some for their buffalo hunt."

Elijah had sent one of the braves to get his rifle from the camp beyond the north ridge. Beau brought it to Peck to look over. He then went to Rob's wagon and put gunpowder and some lead into a box. Beau also put in a couple of skinning knives and glass beads, before placing a bag of corn meal on top of it. The box was brought to the hides that Eli and the braves were sitting on. Beau saw that what remained of the elk had been packed onto their horses for transport to their camp.

"You will join us at out teepees?" Eli asked Beau.

"I will," the mountain man said. "If any of my people want to eat with you, are they welcome?"

"They are," the Flathead chief replied. "We are north below the ridge. We will share meat when the sun gets low."

Eli and his family left with the rest of the braves. Returning to the wagons, Beau found the place concerned about having the Flathead camping so close. Otto and several of the men confronted him.

"We'll have to have extra men on watch tonight," the old man said.

"Jocko shot the elk," Quinn Rogers said. "Why did we give most of the meat to them?"

Frustrated by the statements, Beau was careful with his reply. These men and women had learned about the Plains Indians in newspaper headlines and dime novels. They saw all braves as butchers and rapists of emigrant families. The truth was that most braves were more interested in stealing horses. On occasion they would kidnap women and children from their enemies. These women became their wives and the children were raised as their own, being protected by the tribe.

Beau decide to tell them the benefits of being friends with the Flathead. "As long as we are in the territory controlled by the Flathead we are safe from attack. We have shared our meat and gained their respect. I have been invited to eat with them tonight. They will make medicine to help make their hunt for buffalo a success."

"How far does this territory cover?" Edsel asked.

"From here to the Snake River, which is beyond Fort Hall," Beau said. "Then we will face the Snake River tribes, which are Bannock and Shoshone. My friend Eli warned me about them."

"So, their friendship guarantees we will not be attacked before the Snake River?" Otto asked.

"There are no guarantees," Beau replied, "but we will be known as a friend of the Flathead. There will always be renegades that can not be controlled, but they will be far fewer than the number of friendly Indians we will pass on this trail."

The men seemed satisfied with his explanation. Then the mountain man made an offer. "I will be eating with the Flathead tonight. Any of you that might like to see how they live are invited to join me."

That night Beau showed up with the repaired rifle in his scabbard. Jocko, Hoot Johnson and Edsel Ward came with him. Jocko had been to ceremonial meals before when buffalo hunting, while Hoot and Edsel came more out of curiosity. They were greeted by several barking dogs. Their horses were taken away by young braves, the rifle still in Beau's scabbard. A large fire was burning in the middle of a dozen teepees. There was a stream running behind the camp.

Speaking quietly, Hoot asked Edsel, "I hear they like horse meat. Do you think we'll see ours again?"

Smiling, Beau assured the two men that their horses would be returned safely. Eli met them and motioned the men to sit near him at the fire. The mountain man sat next to the Flathead chief. One of the braves was telling a story of a past buffalo hunt using broad gestures that made it possible for everyone to understand, even if they did not speak the language.

"Will you be spending some time at this camp?" Eli asked.

"Just one night," Beau replied. "Tomorrow we will travel to Pacific Springs."

The springs were a swampy area a day's travel away and 300 feet below the crest of the South Pass. It had been a favorite stop for trappers and earlier travelers, with good water and grazing. It was touted as the first place you could drink water that was flowing to the Pacific Ocean.

Elijah shook his head, "The spring has been grazed clean of grass with too many wagons camping in the area. It stinks of dead oxen that lie everywhere.

I would recommend you continue on to the Dry Sandy River."

"Much of the Sandy will be dry this time of year," Beau replied.

The Flathead chief drew a map in the dirt. Indicating a point on the sketch, he said, "You will find water here. It is three days by wagon."

The location would bring them a little north of the most direct route to the Green River, but because of the need for water and grazing for the stock it made sense. The men continued to talk while the meal was cooked over the fire.

A large pot with elk meat was boiling. The men could see racks with strips of additional meat drying for future use. The women came from within the teepees with wooden bowls and began to fill them from the pot. Saka'am handed them to their guests before giving one to her husband.

Eli nodded to his guests and said, "Enjoy." He then dipped his fingers into the broth, pulling out a piece of meat.

There was the organ meat of the elk, along with strips from the ribs and shoulders. It also included greens and wild onions picked in the area. A thin layer of fat from the elk floated on top of the broth. Jocko and Beau eagerly began to eat, while Hoot and Edsel poked around the contents a bit before taking their first bite.

While being a bit bland, the meat was tender and juicy. Each of the men had been given a piece of cloth to wipe their hands and faces when they finished. When offered Hoot accepted a second bowl full. With everyone's bellies full, and darkness surrounding the camp, a hunting ceremony began.

Out of the night came a brave shrouded in a buffalo skin and a head dress adorned with horns. There was the beating of drums and chanting around the fire. The brave dressed as a buffalo made aggressive moves indicating that it was an animal to be feared. Several other braves slowly surrounded it, carrying spears. They threatened with the spears and dodged their prey as the brave playing the beast attempted to gore them. The chanting and the drums became more intense and suddenly one of the spear-carrying braves leaped forward, pretending to run his point through the buffalo. Then all was quiet while the brave playing the animal staggered and fell, followed by earsplitting cries and chortles from the Flathead.

Not being prepared for the victory cheers, Hoot and Edsel became somewhat unnerved as they involuntarily flinched. Laughing, Beau slapped Edsel on the shoulder, "They are loud so the great spirit will hear them and give them strong medicine for the hunt."

Before the men left, Eli passed around a pipe of peace. Each smoked it, along with the rest of the council. "We thank you for inviting us to share your food," Beau told the Flathead chief.

"I have told my people of your hunting skill, about the time you and I killed the silver tip on the Wind River Range," Eli said. "You and your friend will bring strong medicine to our hunt."

As the four men received their horses from the young braves, Beau saw leather bags hanging from the saddle horns. They were filled with pemmican. He also noticed that the rifle was gone from the scabbard. Swinging up onto the sorrel, Beau waved to his friend, who had once been a slave, and was now a Flathead chief and true mountain man.

They rode in silence until about halfway to the wagons. Then Edsel asked, "The cries at the end. Is that what it sounds like when they're attacking?"

"If you're lucky, you'll have a warning like that," Jocko replied. "Most often they slip up without a sound and lift your hair before you have a chance to move."

"Well, hell," Edsel replied, "that sure doesn't make me feel any better."

Suddenly, Hoot asked, "Didn't you bring your rifle to their camp?"

"No, I didn't," Beau replied. "I did not bring my rifle."

CHAPTER TWELVE

It was the beginning of August when the wagon train reached the Green River. Beau had them set up their camp about 10 miles north of the Lombard Ferry. Good water and grazing were available for the stock. Game was plentiful and fuel for their fires was abundant. The Green River ran deep, with a fast current making this area unattractive for a ferry or fording. Those guiding other wagon trains knew this and kept further south.

The area was perfect for building up the strength of the stock and making repairs for the next leg of the trail. The men spent time hunting and then everyone pitched in to make jerky. The pemmican given by the Flatheads would be saved and used when going over the mountains. For two days Beau hunted and explored the area. He had camped here three years ago and found little had changed. Two miles further north, the river made a sharp bend and flowed into boulder-strewn rapids, with the water cascading down the steep gradient.

The fishing had been good years ago at the end of the rapids and he found it still to be rewarding. The mountain man rode back to the wagons with a stringer of fish that would feed several people. Keeping three plump cutthroat trout for himself, Jocko and Rob, the mountain man got the blackened frying pan out and sliced some side meat into it for the grease. Jocko came back from helping Clem Williams change an axle on his wagon.

"I heard folks talking about the great fishman," Jocko said, with a look of anticipation on his face.

"These will be ready in a couple minutes," Beau told him. "Do you know where Rob is?"

"I saw him talking to the Rogers," the stocky friend replied, tossing down his tools. "I'll go let him know it's time to eat."

While the fish sputtered in the pan, Beau added grounds to the coffee pot. By the time Jocko and Rob returned, there was a meal fit for a king set out on the tin plates. Using his skinning knife to separate the sweet, flaky flesh from the bones, the mountain man ate the fish, a smile breaking out on his bearded face. All too soon, the men were searching for the last remaining bits of meat on the plates.

Setting his aside, Beau wiped his mouth with the back of his shirt sleeve. "I'll ride down to the Lombard ferry tomorrow and check things out."

"Want me to come along?" Jocko asked.

"Why don't you see if you can knock down something big for making jerky?" Beau suggested. "After tomorrow we won't have enough days left to dry the meat."

As the sun set that night, the ladies sat near a fire and worked on their darning and patching. They began to sing some gospel songs. The mountain man sat under the fly tarp hanging from Rob's wagon and listened while cleaning his Hawken and Colt. It brought him back to the days on Crowley Ridge in Arkansas when he'd hear the music coming up from the workers on the plantation.

With the fires dying down and the stars bright in the night sky, Beau crawled under his blankets with the cleaned and oiled Hawken next to him. The stress of the constant travel was slowly leaving his body and he was sleeping more soundly. A smiling woman's face often appeared in his dreams, but he could never be sure who it was. While he felt he knew her, the elusive woman could be Ana, Hanna, or even Ellie.

* * *

The sun was just coming up as Beau rode away from the wagons, chewing on a cold biscuit. He was looking forward to the hour ride to the Lombard Ferry. He had saved his horse the task of swimming the Green River more than once in the past by using the ferry. Once across the river the wagons would have just under a week's travel to Fort Bridger.

Beau was still several miles from the ferry when he started passing abandoned camping areas near the river with the grass grazed off. The place he'd chosen would add a day's travel to the ferry, but the benefits of well-fed stock and rested folks would make up for the day. He rode to a rise to get his first look at the Lombard Ferry.

He let out an audible "Good God." There were easily two hundred wagons backed up at the crossing. They would be waiting at least five days. And that was without figuring any more wagon trains that might arrive before his wagons got there. The area had been denuded of trees and brush to use for cook fires. There was a large, brown area extending a half-mile that had been grazed off.

Riding down closer to the ferry crossing, Beau swung down near four men sitting on a blanket playing poker. "How long before you cross?" he asked.

A man with a broad, flat-featured face looked up from his hand. "We are about two days out," he replied. "Maybe more if the bastards keep getting drunk. By yesterday afternoon they were too damn drunk to hardly work the ferry. Some folks took over to keep them moving and still had to pay the damn $20."

"Isn't that kind of high at $20?" Beau asked. "Last time I crossed it was well under $10."

One of the other card players pointed to a cluster of wagons well back from the others. "You see them folks over there? They're holding out for lower prices and have been waiting a week. If there's a break in the wagons waiting, they might get a better price, but the damn gold in California won't wait."

Disheartened, Beau rode away from the ferry. He had heard rumors about the Mormons building some additional ferries to cross the river, but the fact that everyone was backed up at Lombard gave him little hope that they had got them up and running. As he reached his wagons, Beau continued by riding to the north. The bad news he was carrying could wait. It wouldn't be any worse later tonight and the folks could have another day enjoying life along the river.

Shaking his head and looking at the water, he mumbled, "The damn river that stands between

Oregon and us."

He intended to do some more fishing below the rapids, hoping that the quiet time spent near the water would relieve some of the frustration he was feeling. He was passing the sharp bend when nature called. Swinging down from the bay, he tied it to the brush near the river and stood staring across the water, relieving himself.

He felt a flash go through his body. He was staring at a tall growth of pine growing on a hillside just across the river. "We'll build our own damn rafts." Then he shouted, "We will build our own damn rafts to get across!"

With his heart pounding, Beau was back on the bay and galloped back to the wagons. Several of the men grabbed their rifles as they saw him riding toward them. "You being chased?" Otto shouted.

Pulling the bay up, Beau swung down. "I am not being chased, but we got some work to do."

"Ain't that what we've been doing here?" Hoot asked.

Seeing Jocko walking toward him, the mountain man called to him, "Gather everyone together. We need to have a meeting."

Within fifteen minutes everyone had gathered around. Being just above medium height, Beau wished he was taller or had a stump to stand on to address the folks. "I rode down to the ferry today and got some bad news," he started. "Things are backed up and the prices have doubled."

Seeing the enthusiasm on the leader's face, Edsel asked, "And this is why you came galloping in all excited?"

"No. No, it's not," Beau replied, shaking his

head. "But I got a solution for us. There is a slow-flowing area near the bend just north of us, with a nice stand of pine on the other side. I propose that we build our own ferry. We would be saving over $300 and who knows how many days sitting and waiting our turn."

"I seen that slow-moving bend," Alvin said, "and there is an awfully fast-moving rapid right beyond it."

Feeling good about his idea and almost giddy, Beau replied, "I recommend we don't let the raft go around the bend then."

There was grumbling in the group of people. Doing his best to get serious, the mountain man said, "As your leader, it is my responsibility to watch out for your safety. Sometimes it is beyond our control, but this would not be."

After a bit more discussion, most of the people followed Beau up the river to see the spot he was talking about. As they stood on the bank above the bend, the idea began to take hold with several of the other folks.

"The bank would have to be cut down on both sides," Otto noted.

"The logs would have to be floated across to build a raft," Peck said.

"We would build the raft on the other side," Beau told them. "I have swum a horse across this river many times. After moving our camp near here, we would swim some oxen across to skid logs. Six men, including myself, would go across and build the raft. In the meantime, a landing could be built on this side to load wagons."

The same excitement that had grabbed Beau began to grow in the crowd as they realized the possibility of creating their own crossing. Quickly, the decision was made and everyone headed back to move the wagons. Beau stayed behind and swam the bay across the river. Even the slow current took him and his horse downstream forty feet. He reached the other side just before being caught in the fast-moving rapids.

The hills on the other side didn't leave much room for the wagons once they crossed. A mile south, they moved away from the river and it offered a place to camp. Several large trees would have to be removed to make a trail and some washouts would have to be filled. Road building was not something new to folks traveling west, so it did not worry Beau.

Satisfied with his findings on the west side of the river, he rode along the bank and looked for the best area to bring the wagons out. At last he found an area that wouldn't require much work. He was now in a bit faster-moving water that hadn't reached the bend. By tying ropes to the raft, they could control its drift.

By the time he swam the bay back across, the wagons were coming alongside the river. His intention was to start the project in the morning, but he'd done such a good job of motivating everyone with the wagons that they wanted to start today. There was still several hours of daylight. The men and oxen could cross to the other side and maybe they could fell some trees before dark.

Beck and Ludwig had worked in the woods and were the first selected for the other side. Men from two wagons who stayed mostly to themselves stepped forward. Herb Tucker let Beau know that he and Tano Edwards had lumber jacked in upper Michigan. Sean Rogers was also chosen to go across, and with Beau that made six to cut logs and build the raft.

Packs containing tools, a tent, blankets and ground cloths, a fly tarp, chain and rope, food and what was needed to make meals, were prepared and put on the backs of four oxen that would be taken across. Beau would swim his sorrel across and the others would bring mules or their horses.

Ropes were towed across so the ox yokes could be floated over and later logs needed to build the east landing could be pulled back. With everything ready, the workers going to the far side entered the water with the stock and swam for the other side. They landed well before the rapids. While Sean and Beck set up camp, the other four took their axes and headed for the stand of pine.

Beau wanted to build a twenty-foot-long raft with a width of at least twelve feet. Beck and Ludwig had worked in the logging camps that squared the logs and built rafts to float them down the rivers. For the rest of the daylight hours there was the sound of axes ringing as they bit into the pine trees, followed by the crashing as they were felled. After several trees were down, Beau and Tano continued to select and fell them while Ludwig and Herb bucked them to length.

With the camp set up, Sean and Beck came up with pairs of oxen and started skidding the logs to the river bank. Being ahead felling trees, Tano came down and worked on the landing area clearing the brush and cutting down the bank with a shovel. Fortunately, little would be required in bank preparation on the west side. The raft would be built there, half in and half out of the water.

Beau was working with his shirt off, swinging the sharp axe into the wood. Again, his mind went back to Crowley Ridge when he was working a contract off, clearing land. With sweat glistening on his well-muscled body, Beau stopped for a moment to take a drink from his canteen. Across the river he saw men and women with shovels digging into the river bank, readying it for the logs that would be floated across to build the landing.

Sean had a pot of beans waiting when the work stopped at dark. In a blackened skillet he had fried venison and next to the fire a pot of coffee. The hard work felt good to Beau. He had donned his shirt as the evening air cooled. The men sat around the fire, eating in silence after the hours of hard work. Ludwig had a broad axe near him for sharpening. The logs would be squared only enough to fit together and allow rolling of the wagons on. They would then be notched for the connecting log used to hold the others together.

An auger would be used as a final step to bore holes through the connecting and outside logs to drive pegs to add strength to the raft when being towed in the current. The frame would be built first and lashed together using a clove hitch to start on the connecting log, then crisscrossing the rope over the logs to secure them to the connecting log with an overhand knot. Once the frame was finished, the center logs would be lashed to the connecting log.

There was a cheery fire across the river in the middle of the wagons and the tired men on the west side could hear the excited voices drift across. Beau smiled and thought, *It sure as hell beats waiting at Lombard Ferry for their turn.*

In three days the raft was complete and rough landings built on both sides. The winter ice and spring thaw would wash away any evidence of their work, but it would provide well for their needs. A tree on each bank was kept for a snugging post to let out the rope as the raft was pulled across. Oxen would be used to pull it over. Men with poles would ride on the raft, helping guide it and, in the event that a rope broke, to prevent it from going over the rapids.

Beau, Sean, and Tano rode the raft to the east side on its maiden voyage. An extra connecting log had been put in the center to prevent the wagon wheels from spreading the logs. Alvin Thompson's wagon was waiting to be loaded on the east bank. Two heavy planks had been cut for the wagons to roll onto the raft. With the raft moored to the landing, the wagon was rolled on. The gear and supplies carried in the wagons would be brought across on separate trips. The raft tilted and water washed across the logs and the wagon rolled on. Once in the center the raft was level on the water. With the wheels lashed to the raft, they began the trip across.

Beau let out a sigh of relief when the first wagon was pulled off on the west side. The raft had worked well. The day was spent ferrying the wagons and their supplies to the west side. The Williams' cows even got a ride across on the raft, surrounded by boxes and barrels of supplies.

The tension came back as they readied the stock to swim across the river. Memories of Jon dying in the crossing of the Platte was still fresh in the folks' minds. With shouts and slaps of the ropes, the oxen, mules, and extra horses entered the river. The men on horses continued to encourage them across. One of the oxen took a beeline for the riverbank just above the rapids. Unable to safely go after it, the men watched it get washed down the cascading water of the falls, tumbling as it went down.

Dripping wet and tired, the stock crossed the river and were driven down to the area they would be camping. The raft remained on the east side. Beau saw several men riding up the east bank of the Green River. Not looking forward to another crossing, Beau felt that he should. He swam the sorrel across to the east side. Safely across the river, he swung off the horse and stood near the raft.

The leader of the group pulled up and got off of his horse. "What do you charge to take wagons across?" he asked.

"Well," Beau said, "This is a private ferry. We're not looking for paying customers."

The man seemed confused. "Are you waiting for wagons?"

The mountain man didn't answer. One of the men behind the leader asked. "Would you be willing to sell it?"

Beau kicked the post near the landing, "Could be I would sell if the price was right."

The leader blurted out, "We'll give you $500 for the raft."

It appeared that this group came from a large wagon train. At least Beau hoped so. "I would consider your price and a dozen oxen brung here first thing tomorrow."

The man talked to the others and then turned back to Beau, "It sounds fair to us."

"You'll need to put new ropes across the river before you use it. They are kind of barked up right now." Beau told the man, not wanting them to snap during their crossing.

"We'll bring you the money and oxen this evening and start our crossing," their leader said as he mounted his horse and rode away followed by the others.

Jocko stood on the far side and watched the men ride away. The then called to his friend, "What did they want?"

"They bought the raft," Beau replied. "They'll be back in a little while with the money and some oxen. I'll stay here and wait for them."

The buyers' wagon train had not been far away, because an hour later he showed up with the money and the oxen. He had brought extra oxen to pull the raft on the far side. His men helped swim the oxen across. Jocko and Hoot were there to drive the dozen oxen to their camp. Shortly after the first wagon showed up. Beau helped them load it, taking care not to let the sharp iron rims of the wheels cut the ropes lashing the connecting logs.

With Jocko's help on the other side, the raft was pulled across and the wagon was rolled off. A cheer went up from the folks on the new wagon train. Beau found out that they had sent a man ahead to Lombard Ferry and had been told the backup was a week and it would be $25 per wagon. On the way back, he'd caught sight of the raft.

Reminding them that the ropes should be changed, Beau swam the sorrel back across the Green River for the last time and rode to the camp. Everyone already knew about the deal made on the raft. Otto suggested that Beau and Jocko keep the money as payment for leading the wagons and that the oxen become part of the wagon train extra stock.

Jocko smiled at Beau and said, "It is okay with me, if it's with you."

That night the two friends sat near their fire,

well satisfied with the deal. "I was going to just ride away from the raft," Beau said. "They rode up with a desperate look in their eyes. I realized I had something they wanted."

Beau slept well that night. The nagging worry if the raft would hold the wagons was gone and their work building it had been rewarded. He dreamt that he was walking on the grounds of the plantation back east and there was a girl ahead of him who remained just beyond his ability to recognize her. It was a good dream rather than frustrating because she was leading him someplace. Suddenly, he came out of the woods and was in the high meadow above the Mexican village.

He heard a voice. "Beau. Beau, wake up."

Fighting to stay asleep, the mountain man rolled over and groaned, "Leave me be."

"I'd like to," Jocko said, "but the other wagon train needs room to set up camp. We best get ready and leave."

The dream was gone. Beau was now too wide awake to try and get back to the high meadow. He smiled, thinking, *Maybe it was Ana I was chasing.*

Tossing off the blankets, he reached for his boots and pulled them over his darned woolen socks. It was still dark and there was a pot of coffee steaming on a small fire next to the fly tarp.

"They got six wagons across last night, before it got too dark," his stocky friend said. "They are lined up next to us on the trail. I can hear them setting up to start bringing more over."

The area where the wagon train had camped was a small clearing near the river. There was not room for the other wagons to go around without cutting several trees and moving rocks. As it was, it would require work to cut the trail to meet up with the one to Fort Bridger.

After some coffee and hard bread for breakfast, Beau made rounds, getting everyone ready to go while Jocko rode out looking for the easiest passage away from the camp. The mood was upbeat around the wagons. The last wide river had been crossed until they reached the Columbia in Oregon.

Beau checked out the oxen they had gotten in the deal and was somewhat disappointed in their condition. He wished that he had a week to rest them before getting under way, but the summer was quickly passing and soon they would be facing the danger of snow storms in the mountains. Tano and Herb had to lead their oxen, so Beck and Ludwig were chosen to ride out ahead with Jocko and work on the trail, removing windfalls and felling a few trees.

* * *

Fort Bridger came into sight on the sixth day. The people on the wagon train had been treated to breathless views of mountain ranges and foothills covered with timber. The only complaints during the day were the dust and heat in the high elevations. Most nights were cold. Rainfall was slim in August and, being in the high desert, they often traveled the day without finding water.

The rough, log structures of the fort were a disappointment to those on the wagon train. They also found it poorly stocked and the prices high. There had been a lot of friction between Fort Bridger and the Mormons over the years and their focus had been more on defense than supplies. The fort did have a blacksmith shop and many took advantage of the smithy's forge to have broken items repaired, or missing items replaced.

Beau had hoped to swap some of their oxen with rested stock, but he found them not available. The next opportunity would be at Fort Hall, almost 250 miles away, with the oxen-killing Big Hill still ahead. The mountain man also realized that it would be near the end of August when they arrived at Fort Hall. They would still have around two months, which included mountain travel, before they reached their destination.

Wagon trains continued to pull into Fort Bridger, which created even more shortages and drove prices up for scarce items. Beau kept his wagons at the fort for two days before taking the trail to Fort Hall. The mountain man felt that the continuing competition on the trail for supplies, water, grass, and space for camping was taking its toll on the people in his wagon train. He was thankful for Jocko's hunting skills for bringing game in for their meals, giving folks with the wagon train something to look forward to.

Rob had begun parking his wagon with the Rogers and spending most of his spare time visiting and eating with them. The three wagons owned by the Rogers, and Rob's wagon, were the only ones being pulled by teams of mules. There were four mules in the surplus stock and the four wagons would use them for riding, or if an animal needed a rest or became injured.

The last night before leaving Jocko and Beau spent time at a saloon located in the fort. It had a stone floor and walls of rough-hewn logs poorly fitted together. A plank bar supported by a barrel on one end and some whiskey boxes on the other, ran along the back wall. The door hung open on rusty metal hinges and a windowless opening on one wall served to bring in additional light. There were horns of elk, mountain sheep, mule deer, along with hides and furs adorning the walls. A fireplace on the right wall had a bearskin rug at its front. It was said that many a drunk mountain man had spent the night sleeping on it.

Several rough tables with stools or chairs were spread across the room for card playing, or partaking of a meal from the rustic kitchen. Tonight was venison stew, and the two men ordered a meal and a bottle of whiskey. The clay bowls of stew came with a mug of beer that could have used a bit more time to age. They were sitting at a table scarred from hard use and having knives stuck into it when making a point during heated discussions.

The whiskey was fair to the taste and the back bar was well-stocked, unlike the trading post. It was claimed that Jim Bridger sold guns and whiskey to the local braves. Thinking of his friend, Eli, Beau could understand doing so. The bowls of stew came with hard biscuits. The men soaked them in the thin broth of the stew to make them easier to chew. The stew was wolfed down and the two men began working on the bottle.

When the bartender came over to clear the dishes from the table, he gave them a wide smile showing yellowed and chipped teeth. "I got women in the back if you two were interested in some after-supper fun."

"Not right now," Beau said. The mountain man figured that they came from one of the local tribes and their pay was beads and other trinkets.

There was a full moon in the night sky when Beau and Jocko headed back to their camp. Without Rob's wagon for the fly tarp, they had staked it to the ground at one end and supported it on four-foot poles on the other. Both men were smoking short cigars purchased at the fort. Beau tripped on a guy line holding fly tarp and almost took a tumble. Laughing, he stumbled over to their smoldering fire and sat heavily. Their dirty mugs sat near the pot of stale coffee.

Pouring himself a cup of the tepid brew, he turned to Jocko. "When we get to the Three Island Crossing on the Snake River, miles could be saved traveling on the north side. You think we should plan to cross?"

"Hell, I don't know," Jocko said. "It's a month away from here. What the hell brought that up?"

Taking a drink of the coffee, Beau said, "Well, I just been thinking."

"What you've been doing is drinking," his friend replied. "Drinking and letting yourself worry about things too far out to have on your mind."

"Okay then," Beau said, chuckling, "should we go back and visit the women in the back room?"

Laughing at his inebriated friend, the stocky man replied, "I think we should get some sleep. Besides, Lisa wouldn't care much for me carrying on like that."

Tossing the mug down and crawling toward his blankets, the mountain man said, "No, I imagine she wouldn't. The girl in my dream wouldn't like it either."

CHAPTER THIRTEEN

Beau's head was heavy as he led the wagon train out of Fort Bridger. The 15 wagons stretched out on the trail. While he was suffering from the night's drinking, he had managed to get rid of a lot of the stress he'd been carrying. Jocko was a good friend and knew how to get him laughing.

Otto's wagon was the first one in line and Beau swung off the sorrel and walked alongside the old man. "I heard you cackling all around the camp last night."

"I did have a few drinks," the mountain man admitted.

"It's the devil's brew," Otto told him. Changing the subject, he asked, "Does the Bear River go all the way to Fort Hall?"

"It winds back and forth between the mountains and takes us to the fort," Beau said.

"We been competing with the California wagons since Missouri," the old man said. "When do we get rid of them?"

"A couple days out of Fort Hall the California

Trail heads south and we keep to the west," Beau told him.

"I been hearing talk that some of our wagons are going that way," Otto told him.

"I would expect some will," Beau agreed. "Then again, we might pick up some wanting to go to Oregon."

"We're getting low on oxen," Otto said.

Their conversation continued touching on the condition of stock and the wagons and general stuff. What the mountain man got from the visit was that the old man wanted to warn him about some wagons splitting off. Beau was pretty sure the Rogers would no longer be with them after reaching the Parting of the Ways, and maybe even Rob. That would put him down to 11 wagons and make them a more likely target of the Bannock or Shoshones.

As the wagons worked their way north and west toward Fort Hall, they were often away from the Bear River and in arid areas. Many of their cook fires were fueled with sage brush. They continued to lose the occasional ox. Beau had gotten some grain at Fort Bridger and was able to give it to his horses for several days.

Those with trail guides began to talk and spread the word about the Big Hill. It had the longest climb and descent of all the hills on the trail. Peck Wilson began preparing the wagons days before they reached the hill. Most of the wagons had brakes, which pushed a metal shoe against the iron tires of the back wheels. They would barely prevent the loaded wagons from coming up against the heels of the oxen and mules.

The extra stock being driven alongside the wagons would be needed to help on the long pull up the Big Hill. A week away from the hill, Mary Ward, who was helping to drive the extra stock, let Beau know that two oxen had dropped out during the day. They had just stopped walking and stood with their heads hanging and the loose hide on their bodies twitching.

Beau had noticed gray and black flashes of wolves following the wagon train. It was unlikely they were going hungry with all the dead oxen along the trail. He worried that they might be watching the young people walking alongside the wagons. That night the count of the extra stock was 10 oxen and four mules. Mrs. Williams' milk cows were still with them, although one had dried up. She believed it was carrying a calf.

It was a bright, sunny morning when the wagons started up the long ascent of the Big Hill. All were outfitted with a log to drop behind the back wheels, to help chock them should the wagon have to stop and rest their animals. An advantage was that they were all on the light side of their supplies and it would only be a day to Clover Creek after they got off the hill, so only enough water for a short period was carried in the barrels.

The wagons stopped several times to give the animals a breather. Beau had his saddle on the bay and was walking it up the hill alongside the wagons. Jocko had ridden to the top to see how many wagons were on the way down the far side. Looking back down the hill, the mountain man saw a wagon train with 60-plus wagons a mile out from the base. There was no way he wanted to let them catch up. The stock with his wagon train needed any grass that could be found at the next couple of stops.

It was three hours before the last wagon was at the top. Several of the people exclaimed when they looked at the other side of the hill. "How can we hold the wagons on the way down?"

Beau was thankful that the hillside was empty. A wagon train ahead of them was just disappearing into a swale ahead. "We'll take one wagon down at a time," the mountain man told the folks. "If your brake doesn't work well, I would recommend lashing your back wheels."

The beauty of the wide expanse below was lost to the severity of the hillside. Extending beyond the Big Hill were golden, rolling foothills covered with grass, patches of sage and some scrub pine.

There was no way the oxen or mules could hold the wagons back, so one team was used to bring the wagon down. If a wagon got loose, fewer animals would be hurt. Clem Williams was the first to start down. Peck had the brake working fine and Lucy pulled on the lever, causing the wheels to skid as they started down the hill. His children walked down behind the wagon, leading their cows and stock.

The hill was grass and dirt-covered granite. The wagons bounced in the ruts from previous descents. As the Williams wagon reached the bottom, Beau sent the next wagon. It was Kimi and Helena. Kimi sat in the wagon, working the brake lever and tapping the oxen with a rod, while she followed the wagon leading the extra oxen. A gasp would go up from those at the top each time the wagon going down would lurch to the side or hit a severe rut.

As the afternoon wore on, the wagons continued their descent. The first wagons of the train behind them started reaching the top. It was Edsel

Ward's turn to start down. Mary gave a hopeful grin back at those still waiting their turn. At the bottom Jocko was having them hitch the rest of their teams, move away to line up and be ready to move when the last wagon got down.

Again, there were exclamations when Edsel's wagon hit a rut. It was deeper than the others. The wagon rocked dangerously to one side and then the oxen jerked it ahead. The back wheel snapped off the axle and the wagon dropped to one side, dragging the back corner. The loose wheel rolled down the slope, gathering speed. It was going toward the wagons hitching their teams! Anyone hit by the wheel rolling down the hill would be killed!

Those left at the top of the hill began to shout and warn those below. Beau pulled his Colt and emptied it in the air. Finally, some at the bottom looked up and everyone rushed to take cover. The wheel hit a boulder and became air born, flying over a hundred feet before bouncing back off the ground. It began to tumble sideways and finally came to a stop just short of the bottom.

Beau stood on the top, his heart pounding and sweat running down his face. He had never felt so helpless, watching the wheel bear down on those below. Unable to do anything else, Edsel's wagon continued down the hill, his back corner dragging. The tail gate fell off when going over a bump and a few of the items began to fall out. Mary picked up what she could as she led the stock down.

As the next wagon started down, Beau reached into his possible bag and began to load the Colt. He had a couple of bottles in his gear on Rob's wagon. He figured he'd have a couple of stiff drinks tonight. With the Colt back in his broad belt, he pulled a twist of tobacco out of his bag and tore off a chew. Three more wagons and he could relax.

By the time the last wagon was at the bottom, and with the help of the Grafs, Edsel had replaced his axle and had a wheel on the wagon. Jocko had ridden up the hill and collected items that still remained, including the tail gate. As the wagons rolled away from the Big Hill, nobody looked back. It was a hill they wanted to forget.

On the second day they reached Clover Creek, in the Bear Lake Valley. It had seen lots of traffic from wagons going to California, but still had adequate grazing and wonderful, clean water. Wood was gathered and a large fire was built in the center of the wagons. The group needed a boost to their spirits. They were less than two weeks from Fort Hall, where needed supplies could be purchased, and they had the Soda Springs to look forward to along the way. As the sun set, Tano and Herb brought out their fiddles and soon several people were gathering to listen. A few even danced.

Beau brought out the remainder of his whiskey to share. A keg of hard cider was tapped that Alvin had hidden away in his wagon. The Dutch ovens were filled with sweet bread to be enjoyed after a meal of roasted deer on a spit over the fire. It was after midnight when the fire burned down and the music stopped. Everyone had eaten and drank their fill and were tired from singing and dancing. Groups of men and women sat in conversation, laughter breaking out when someone said something funny.

After having traveled across the Wyoming desert and tackling the Big Hill, the folks needed a rest.

Jocko had found them a good camping spot and Beau decided to stay for three days. Much of the time would be spent doing laundry, bathing, repairing wagons, yokes, and harnesses, as well as lubricating axles. While it seemed like a lot to do, it could be done at an easy pace, with several chances to sit and enjoy looking at the green of the valley.

The last evening, Beau and Jocko sat under the fly tarp, cleaning their rifles. "We are in the Bannock area now," the stocky man said.

"Them and the Shoshones," Beau said. "We'll have to keep closer watch. I must admit, I've become lax knowing we were traveling as friends of the Flatheads. That protection is pretty much gone now."

"I passed some men traveling from Fort Hall to the Green River," Jocko said. "They spoke of an emigrant that was killed when he fell behind his wagon train looking for some lost horses."

"That would be a fool thing to do along the Snake River," Beau replied, "but he still didn't deserve being killed."

Beau thought about the miles he'd traveled alone in Indian territory. More than once he'd ended up in a run for his life with braves on his heels, looking to take his scalp. Once, he'd held some off while hunkering down in a buffalo wallow. They'd killed his packhorse loaded with a winter's trapping. Beau was saved by a wind that came up that night and he'd led the sorrel away with the cover of a dust storm.

The mountain man knew that if a person traveling alone watched and listened for things that were out of place, trouble could most often be avoided. Looking around the wagon train, he knew the rules of avoiding trouble had to be replaced with being prepared to take on the trouble when it appeared.

Those without hangovers were smiling the next morning while the gear was put away and the animals hitched. Beau made his rounds of the wagons, reminding everyone to stay close and have their rifles or revolvers at the ready. He reminded them that they were now out of the Flathead territory. He found Aarno and Kimi filling their water barrel from a spring near the river. Helena's children Theo and Lilith were doing their best to try and help. Beau knew that the children liked to wander away from the slow-moving wagons and he stressed to Kimi that they be kept close.

As the wagons got ready to pull out, Beau and Jocko sat on their horses. "I want you to keep in sight of the wagons when riding out," the mountain man told his friend.

"Hard to hunt that close to the noise of the wagons," Jocko told him.

"If we're attacked, I'll need your rifle in the fight," Beau replied. "I don't want Bannock braves cutting you off."

"You are worried, aren't you?" Jocko asked.

"I try and only show it to you," Beau said smiling. Then, getting serious, he added, "It's not if we are attacked, but rather when we get attacked."

"Do you think they're watching us?" Jocko asked.

"What I know is they're always watching the trail, looking for those being careless," the mountain man said. "I don't want them to take notice of us."

Jocko knew that his friend wanted to give any watchers the impression that they were traveling as an armed camp and would inflict serious injuries on any attacker. The stocky man rode ahead on the gray, more alert of his surrounding and a bit less focused on game trails.

Often the extra stock would fall well back of the wagons, being allowed to graze on any available grass. They would generally catch up during a midday rest or when the wagon train made evening camp. Beau could no longer allow them to lag behind. For most of the trip west, the least able to defend themselves had herded the extra stock. From now on, he insisted they stay alongside the wagons, or just a short run from the last wagon. He put two armed men with the extra stock and he told them, in case of an attack, to leave the animals and just save themselves.

Traveling up the Bear Lake Valley was beautiful, making it hard to believe that there could be danger around them. The folks had done as he asked and traveled as a close-knit group. He was pleased to hear that most of the conversation was about what they could purchase at Fort Hall rather than about being attacked. Lucy Williams had read in the guide about the bubbling springs they were headed for and was describing them to her children.

It was mid-afternoon on the third day when they reached Soda Springs. The sounds and smells of the many springs brought out expressions of wonder. One of the favorites was a spring that appeared to be boiling, but the water was cold and naturally carbonated. Several of the folks sat near the springs with their mugs, dipping them in and drinking several times. Lucy Williams had a can of peaches and opened it at the springs. She poured some of the juice into the children's mugs of bubbling water, making a flavorful drink.

Several of the men added whiskey to their

mugs, making a pleasant beverage. Beau would have liked to spend a few days here also, but they had just had a break at Clover Creek and the cold weather of fall and winter wouldn't wait. They left Soda Springs the next day, just ahead of a large wagon train headed for California. It was filled mostly with men headed for the gold fields, and they tended to get rather rowdy when unwinding during the evening.

Fort Hall was reached September 1st. The sight of the adobe walls sent a ripple of excitement through the wagon train. It was Saturday afternoon and the fort was as busy as any other day of the week in the big cities back east. The gates of the fort were wide open. Several teepees were erected outside the walls, with their occupants sitting near them. Several had leather goods and other items to sell.

Just beyond the fort, Jocko had found a good spot to set up camp. A short distance away there was a clear-flowing stream. The fort had been built in 1834, and since then most of the trees had been cut for building or firewood. When the Hudson Bay Company had purchased it from Nathaniel Wyeth in 1837, the walls were covered with the adobe bricks.

In the early years the British-owned company had tried to discourage the emigration of Americans, even going so far as to have abandoned wagons near the fort and telling those traveling that they'd have to use pack animals to continue west. Finally, the unstoppable flow to America's west was accepted Fort Hall was now an important stop for supplies.

Most of those on the wagon train spent the evening going through their supplies, taking inventory of what they had and making a list of things needed. Beau intended to purchase rope to replace that left at the Green River raft. He also hoped to do some trading of oxen. Too many of theirs were walking bones draped in a hide. The terrain ahead of them would be the most difficult of the trip, with narrow mountain roads and steep climbs. They would face desert conditions for several days after leaving Fort Hall, and then they'd have to decide whether to cross the Snake River at Three Island Crossing.

The next morning, Otto gave a fire and brimstone sermon, hoping to discourage the purchase of whiskey at the fort. After the last hymn was sung, several of the people headed for the fort to find out what supplies were available and how expensive they'd be.

As a courtesy to Otto, Beau stayed clear of the saloon within the fort. They would be camping there for at least four days and there was plenty of time to enjoy the whiskey another day. Today he was more interested in checking on replacement oxen. He was pleased to learn that a pasture behind the fort had over a hundred animals. The price was $10 per animal in a swap. They were $20 each if purchased outright.

A buckskin-clad man with a stained, white beard took Beau to the pasture to look over the stock. The price of a yoke of oxen had been $25 before the gold strike in California. The demand had driven the prices up, if they could be found at all. The animals were in good condition, having plenty of water and grass.

Before heading back for the wagons, he stopped at the fort store. The long, narrow building was packed to the ceiling on both sides with goods needed by those traveling to the gold strike. The smell of new rope, leather, lamp oil, and spices filled the air.

Most of the traps and things used by the mountain men had been replaced with picks, pans, and shovels. The store had a good stock of boots and warm clothing.

Beau saw a sawbuck saddle for holding packs and picked it up. He went to the shelves stacked with boots and found a pair that fit. Next to the boots were stacks of woolen socks and he selected three pairs. Carrying his purchases to the long counter at the front, he reached into his possible bag and took out a small, leather bag holding his money. Before paying, he included some twists of tobacco and a bag of grain.

The owner was a heavy-set man with a Scottish accent. He had white hair and a ruddy, red complexion. The man smiled and asked, "You headed for California?"

Shaking his head, Beau replied, "I'm leading some folks to Oregon."

"Had some wagons heading that way a few days ago," he said as he tallied the items. "Most coming through are after the gold."

After paying the man, Beau handed him a list of items he still needed, which included the rope. "I'll be back for these in two days," the mountain man told him.

Walking back to the camp with the grain sack over one shoulder and the sawbuck under the other arm, he saw that several of the folks were near the center of the wagons, about to partake in a Sunday meal. Lucy Williams called him over to join them.

After putting his purchases next to the fly tarp, Beau joined them. He told them about the oxen available in case anyone wanted to swap theirs out. He noticed that the Rogers and Rob were not at the meal. Sitting in the sunshine on the blankets, enjoying a

Sunday meal, created a good feeling in the mountain man. He began to think his decision to make Oregon his future home was the right one, rather than the lonely life in the mountains.

Once the food was eaten, Beau pulled a twist of tobacco out of his possible bag and shared it with those who wanted a chew or smoke. Using his skinning knife, he chopped up enough to fill his pipe and lit it using a brand from the fire. Smiling, he thought, A *Sunday meal, a smoke, and friends, this is the life.*

The days at the fort went by quickly. Everyone had purchased goods they needed. Several replaced some or all of their oxen. The Rogers and Rob let him know they would be staying behind and joining a wagon train heading for California. Unfortunately, there were no additional wagons looking to go to Oregon. They would now be down to 11 wagons and fewer rifles.

There was a traveling troupe putting on a play at the fort and most from the wagon train had gone to see it. Beau stayed back, busy separating his gear from Rob's wagon. Sudden shouts caught his attention. He looked toward the noise and was shocked to see a full-blown brawl going on near the Rogers' wagons.

Putting the Colt into his belt, Beau ran across the center area to break up the fight. Aarno Hanson and Quinn were sitting on a rock. The old man had his Hawken across his knees. The two were watching while Kimi and three Rogers brothers went at it.

"What the hell is going on here!" the mountain man demanded.

"Stay back, Beau," Aarno warned him. "It's under control here."

It was evident that the raw-boned Kimi was

holding his own against the three brothers. Duncan and Sean were down at the moment, and it was one-on-one between Kimi and Art. Beau had been to a few professional fights in his life, but had never saw a fighter move as quickly and effectively as Kimi. The man ducked and dodged while landing blows on his opponent. Sean started to get up, tripping Art, and the raw-boned man stepped back, giving them both a chance to get back up.

Suddenly, Quinn said, "Enough! Enough of this nonsense."

Beau was almost disappointed, because he was starting to enjoy watching the sparring. The elder brother, Quinn, reached out his hand to Kimi. "You made your point and Sean here was wrong."

In awe, the mountain man watched as the men shook hands and the Rogers headed toward the fort, wiping the blood off their faces with their neckerchiefs. Kimi looked at his father and said, "I didn't need you to stand by with your rifle, pa. I could handle them."

Beau noticed that the Rogers women, Helena and the children were gone to the play. Other than he, Quinn, and Aarno, there had been no witnesses. He spoke up, "What was the fight about?"

Kimi shook his head and said, "Nothing." Then he headed for his wagon.

"The young Rogers boy insulted his wife," Aarno replied. "He asked her to spend some time with him. I guess he thought she was still on the waterfront."

"If they'd have beat your boy, would you have used the rifle?" Beau asked.

"Nope," the old man said. "As long as the fight remained clean, and no kicking a man that's down. If Kimi went down, he'd have lost and would have had to accept what was said."

The mountain man headed back for his camp, hoping that in any skirmish Kimi was on his side. He was quite the fighter. Beau also knew that he couldn't tell anyone about the fight. Helena's past would then come out, and soon a line of tough guys would be trying their hand against the raw-boned kid.

After the troupe had finished everyone wandered back from the play. Not a word was said about the fight. The Rogers and Rob hitched their wagons to move to the other wagon train. They received hugs and well wishes from folks on the wagon train. It was like family moving away. Once again, Kimi shook the men's hand and wished them a safe trip to California.

Rob thanked Beau and Jocko for letting him come with the wagons. He had fully intended to go to Oregon, but hearing the Rogers talk of gold just waiting to be picked up had gotten to him and he had to go see for himself. The mountain man felt that he was a good man, and unless he fell into the wrong type of crowd again he'd do well where ever he went.

Beau put the rope and bigger items into Aarno's wagon. The rest he'd carry on the bay, using the sawbuck saddle. Jocko also put packs onto his mustang. That night wood was gotten from the hills nearby and a big fire was built. A meal topped off with some pies made from dried fruit gotten at the fort was enjoyed. Then the now smaller circle of wagons were packed with any loose gear and readied to leave in the morning. The new oxen had had their yokes fitted and the wagon axles had been lubricated. There was nothing left to do but have a smoke and a few drinks of the Scottish whiskey.

CHAPTER FOURTEEN

The beauty of the Bear Lake Valley and the security of Fort Hall were all too soon behind them as the wagons pulled back out onto the trail. They were following the Snake River, which cut through a rolling, arid landscape. Large boulders and granite outcrops could be seen. The river hugged the south side and had cut deeply into the wide basin they were traversing. Much of the time the Snake River was far below the trail and difficult to reach.

Up until leaving Fort Hall, Beau had ridden most of the time, rotating between his two horses. But now, having to carry packs on one of his horses, he kept the other saddled and ready for emergencies while leading the one with the packs. They were also facing the most difficult part of the trip through the mountains, and by walking he could gauge the fatigue in those with the train who had to walk all the time leading their oxen. Jocko continued to ride, being the eyes and ears of what was ahead for the wagon train.

On the third day out of Fort Hall the trail ran

through a narrow opening in the rocks, wide enough for only one wagon at a time. The granite towered above the wagons on both sides and the people clutched their rifles, fearing that the Bannock or Shoshone might be hidden above, waiting to shower them with arrows and musket fire.

The men had their wives and children ride inside the wagons, enduring the jarring bumps of the rough, rocky trail. The sun burned down on the wagon train and the condition of the trail prevented them from hurrying through. In years to come, this narrow passage would be called the Gate of Death, from massacres in the area.

Finally, out from the granite cliffs, the passengers in the wagons climbed out, preferring walking to riding. Several people were limping as they attempted to break in the new shoes purchased at the fort. That evening they made camp near the steep banks of the river. Buckets suspended on ropes were used to retrieve water for cooking and the stock. Another larger wagon train rumbled by, looking to get ahead on the California Trail and take advantage of the remaining grass.

Their cook fire was sage brush or dried oxen droppings. Above them, out of reach, in the cliffs they could see timber and brush. Below them in the river gorge were areas with driftwood piled up. Tomorrow they would reach the Raft River, where those going to California would go south, following the Raft River basin, while those going to Oregon would continue along the Snake River. Much of the pressure for grass would be relieved.

Jocko and Beau ate stale biscuits gotten at the fort. Dunked in hot coffee, they were chewable. "I saw a couple of heads in the rocks above us," Jocko said.

Pulling his new boots off and rubbing his sore feet, Beau replied, "I caught movement a couple of times myself. With luck they'll take a liking to the wagon train that passed us."

"Do you think we'll lose any more wagons at the Raft River?" the stocky friend asked.

The mountain man sighed and looked at the wagons nearby. "The men with wives will continue to Oregon. Otto's bunch and Hoot's might be waiting to make a last-minute decision." Then he shook his head. "I don't think we'll lose any."

The Raft River was just a couple of hours down the trail from their campsite. The next morning, they found the spot churned to dust and littered with oxen droppings. Many had stopped there to spend the night before heading down the narrower basin of the Raft River. The wagon train that had passed them the night before was just disappearing to the south. Crossing the broad river, the Oregon Trail continued straight ahead. There were no fresh tracks on the well-worn trail. Oregon had lost most of its traffic since the gold strike in California.

So much the better, thought Beau. Today the sorrel was saddled and tied to the back of the lead wagon. The mountain man walked ahead of the wagon train, leading the bay with his packs, the Hawken cradled in the crook of his arm.

The wagon train was traveling on the south side of the river, still a week and a half from Three Island Crossing. The route along the north side of the Snake River was shorter, had better water and grazing. It also had easier terrain to traverse. The problem was, there were few places where the river provided an opportunity to cross. Three Island was one of the first. The water between each of the islands was deep, with a challenging current. The saving grace was that each of the islands gave the oxen a chance to rest before the next fording.

Another danger was that the churning current created cuts in the river bottom, which could damage or tip a wagon. Since the crossing had been used, several emigrants had met their deaths in the river. Beau felt that the advantages of the north side outweighed the challenges of crossing the Snake River. It could be made safer by using ropes to help control the pull of the current.

Staying on the south side of the river also had its challenges, with little distance between the river and the basin walls. There were also a couple of ridges that had to be climbed over, which had taken more than one life. Beau also felt there was more chance of attack with the wagons being forced to travel closer to the granite or sandstone cliffs along the river.

As the wagon train rolled on above the Snake River gorge, Beau looked back, making sure they weren't stringing out. Smiling, he noticed that they were keeping tight and the barrels of ready rifles stuck out of the front of every wagon. Some of the folks had two rifles.

While taking a midday rest, clouds that had been threatening rain for two days finally let loose. The water was welcome in the arid basin they'd been traveling through. Hoping it was just a short burst, everyone climbed into their wagons and sat listening to the rain beating on the canvas tops. Beau had taken cover in Aarno's wagon.

The old man offered him a chew from his twist of tobacco. "We might be here for a while," he said with a certain amount of inner wisdom.

Tearing off a piece with his teeth, Beau rolled the tobacco into his cheek. After he spat out the back of the wagon, he said, "You might be right. We'll give it a few minutes and then, raining or not, we have to move on."

The more Beau got to know Aarno Hanson, the more he liked the old man. He had a practical way of looking at things. He and Jocko had taken to eating their meals at the old man's wagon. Kimi and Helena with the children were always camped nearby, and it was entertaining to watch the carefree children at play.

"Do you think we'll have snow crossing the mountains?" Aarno asked.

The mountain man had traveled the high country extensively this time of year, trapping and hunting. He looked at the old man. "We'll see snow for sure. I just hope we don't see too much of the white stuff."

Clenching his pipe in his teeth, Aarno said, "If we do, we got warm clothes and, with a little luck hunting, enough to eat." Grinning, he added, "We can also eat the oxen before starving. As far as Mrs. Williams' milk cows, those we can't eat. They'll be needed to give milk for all the babies that will be born to the families on this wagon train."

The two men sat talking for another hour while Beau hoped the rain would slack off. He wondered how Jocko was faring out ahead of them. He hoped that his friend had found some kind of shelter. Finally, Beau grunted, "We got to get started. Time to break out the rain slickers."

The mountain man had his in Aarno's wagon. He dug it out of the gear and pulled it over his head. With his drooping, leather-brimmed hat firmly on his head, Beau climbed out the back of the wagon. His feet slipped on the muddy ground and he grabbed the tailgate.

"You best be careful how you step," the old man cautioned him.

With their heads leaning into the blowing rain, the two men walked along the line of wagons, letting everyone know they were moving on. The rifles had to be put further into the wagons, making them less accessible, but Beau figured that the Bannock and Shoshone would be sitting tight in this rain rather than looking for a fight.

Leading his sorrel with the pack and with the gray saddled and tied to the lead wagon, Beau walked in front of the wagon train, feeling the pelleting rain finding its way under his slicker. He saw Jocko trotting towards him. To protect himself from the rain, the stocky friend had on the buckskin jacket he'd gotten at Fort Hall. Swinging down from the horse, he walked alongside Beau.

"Before the rain started, I saw plenty of tracks about a mile ahead of us," Jocko said.

"Did they look like they were passing through?" Beau asked.

"Nope," the stocky man said. "They was milling around and sort of waiting. Almost like it was a meeting. They hadn't been gone long when I came across them."

"How many do you figure?" he asked his friend.

"Fifteen, maybe twenty riders," Jocko

answered. "I'm willing to bet they was setting up for an attack and the rain ruined their plans. There were plenty of big boulders for them to hide among."

Something about his friend's story bothered him. Keeping his voice level, Beau asked, "What were you doing that far ahead of the wagons?"

"It will do little good to ride near the wagons," Jocko said. "We'll be attacked without warning. I have to be further out to search for sign."

"What's to stop them from taking your scalp for a prize?" the mountain man asked.

"The wagon train is the prize they want," Jocko said, matter-of-factly. "Why would they risk warning you by trying to kill me first? Even with a few arrows in us, the horse and I would get back to you."

Beau looked at his confident friend. He knew Jocko was right. Riding well ahead of the wagon train was necessary, but he didn't like the thought of his friend risking his life. As far as the mountain man was concerned, they couldn't get to the Three Island crossing soon enough. On the north side there was more room to stay away from boulders and cliffs.

That evening the rain kept falling. Beau had them park the wagons in a half-circle, using the Snake River to protect their backs. All the stock was kept within the wagons, making things close with the wet, steaming bodies of the oxen and horses. He instructed the folks to have a quick, cold meal and as soon as darkness set in, they were to get yokes on the oxen.

Standing in the rain near Aarno's wagon, Otto asked, "Why are we moving in the rain? Come morning the weather might break."

"That is why we are moving tonight," Beau replied. "We are being followed by some Bannock or

246

Shoshone braves that are intent on hitting us. We would have already been attacked except for this rain. When the weather breaks they will come. For the past ten miles and as many in front of us, the cliffs crowd the river, and that's what they've been waiting for. The rain saved us today, and can do the same tonight while we make for the area where we have more space between the river and cliffs."

Edsel asked, "Once we get to the wider area, will that prevent them from attacking?"

Beau looked at the several men standing in the rain. He regretted what he was about to have to say. "No, it won't. We will be attacked. They have been following us since we went through the narrows. By now they think they know our weaknesses and are just waiting for a place to attack."

"We're set up pretty good right here," Otto said. "We can use stuff from the wagons to make better fortifications and be ready for them."

"They'll be picking us off from the rocks above us," Beau explained. "The wagons will be set afire with burning arrows and every time we poke our head out to aim our rifles, we'll be showered with arrows or have a musket ball sent at us."

"So we're trapped," Clem said. "Here, or down the trail, they will get us."

Not wanting the people to feel defeated, Beau said firmly. "The move tonight will make them come out of the rocks to fight and give us the advantage. We have better firepower and, by God, more will to fight for our friends and families. Now have your teams ready in a half-hour. Keep the noise to a minimum. We'll give them a surprise come morning when they climb into the rocks near us and find we're gone."

Like ghosts in the night, the men got the oxen into their yokes and pinned the wagon tongues to the yoke rings. The spare oxen and horses were tied to the back of the wagons so they wouldn't have to be driven. Quiet as drifting fog, the wagon train pulled away from their camp. The pouring rain helped mask any errant noise or the creaks of the wagons and the jingle of the trace chains.

Beau, leading his bay with packs, set the pace. The normal plodding of the oxen was not acceptable tonight. The drovers used their rods to hurry the tired animals on, having to forgo the voice commands. Jocko rode to the back and kept an eye over his shoulder in case the braves were alerted and decided to fight rain or shine.

Through the night they moved along the Snake River, anticipating an attack at any time. Those not driving the oxen lay on blankets in the wagons, trying to sleep while enduring the jolts along the trail. A fire had been left burning in the campsite, in case any of the braves climbed out of whatever shelters they had and looked over the rocks. The extra men and some of the women climbed out of the shelter of the wagons and relieved those driving the oxen.

The mountain man continued to lead the tight line of oxen and wagons along the trail in the darkness. Despite the cold rain, Beau was sweating under his slicker. Tonight would have been a full moon, but the heavy cloud cover prevented light from getting through.

While walking he planned their defense. He hoped to make it to the wider area by daybreak, allowing them to stay out of range of arrows. He remembered a sort of plateau near the river that was broad enough to set up camp, and that would give them high ground if the attack was on horseback. It would also make it more difficult to crawl up close before being seen.

Several times Beau wandered off the trail, coming up against loose rocks on the side of the trail. He zig-zagged until he felt the ruts of the trail under foot. A few hours before sunup, the rain began to slacken. Behind he could see the black silhouettes of the teams and wagons. Jocko came to the front of the train, riding the mustang. He walked the horse alongside Beau.

With a hoarse voice, the mountain man asked, "Would you ride ahead? There's a low plateau next to the river. Let me know how far it is from here."

Jocko urged the mustang to a trot, quickly disappearing into the drizzle. Beau let the lead wagon catch up with him. Web Johnson was leading the team. "I want you to keep everyone moving," he said. "Jocko is out ahead, scouting a good place to stop. I have to go to the back and make sure nobody gets left behind."

The mountain man tied the bay to the back of the wagon and led the sorrel away from the wagons. Tightening the cinch, he swung into the saddle. The relief on his tired legs was beyond explanation. He rode by the people driving the oxen, assuring them that they didn't have much further to go. Arriving at the back, he stopped and sat in the drizzle, listening for any sounds that weren't made by the wagons. He strained his eyes in the darkness, trying to see any movement.

The sound of the wagons was fading when he thought he heard something coming toward him. Sitting on the horse, he felt exposed and swung down, leaning against his horse. His tired legs had stiffened and didn't want to support him. Hanging on to the saddle horn, he waited, listening. He was definitely hearing something. Sliding his Hawken into the scabbard, he pulled the Colt from his wide belt. Using the sorrel to shield his body, Beau stood ready with the Colt cocked. Suddenly something dark loomed toward him. Relief flooded over the mountain man. It was one of their oxen that had gotten loose from one of the wagons and it was trying to catch up with the others. He was thankful it hadn't started lowing.

By the time Beau herded the stray ox back to the wagons, the rain had stopped and the gloom was just beginning to be cut by the rising sun. Young Charles was in the last wagon and he climbed out to grab the trailing rope of the ox and tie it to the back of their wagon. Riding to the front of the wagons, Beau saw Jocko coming in the distance.

As he rode up the stocky friend said, "Another mile and we'll be at the plateau."

Slowly the morning sun made the landscape visible and Beau was relieved to see that the cliffs were now beyond the range of the bows. Scattered rocks and boulders littered across the basin would give some cover to the attacking braves.

The plateau was grass-covered and had a dip, or bowl toward the river, offering cover for the oxen and horses. Again, the wagons were put into a half-circle, using the river as their back cover. Several boxes were pulled from the wagons and placed on the ground to give additional cover for those lying under the wagons firing.

Jocko and Beau rode around the space between the river and the cliffs. There was one wash that could be used by the braves to crawl closer. The cliff cut away to the east and that would give the Bannock and Shoshone a good place to move in without being seen. But even from that point they wouldn't be able to use the bows or muskets.

Riding back to the wagons, Beau called a meeting. "Right now, the braves have to come at us from the east. There's a depression they can move in along our front, but they will still be out of range for their bows. If they come at us on horseback from the east, they will be within the range of our rifles before they can return fire. Right now, I expect them to work their way to the front and crawl close before attacking."

Otto asked, "If we hitch up and make a run for it, could we get to safety?"

"Our oxen are played out," Beau reminded him. "We are in the best location to defend ourselves on this rise. If we try and run they will catch us in the open without a way to do so."

The mountain man asked Otto, Jocko, and Hoot to join him as they set up defenses. At this time, they did not expect an attack from the west, but he asked Hoot to take charge in that area in case the braves found a way to come at them on horseback. Jocko would be in charge of the center, while Otto was on the east. He wanted those with rifles to work in pairs, with one firing while the other was loading. That would keep one rifle at the ready at all times.

He assigned five men led by Otto to the east, seven with Jocko to the center, and five with Hoot to the west. Beau would work his way back and forth to any area needing assistance. He had two women helping load rifles on the east end, three in the center, and two on the west. Young Charles would load and shoot in the center. Mary and Cora would be taking care of the six younger children and assist with anyone who was wounded.

The mountain man saw worry on their faces as they prepared the wagons for the coming attack. The waiting would be the toughest part. Once the action started, he was confident that they would fight. Beau just prayed that their preparation and having the high ground would be enough.

Beau set up guards to watch for any attack. The rest of the people were told to get whatever rest they could. There was always a chance the braves wouldn't attack with the wagons so well-positioned, but the mountain man figured that the move last night would make their leaders determined. They would want to make some kind of strike before they lost the faith of their followers.

The morning dragged on, the air remaining cold. The mountain man had gotten one chilling realization as the sun had burned off the haze. The mountain tops to the south were now snow-covered. There was no doubt that part of their trail west had also gotten snow. When others on the train began to wake up to take their watch, they exclaimed at the beauty of the mountain tops. Beau just agreed with them.

It was the young Charles Williams who gave the alert when he saw movement near the wash. "Over there!" he shouted. "I saw one near the boulder shaped like an egg."

Within moments, everyone was up and ready. "When do we start shooting?" Alvin Thompson asked.

"If you see something move, shoot it!" Aarno growled.

"He's right," Beau said. "If you see a target,

fire. Don't shoot at shadows. Once you squeeze the trigger, you are defenseless until the rifle is reloaded."

The mountain man had barely gotten the words out of his mouth when someone fired. A few braves were working their way closer, using whatever cover available. Their dust-covered bodies blended well with the fast-drying ground. Clem and young Charles both held rifles. The young man had a flintlock while his father's rifle used caps.

The flintlock fired and the shadowy shape Beau was watching disappeared. The boy had a sharp eye. "You think I hit it?" Charles asked, his voice excited as he reloaded the flintlock.

"Forget thinking about what you might have hit, son," Beau said. "Just keep looking for things that don't belong and put a shot in it."

Sporadic firing continued from those defending the center. Some of the rifles were being loaded with ball and buckshot. It would tear up a sage brush while sending dust flying around it. The men were told to fire at any suspected movement or cover that could be used by the braves. Twice, the shots scored a hit on braves still a good distance from the wagons.

Suddenly, something appeared at the top of the cliff. Two braves sat astride their ponies, looking over the basin. Clem had a spyglass and handed it to Beau. The mountain man quickly realized that they were directing the attack!

One of the braves was carrying a lance and held it out with a motion to the east. He then made a motion to the west. Handing the glass back to Clem, Beau had Aarno move from the center to the west position. "Whatever happens behind you, stay here," he told the man. Then to Hoot, "It is a short run from the cliffs to you. I think there are riders somewhere that we can't see. When they do come, they'll be riding hard."

With Aarno to add to their firepower, he then ran to see Otto. "There will be riders coming from behind the cliff. At that distance, they'll be a distraction to get us looking to the east. Don't start shooting until you're sure they're in range. Aim for the horses."

With both ends alerted, Beau took a position in the middle, pairing with young Charles. "Once the riders come at us, we can expect an attack from the wash."

"Are we going to let the bastards on the cliff sit there, directing the attack?" Jocko asked.

"It would be quite a shot to hit them from here," Beau said. "They're near a quarter-mile and uphill."

"I fired a couple at the cliff earlier and the drop was about two feet," the stocky man said. "We could make sitting up there damn uncomfortable for them."

Suddenly there were shouts from the east, "Riders coming!"

Beau nodded to Peck and Jocko. "Let's see if we can hit something up there. On the count of three."

The rifles roared, sending lead at the two braves on the cliff. One rider twisted and fell from the pony. The other's horse bucked back, falling over and sending the brave sprawling into the dirt. Then shots echoed in the basin from the rifles near the east wagon. Fighting the urge to send some of his men to help the others, Hoot searched for a target.

Then braves appeared from the west, riding

low and already in range of the rifles. Aarno shouted, "Here they come!"

A moment later Hoot yelled, "It's our stock! They're after the oxen!"

The strategy became clear to Beau. The intent was to divert attention away from the west, allowing the riders to close in quickly and get to the oxen, driving them away from the wagons or, even better, through the wagons. The eastern riders had been a diversion, intending to come in after the oxen had been stampeded. Beau knew that the next punch was coming and it would be from the front.

"Get ready" he told those in the center. He had barely gotten the words out when a shower of arrows came in, followed by 8 to 10 braves armed with bows, tomahawks, and knives, ducking and dodging as they ran at the wagons. They had a hundred-yard gap to cross and had expected all attention to be on the riders. The first two volleys from the center knocked down six of the braves, wounding them. The braves were forced to dive for any cover they could find.

"Put a ball in anything that moves," Beau said as he ran to help Hoot. From behind he could hear shots from those on the east. Continuous shooting by the men working in pairs, and with the ladies loading, had turned the attack from the west. Several ponies were down, or running rider less. The remainder had turned away, putting distance between themselves and the rifles.

Arrows continued to fly toward the wagons from the front, shot by braves who had found cover within range of their bows. Musket balls also splintered the wood on the wagons. Beau looked back at the wagon train's defenses and saw that at least three of the men were down. Edsel, Mary, and Cora were working on them.

He moved back to those defending the center. Most were loading with buck and ball, tearing up any cover they could see. Beau saw one brave lying just outside the wagons. He had taken a full load in the chest, his blood soaking into the dust and sand.

Beau looked to see if the riders on the cliff had re-appeared when he caught sight of someone climbing the rocks of the cliff to be a spotter for those on the ground. He pointed it out to Jocko. The stocky man took careful aim and pulled his set trigger. He then touched off the hair trigger. Fire belched from the Hawken. A second later the brave climbing the rocks stopped, then, losing his grip, he fell, bouncing off the boulders below.

The wagons were well-positioned to be defended. For the next several minutes there was a life and death struggle between the attacking braves and the people defending the wagons. The women helped with the loading of rifles and, when needed, would shoot to increase the firepower. When Alvin was knocked down by a musket ball, Tilly took his place and continued to fire while Edsel checked his wound.

Finally, the attack broke. Searching fire continued from the wagon train until Beau ordered them to stop. Young Charles came over to Beau, the side of his face blackened by the powder burning in the pan of the flintlock.

Wide-eyed, he said, "I might have killed one."

"Odds are you wounded one," Beau assured the young boy. "Even if they fall down, they probably crawled to safety."

"I hope so," the boy said.

"Another thing that is very important," he told the boy. "Their full intension was to kill every one of us and take anything of value. Your sharp eyes in the beginning might have saved many lives."

With the shooting stopped, Beau learned that three of the men had been wounded. One woman had been hit. Then, to his dismay, he learned that Beck Graf had been hit behind the ear with a musket ball and was near death.

The wagons continued to be guarded by the men while the wounded were given care. The guards' faces were grim as they searched for any movement. Peck had caught one of the ponies that had run within the wagons. Beau had the dead brave near the wagons slung over its back and sent it running west.

Clouds had come in during the attack and with the late afternoon temperatures dropping, large snowflakes began to fall. Beau was thankful that the snow hadn't started before the attack. It would have made seeing targets difficult. Twice there'd been shots by nervous guards.

The Shoshone, or Bannock, that had attacked them were late heading to their winter camp. This snow just might prevent a second try at the wagons. Beau was exhausted as he walked along the wagons.

A fly tarp had been put up near Otto's wagon. Beck lay on blankets with his brother and father near him.

"Has Edsel seen your son?" Beau asked the grieving Otto.

"He come and done what he could," the old man said. "He got the bleeding stopped but couldn't get to the ball."

The mountain man noticed that Ludwig's

shoulders shook as he wept. "They got coffee at the fire," Beau said. "Can I get you some?"

Otto looked up with tear-filled eyes. "You done everything you could to get us ready. It was just bad luck. The ball went through the wagon canvas and got Beck. He was going after more caps. The brave didn't even see what he hit."

"I'll get you some coffee," the mountain man replied.

It was still snowing when darkness fell. After checking on all those needing attention for their wounds, Edsel checked the oxen and found three with arrows sticking out of their sides. He was able to get the arrows out and put grease on the wounds.

Beau found Helena near her wagon, crying. Kimi was on watch and the children were in the wagon sleeping. "I can relieve Kimi and let him come to sit with you," he said.

"I'll be alright," she told him. "I'm just thankful that my children or husband weren't hurt. It's nerves coming out." He sat talking with her for a few minutes before going to relieve Kimi. Helena was a strong woman, but having her husband near right now was something she needed.

By midnight the snow stopped as the clouds cleared. The air felt frigid. The cook fire was banked and the stars gave a feeble light on the snow-covered ground. Beau got a start when he saw the shadowy figures of two wolves passing by near the wash. He finally crawled into his blankets to a night of restless sleep. The eastern sky was beginning to get light when Jocko shook him awake.

"Beck passed during the night," he told his friend.

Beau pulled on his stiff, frozen boots. He saw that the fire had been started and pots of water had been put on for coffee. "We got to ride out this morning to see if there's any sign of the Indians."

"The snow will probably have them riding for winter camp," Jocko said.

"I tend to agree with you," the mountain man replied, "but we got to make sure."

After coffee and hard bread, the two men rode out with revolvers in their belts and their Hawkens across the saddles. There was about four inches of fluffy snow on the ground. The air was cold and the sky clear and blue. The mountains all around them were shrouded in snow. They rode wide of the wash and headed to the east of the cliff.

The snow was without tracks as far as they could see. Around the edge of the cliff, they found a narrow trail that led to the top. They rode slowly, emerging above the wagon train. Snow covered one of the horses that had been killed by the volley of fire. The cliff sloped down to the south, showing how the braves were able to get to the west side without being seen.

The view from the cliff of the snow-covered basin and outlying mountain was spectacular. Beyond the river and to the west were rolling hills. Sage brush protruded from the snow cover, their tops crowned with clumps of the white stuff. The only tracks, other than their own, were those of the two wolves along the wash. There was no sign of life except around the wagon train. The braves had left and had taken their dead with them.

Beck was buried in the afternoon. Otto stayed near the grave, praying for his son. Ludwig had returned to their wagon to get it ready to roll. Beau went to stand with the old man. He knew they had to continue west, and he was searching for the words to tell the grieving father.

Suddenly, Otto spoke without looking up. "I know we have to leave in the morning. I'll be ready."

"I'll help Ludwig get your stock and other things ready," Beau said as he headed back to the wagons.

He met Edsel who was making his rounds, checking on the wounded. "Otto collected dirt with his son's blood to bury in Oregon," the doc told him. "The old man told me it would help to know that a bit of his boy was under the dirt near their new home."

"Then we best make sure that dirt doesn't get lost," the mountain man said.

CHAPTER FIFTEEN

Early the next morning the wagons left the plateau that had provided their defense. Three Island Crossing was eight days away, through a series of hills. The temperatures had risen enough to start melting off the early snow. Bloody bandages on several people were a reminder of the attack they'd survived. A total of eight had injuries requiring dressing. Young Charles had been creased by an arrow and proudly displayed his wounded arm while carrying his loaded flintlock.

Five days after the attack, the wagon train reached Salmon Falls. The people with the wagons were unsure if they should go wide of the falls or not. At Salmon Falls there were Shoshone and Paiute catching the plentiful, spawning salmon. After gutting the fish and saving the eggs to be eaten immediately, they dried or smoked their catch. They used the fish to trade for items with other tribes, trappers, or wagon trains. Even though the people were hesitant, Beau convinced them to stop. Otto chose to stay away from the Indians, not trusting himself. The loss of his son by one of their brethren was too painful, even though these Shoshone that were selling fish were probably not the ones who had attacked the wagon train.

While talking with a tribal elder, Beau found out that the young brave leading the attack had been killed. The others had stopped on their way to the winter camp, many with wounds. The elder brave he spoke with shook his head. "The young forget that this is the time to prepare for the coming winter."

The mountain man traded for several smoked fish and some freshly caught salmon to eat that night. "The fish is appreciated," Beau told the old man. "Come morning, we will leave and soon will be away from your land."

The old brave wiped his hands on his buckskin britches, looking at the wagons. "Their medicine must have been weak," he said. "So few wagons. So many died."

Glad that the old brave hadn't been leading them, Beau thought, *Maybe our medicine was stronger.*

Leaving Salmon Falls, they entered rolling hills between the river gorge and the mountains. They camped below the hills to help cut the cold, blowing wind. The stock could be driven down to the river for water, but what was needed for cooking and drinking had to be carried up the slope from the river.

Jocko rode ahead in the hills to make sure that the braves who had attacked them didn't decide to use these hills to surprise the wagon train. The wagons wound through and over the seemingly endless hills, with parts of the trail cut into the sides by previous travelers.

Finally, the wagon train descended along a cut in the sage brush and grass-covered hill to the crossing.

In the distance they could see scattered trees with their leaves bright yellow or the occasional, dark evergreen. There was a flat, grassy area near the river for the wagons to set up camp.

Beau was aware of two crossings in this area. About two miles west was another crossing called Two Island Ford, but the water was deeper and the currents stronger. The Three Island Crossing would require some swimming, but most of the way the animals would have contact with the bottom, even though the wagons would be floating.

They wouldn't actually cross all three islands. After crossing the first island, they would then cross the channel to the second. Then they would go to the eastern tip of the second island and from there they would head for the north bank. While they'd be in the water longer, it did not have the faster current that flowed past the third island.

After setting up camp on the south side of Three Island Crossing, Beau brought out several blocks of tar carried in Aarnos' wagon. These were set near the fire, with one melting in a pot. Calling the folks to gather, he addressed them.

"Adding wood blocks under the wagon axles will not help at this crossing. The wagons will have to float from island to island," he told them. "I need all of you to empty your wagons and seal them with tar. We have enough rope to help lead the oxen and guide the wagons."

What the mountain man did not tell the folks was how many stories he'd heard about people and wagons at this crossing being washed downstream into stronger currents and deeper holes, ending up drowning. The danger was real, but miles saved, better terrain on the north side of the river, plus the plentiful forage for the animals made it worthwhile.

The smell of hot tar was carried through the camp by the cool, north breeze. All the wagons had their goods stacked near them, covered with canvas in case of a change in the weather. Tomorrow was Sunday, so they'd spend an additional day on the south side. Beau looked at Otto sitting near his wagon, by all appearances a broken man, mourning the loss of his son. Ludwig had a pot of hot tar and a flat stick and was attempting to seal the cracks for the crossing.

Sitting next to the old man, Beau asked, "Do you want me to ask Edsel to give the sermon tomorrow?"

Otto looked at him with bleary eyes. At first, the mountain man thought the man hadn't heard him. He was about to repeat the suggestion when Otto straightened up. "I want to apologize for the way I've been acting. You need us to be strong and do our part. I will give the sermon tomorrow."

"You've been an important part of this wagon train," Beau told him. "You deserve time to remember your son."

As they talked, Beau saw some of the life come back into Otto's eyes. Continuing to make his rounds, Beau noticed the old man helping Ludwig with the tarring. Only Alvin Thompson and Web Johnson remained disabled by their wounds. Edsel was sure they would heal with time. Jocko was going to take the Thompson wagon across the river.

The next morning, everyone gathered to hear Otto's sermon. The old man spoke with a bit less fire and brimstone, but replaced it with hope and talked of their future and doing the Lord's work in Oregon. He then spoke of his son, his voice becoming labored, bringing tears to many eyes. Everyone realized how easily it could have been one of their loved ones who was killed.

After a Sunday meal, including hot cornbread and sourdough biscuits, the rest of the day was spent putting their supplies and gear back into the wagons. Beau had requested that the canvas tops be removed from, or rolled up on, the wagons in the morning. If a floating wagon was to be upset by a rock or hole on the bottom, he didn't want anyone inside being trapped under the cover.

The wind was cold and damp that night and everyone was sleeping in their clothes, snug within their blankets. Beau awoke several times, thinking about the crossing. He knew it was the right thing to do, but what if someone was lost in the river?

A cold rain with some sleet was falling the next morning. Beau stood near the river looking at the three, crescent-shaped islands. The first two crossings were about 150 feet each. From the eastern point of the second island to the far bank was three or four times as far.

Past travelers had cut down the bank, entering the south side of the river, making it easier getting into the water. The temperature would rise enough as the hours passed, preventing the precipitation from becoming all freezing rain or snow.

He ran his hand down the barrel of his Hawken, knocking off the pellets of ice that had formed on contact. Beau heard footsteps behind him and turned. Jocko walked, hunched, ducking his neck under his collar from the morning chill, his buckskin coat dark from the rain.

"Damn miserable weather," his stocky friend complained.

"It sure as hell ain't making the river water any warmer," Beau replied.

"Folks are starting to stir near the wagons," Jocko told him. "I figure they'll wait for the last minute before pulling the tops off. They'll be hoping the rain stops."

It was the 24th of September and early for such cold, wet weather. Beau had expected frosty mornings and some cool days during their September travel across the high elevations along the Snake River, but he hadn't expected snow and freezing rain. He hoped that the cold weather would be followed by fair winds, making the crossing of the higher passes easier.

The cold rain continued and he finally had to order the tops off the wagons and then, with a rope in tow, he swam the sorrel to the first island. Hoot accompanied him with a second line. The plan was to have riders in the water while the wagons came across. Two teams of oxen would be used on each wagon and the drover would wade across in water as deep as his chest, controlling the animals.

After saying a prayer at the south bank, Otto's wagon entered the water. Ludwig walked alongside the oxen while the old man and Slim Johnson rode in the wagon. Beau and Hoot kept the ropes tight as the oxen and wagons reached the deeper water. The wagon rocked and rolled on the top of the water while being swept downstream.

Otto shouted encouragement from the wagon while Ludwig pushed his way through water, using the rod to prod the animals on. Hoot pulled on the rope tied to the wagon. He was as far upstream as the length of rope would allow, fighting to slow the drift of the wagon. Seeing that Ludwig was having no trouble controlling the oxen, Beau dropped his rope and went to help Hoot.

Finally, the wagon wheels engaged the bottom, almost throwing Otto from his seat by the jerk of the wagon straightening out behind the oxen. Soon the wagon and oxen were on the first island, cold water dripping from the animals and wagon. Hoot and Beau quickly coiled up the ropes and crossed on their horses to the second island, trailing the ropes behind them.

Otto and Slim climbed down and untied the trailing ropes on the wagon, then got ready to help the next one across. While Web had a wound that had cracked a bone in his right arm, he insisted on driving the oxen across. He argued that while he could not pull on the lines, he could handle a rod with his left arm driving the oxen. He also pointed out that his wound was well-scabbed over and water shouldn't hurt it.

The Johnson wagon started across with Web alongside the oxen, holding his right arm high out of the water and driving the oxen with the rod. Meanwhile, the Graf wagon started across to the second island. While the wagon still swung downstream, the water was not as deep and it was floating for a shorter time. Soon there was a wagon on each of the islands. Hoot and Beau led the Graf oxen to the eastern tip of the island while Ludwig walked alongside, catching his breath.

It was not practical to string lines across from the second island to the far bank. Beau and Hoot would remain on their horses in the water to help out if a wagon got into trouble. Beau held a rope that was tied to the wagon, riding upstream from it. This worked out when the wagon first started to float, preventing some of the drift. Once his horse was forced to swim, he had to let the rope go to prevent his horse from being rolled.

Hoot had to fight to stay on his horse as it began to crow hop as it fought to maintain footing on the bottom of the river. After driving the team back upstream a short distance, the first wagon finally reached the exit on the far bank. "Drive the team to the flat area beyond the river and get a fire going," Beau told Ludwig before heading back across to the second island.

The mountain man knew that those driving the oxen across would be nearly frozen by the time they got across and would need the heat. After three hours, six wagons were across. The rain had stopped and a break had to be taken to rest the riding stock. The extra oxen had already been moved across the river.

Hoot and Beau stood near the fire, warming their legs. Beau had switched the saddle from the sorrel to the bay. Edsel's wagon was across and he pulled out a bottle of brandy, giving the chilled workers a drink to help warm their insides. He had just finished checking Web's arm and was pleased to see that the water had not reached the wound.

After a half-hour of huddling near the fire, Beau, Hoot, Slim, and Jocko climbed onto their horses and entered the river, crossing to the second island, where two wagons waited to cross. Clem Williams was the next wagon to cross. Lucy and the four children sat in the wagon. Young Charles was upset that he hadn't been allowed to ride a horse across the river. His mother told him that Edsel was worried that he might get his wound wet. Reminding him that he had been wounded fighting the Shoshone brought a smile to his face.

Peck's wagon was the second from the last to cross. While drifting downstream on the way to the far bank, his back wheels ended up hung up in some rocks. He stood waist-deep in the water with the wagon directly downstream behind the oxen. Carrie sat in the wagon, her face white as she hung on for dear life.

Jocko and Beau were trying to help him. "Toss me a couple of ropes," he called to them. Grabbing the ropes, he tied them to the yoke ring. "Take up the slack and help me get them off the rocks," Peck requested.

The two men began to apply tension to the rope while Peck shouted at the oxen and prodded them with the rod. Suddenly, there was a snapping sound and the front axle came loose as the king bolt broke. The oxen lurched forward with the front wheels and tongue of the wagon, while water splashed over the front of the wagon box as it dipped down.

Free from the oxen and the weight of the front wheels and axle, the back wheels became free of the rocks and the wagon began to move downstream. Carrie screamed with fear, realizing the danger of her situation. Peck had his hands full with the lunging oxen as they tried to break for the far bank, the tongue and axle in tow.

Jocko and Beau did not hesitate as they dropped the ropes and went to Carrie's rescue. Jocko came by the slow-moving wagon, grabbed her outreached hand and pulled her onto his horse. Beau carried a second rope on his saddle, quickly made a loop and tossed it over the exposed seat of the wagon.

Wrapping it around the saddle horn, he set his horse against the moving wagon. The bottom was still dragging over the rocks and it was not difficult to stop.

Within moments, two other riders were near the wagon. Slim had run into the water and took over bringing the frantic oxen to the river bank. Peck waded back to the wagon, swearing at himself for trying to pull the wagon off the rocks.

The riders began grabbing goods out of the wagon and taking them to the river bank. The first thought was to abandon the wagon in the river. Peck convinced them that the wagon could be easily fixed if it could be gotten out of the water. With the help of several riders and ropes, the wagon was towed backwards out of the river and pulled onto the bank at the closest point. It bounced over rocks and brush as they got it to an open area.

Four men lifted the front of the wagon while Peck put his wheel jack under the front. He was then able to survey the damage. He crawled back out from under the wagon, smiling. "Just needs a little fixing and a new bolt," he announced.

With everyone safely on the north side of the river, wood and brush was added to the fire. Several men stood around the flames in their wet long johns. Clothing was draped everywhere to dry. The sky had cleared and the sun was shining. Edsel walked around to share his brandy with the chilled men.

Beau knew they would have several more rivers to cross before reaching the Willamette Valley, but none as dangerous, yet as beneficial, as this one. He was thankful that nobody had drowned or even been hurt during the crossing.

As soon as Jocko got into dry clothing, he rode

out with his Hawken to see if he could bring in some meat for the wagon train. Beau admired his friend for all he had done to help him lead the wagons and providing meat for the folks.

He noticed Carrie standing with her hands on her hips, scolding Peck as she watched the front axle being pushed back under the wagon. Soon the wagon would be fixed and the stack of items that had been pulled from it could be put back into the box.

Just before dark, Jocko returned with two pronghorns slung over the back of his saddle. He dropped them to the ground near the fly tarp Beau had set up. "Just west of here the storm washed out part of the trail. If we go around the north side of the first hill, we'll add a couple miles, but we won't have to spend time fixing the trail."

Pointing to the pronghorn, Beau said, "I am glad you had some luck. The wagons are beginning to run low on supplies. We are about two weeks from Fort Boise to replenish."

"We still have the pemmican," Jocko said. "If the snow slows us down in the Blue Mountains or Cascades, hunting will be poor and it might be all we have to eat."

"It's the last week of September," the mountain man said. "We have just over a month of traveling before we reach the Willamette Valley. We best be on the Barlow Road before the end of October."

The next morning the wagon train headed west on the north side of the Snake River. Again, they faced rolling hills covered with sage and brown grass and often camped away from water. Other than sage brush, firewood was scarce. When they found trees or thick brush along the tributaries flowing into the Snake River, the folks took advantage of it and filled the canvases slung under the wagons.

Wes' and Alvin's wounds healed quickly, making everyone capable of doing their share on the trail. While the terrain ahead of them seemed endless, the moods were positive. The guide books that some had gotten gave little information after Fort Hall. Many had been written by the Mormons and focused more on the California Trail, which went south.

When the wagon train reached Bonneville Point, the folks had their first glimpse of the Boise River Valley. The tree-lined river valley offered grazing, firewood and water. The area was known as the wooded river. The leaves had changed to fall colors and there was a blanket of them beneath the spreading limbs.

Camped near a stream, they built a large fire and broiled steaks from an elk that Jocko had shot. Life was good for the moment and the weather had remained fair. In a few days they would be at Fort Boise and many were looking forward to purchasing supplies. Tano and Herb played their fiddles while Tom Wolsey and Beth led with the dancing.

Beau had continued to keep the wagon train on alert in case of an attack. Most of the tribes were in winter camp by now, but there was always the chance of hunting parties that might try to steal horses or even take a scalp. Rifles remained loaded and close by, and the horses were kept within the wagons at night.

The Williams wagon was in the lead when Fort Boise came into view. Young Charles was the first to call out the smoke of their fires while riding in the wagon. He had been sitting on the seat with his flintlock at the ready, on watch for danger.

The fort was much smaller than Fort Hall. The folks also found that while flour, cornmeal, and other staples were plentiful, they were quite expensive. Many had to cut down the list of items they had intended to purchase and stick with necessities only.

After the wagons were situated in the camp, Beau and Jocko walked to the fort. It was mid-afternoon and they were interested in a bath, a haircut, and a few drinks. Smoke and steam rolled out of one of the log buildings, where a large caldron filled with water was heated over an open firepit. They entered the barber shop carrying bottles of whiskey.

"We need our hair trimmed, a hot bath, and then you can direct us to a place that serves a good meal," Beau told the owner.

As the man sat him into the wooden chair that served as a barber chair, he said, "It will take more than a trim to make you boys look civilized. A clip and bath will be four bits."

Jocko laughed, "The damn bottle cost less than getting civilized."

By the time they arrived at the eating establishment, which consisted of a few long tables with benches, the two men had made a dent in their bottles. The fare was some type of roasted meat, rice, and, a course bread. The aproned owner had told them the type of meat, but feeling no pain due to the whiskey, neither could remember what it was as they chewed the stringy roast.

It was Saturday, and business at the fort was brisk. Beau and Jocko staggered back toward the wagons, freshly washed and clipped, bellies full, and feeling giddy from the whiskey. They would be back on the trail by Monday, and figured they'd have Sunday to heal from a night of merriment.

While purchasing the whiskey, Beau had met a freighter who had just come over the trail from Portland. He had told the mountain man that the trail was in good condition and all passes were still clear of snow. He had mentioned that the tolls on the Barlow Road would be about $3 per wagon.

Sunday morning came with the familiar headache and queasy stomach that resulted from a night of celebrating. Beau and Jocko were sitting near their small fire, nursing mugs of coffee when Otto came by.

"Services are in one hour," the old man told them. "I heard you got a bath with the haircuts. By the smell of you two, you wasted your money."

Watching Otto walk away, Beau said, "I am glad to see that he's back to his old self."

"Do you think he'll be preaching about the evils of drink in the sermon?" Jocko asked. Despite the hangovers, both men nodded and laughed.

CHAPTER SIXTEEN

The wagon train endured two days of cold rain after leaving Fort Boise. As Beau had been told, the trail was good, and the wagons were making 15 miles on many days. The fort had been a disappointment for most of the people. While whiskey was cheap, supplies were not. Good grazing in the Boise River Valley had the oxen in good shape for the challenge of the Blue Mountains.

The Snake River continued north and had cut a gorge into dark volcanic rock, forcing the wagon train trail to climb onto a plateau to the west. Once on the plateau, the people got their first view of the Blue Mountains. They appeared to be a formidable line of snow-covered rock, rising thousands of feet above the plateau.

The wagon train soon went from thick grass and wooded streams to a semi-arid landscape. It was covered with sparse grasses, greasewood, and sage. The trail tended to wander somewhat as it searched out water and avoided pinnacles of rock.

As the wagon train approached the mountains, they began to experience some of the foot hills and narrow trails running along ridges, exposing steep drops. Finding acceptable places to camp became more difficult for Jocko. He had to make sure he didn't ride beyond the distance that the wagons could be driven in a day. On horseback, he could travel the 12 to 15 miles in a few hours if he kept the horse at a trot.

The last day in the foothills, they were camped below the towering Blue Mountains and the air was cold. The pond nearby had ice along the edges that had remained throughout the day. A large fire, fueled by sage, burned in the center of the wagons. Everyone was huddled around for warmth, drinking coffee made with water that had a sulfur taste. Even the children drank the coffee with a bit of honey, to sweeten it and make it palatable.

Beau addressed the group. "Tomorrow we start the climb through the mountains . . ."

"What have we been climbing through the past couple of days?" Alvin asked.

Smiling, the mountain man replied, "While they might have felt like mountains, they were just the foothills leading up to the Blue Mountains."

There was a rumbling in the crowd as they kidded each other about the past days' travel being only foothills. Beau cleared his throat to get their attention. "Like I said, we are about to start through the mountains. While it will be the most difficult part of our trip, the next 100 miles has had the trail improved a lot since the first wagons came this way. When we're not traveling on narrow ridges, we'll be in winding valleys or sidehills that you'd swear the wagon won't stay upright."

"Is there any good news about the next 100 miles?" Hoot kidded him.

Grinning, Beau replied, "I just gave you the good news."

"What!" Web exclaimed.

"I'm sorry," the mountain man said. "I probably should have started with the bad news. We can expect ice and snow in the mountains. Elk, deer, and bears have all left the high country and it is unlikely we'll have much fresh meat. The next place we can depend on finding supplies to purchase is the Dalles near the Columbia River."

"Do we reach the Dalles after we get over the mountains?" Peck asked.

"We got 100 miles of mountains and then another 100 miles across some mighty dry ground before the Dalles," Beau told him. "What we need to do is look over your food supplies. Figure out how to make them last three weeks. The pemmican is company food and that will be the last thing we eat."

"I thought our belts and boots were the last thing we eat," Hoot said, laughing.

"I have been close to doing so some of the winters," Beau admitted.

"What if we get snowed in?" Lucy asked. "I read about the Donner party eating each other to survive."

"They were stuck in the mountains for the winter," he told her. "This won't happen to us. Years back, a woman and her two children crossed these mountains through blizzards and deep snow. It can be done, and Jocko and I know how to do it."

After answering a few more questions, the folks went to look over their supplies. Beau knew that the meals would be smaller and the baked goods everyone had been enjoying would become a memory. While not discussing it, he realized that if they were snowed in, the wagons would have to be abandoned and most of the stock would starve. Beau figured they had enough to worry about without adding that information to his warning.

They broke camp shortly after daylight. The pond was completely frozen over and axes were used to chop holes to water stock. Steaming breath rose from the animals as they pulled the wagons away from the pond. Everyone was walking, finding that it helped them keep warm. Beau led the bay with his packs while his sorrel was tied to the lead wagon.

For the first couple of days in the mountains, there wasn't much different than what had been experienced in the foothills. They awoke on the third day to rain. The wagon train trudged on, with mountains rising on all sides. The folks walked alongside the wagons, using them as windbreaks. After the two days of cold wind and stinging rain, the weather improved. Threatening clouds remained in the sky, but the rain or snow they carried remained aloft.

The smaller wheels at the front of the wagon made pulling more difficult, but allowed tighter turns along the mountain trail. While none of theirs were small enough to make a 90-degree turn, with care they sufficed to handle the sharp bends on the trail.

Jocko rode ahead, looking for mountain meadows, or valleys with grazing. Though he was always on the lookout for game, he hadn't had any success. The worry of being attacked by tribes was all but gone in the mountains, but it had become a habit to keep the rifles ready. One saving grace in the mountain travel was the plentiful supply of wood. Another 2,000 feet up it would have been scarce, but at the level they were traveling the trail wound through and around plenty of trees.

A snow storm hit them about halfway through the mountains. For two days they camped in a grove of aspen as the blowing snow filtered through every crack and opening in the wagons, leaving a layer covering everything. Beau and Jocko had fashioned a tent out of the fly tarp and stacked their packs at one opening, and had a fire for warmth at the other.

The mountain man saw the worry on everyone's faces as they sat near their fires, trying to keep warm. He knew that they had plenty to worry about, but it was mid-October and early for the passes to be snowed in. Too much talk about the Donner party was being discussed at the fires. Beau reminded them that they had more than enough meat in their stock if the snow didn't stop, and with a week of walking they could be out of the mountains.

He was thankful when the snow stopped on the third day. Beau knew they would be facing drifts, but the accumulation was not much over a foot. The camp awoke to a winter wonderland. There was sunshine and the snow sparkled. Their stock had spent the storm chewing on tender branches of the aspen and were ready to travel.

The folks now faced another danger and that was snow blindness. Beau had them cut strips of thin cloth with slits and cover their eyes. As the oxen were hitched to the wagons, the snow crunched under the men's boots. The children played in the snow while waiting to move out. Beau asked them to stop, reminded everyone about the danger of sweating in the frigid temperatures. He would keep the pace of the wagons slow enough to help prevent that from happening.

The wagons started with their axles complaining due to the tar and grease mixture being frozen. Soon they would warm up enough to quiet down. The trail was blocked, with chest-high drifts in some places and the ground was bare in others. The wind picked up particles of snow, which stung any exposed skin on the people's faces.

They drove the extra stock ahead to help break trail. Jocko walked along with Beau to keep his feet from freezing. That night they camped in a narrow valley, with the wagons strung out. Axes rang out in the dusk as windfalls were chopped up for the fires. Ice on top of the water barrels had to be broken to make coffee. Some didn't bother and just used snow.

A large pot of beans was boiled for a community meal. Side meat and molasses were added to give it taste. Edsel warned everyone about frostbite, having seen the results of it from his days in the military.

Beau estimated that they would be out of the mountains in another four to five days of travel. He was hoping that any more snow would hold off until then. It had been difficult to keep to the snow-covered trail with the glare of the sun. He had traveled it three times in the past, but never in the snow. Tomorrow he'd send Jocko ahead to make sure they didn't make a wrong turn.

The next morning offered some cloud cover. It would help with the glare, but there was the fear of another storm. The wagons pulled out, having a long, uphill climb along a slippery ridge. As the lead wagons packed the snow, it made it worse for those coming behind. Beau made sure that everyone walked clear of the wagons, should one slide.

Lucy Williams was walking behind their wagon with her children and Clem drove the oxen. Young Charles had asked his father if he could drive today, but his mother had insisted he stay with her. He made sure he was a few steps ahead of the family and carried his flintlock at the ready.

There was a shout, and Beau turned to see snow sliding from the hill above, just in front of the Williams wagon. His eyes went large as he saw the cause. A mountain lion had been stalking the wagons from above and had started the slide. It was now on the trail in front of Clem, snarling. The man fought to control his oxen as more snow slid down, hitting the wagon.

As though in slow motion, the wagon slid sideward and went off the edge of the ridge. Clem clung to the lead rope, slipped, and fell on his back. Suddenly, the wagon and the team of oxen next to it disappeared over the ridge, the trace chains breaking, leaving the remaining two teams on the trail.

There was a rifle shot and the mountain lion spun around and started back up the hillside only to collapse and roll down in front of the struggling Clem, leaving a trail of blood in the snow. It was Young Charles who had shot the cat. Lucy and the other children stood frozen in place, screaming. Peck, who was right behind them, dropped his lead rope and ran forward to help.

For the next several minutes there was confusion as the wagons stopped and people called to find out what had happened. The snow-covered ledge was narrow, with drifted snow against the granite wall, preventing others from coming forward and helping. Clem stood holding the lead rope and was shaking. He had just watched his worldly possessions go over the ridge and fall into a canyon several hundred feet below. Lucy and the three girls ran to him and she grabbed ahold of her husband, crying. When she had seen the snow hit the wagon, she had been sure he'd be pulled over the side.

Young Charles stood over the dead cat, his eyes filled with tears. "I got the damn thing," he said as Beau came up. The quick action of the young man, in shooting the cat should have been cause for celebration, but the tragedy of the wagon going over the side eclipsed it.

As he went by Charles, he patted his shoulder and said, "You done good, lad."

The wagon train was in no position to remain stopped on the ridge and, despite the loss of a wagon, had to keep moving. Peck and Young Charles dragged the cat and threw it into the back of his wagon. Shovels were taken out and the snow remaining from the slide was pushed over the side. Below, the wagon and two oxen could hardly be seen among the trees and sliding snow. Everyone knew it would be impossible to salvage anything from the wagon.

Still in shock at what had just happened, the wagons continued up the ridge, Clem leading his remaining four oxen, staring ahead, clutching the rope. Still crying, Lucy and the children walked alongside him. Nothing could be done and there was no reason to stop as they reached the top of the ridge. With only the occasional sound of a drover barking at the oxen, everyone walked or rode in silence.

A few miles beyond the ridge, Jocko had found a place to spend the night. Tears flowed freely as the women consoled Lucy. In silence, the camp was set up and a fire started. Jocko had missed the tragedy and stared in awe at the large cat that was dragged out of Peck's wagon. Young Charles couldn't help but look proud as the men went by, congratulating him on a fine shot.

No one on the wagon train had eaten cougar before. This large male, weighing about 180 pounds, would make more than one meal for the folks. Jocko helped young Charles skin the animal and then cut up the meat to be shared with the wagons. Beau watched as the young man and his friend scraped the hide and stretched it on a frame made of pine branches.

Aarno called Beau over. "Kimi and I don't need two wagons and I want to loan mine to the Williams."

"That would be good of you, but it has all your supplies," the mountain man replied.

"He got four young'uns and a wife to feed," the crusty old man said. "They need it more than me. I'll get by with a bit here and there."

The Williams family was sitting together by the fire. Beau carried his extra rifle as he and Aarno walked up to them. "Aarno here wants to let your family have the use of his wagon and supplies for the rest of the trip," the mountain man told them. "I got this here extra rifle for you to have."

Hearing the offer, a cheer went up from those standing around the fire. Offers of blankets and clothing came quickly from the others. Several invited Aarno to share their fires for his meals. Beau walked back to his fire with a feeling inside that he couldn't explain. It was warm and tugged at his heart. These people had grown close. It was something he had never experienced while trapping and hunting in the mountains. He was sure his friend Elijah had found it.

The next few days the snow held off and the wagons made good distance. Clem's family was using Aarno's wagon. It appeared Clem hadn't gotten over the shock of the loss yet. He'd lead the oxen and set up camp, but spoke only when spoken to. They were coming to the foothills on the western side. A good spot had been found at mid-afternoon and Beau decided to give everyone a spell. Otto announced that there would be a sermon later that evening to make up for traveling on Sundays.

Beau noticed Lucy Williams walking around her wagon, checking on things. He walked over calling to her, "If there is something you can't find, maybe I can help you."

Turning to him, she had tears in her eyes. "Is something wrong?" he asked.

"Father is gone," she said. "He took the rifle and walked off into the woods."

"Maybe he went hunting," Beau suggested.

"His shooting bag is in the wagon and so is his money belt," she said, her voice cracking.

Speaking softly, he told her, "I'll go find him. Now don't you be worrying. Your husband's a good man and he loves you and the children."

Hurrying back to his fly tarp, Beau pulled out his Colt Paterson and headed out, following the tracks leading away from their wagon. A river ran near the wagons and had cut a gully. The tracks led down to the river, crossing on some rocks. There was one spot where Clem had slipped into the water. For almost a mile the mountain man followed the man as the tracks wound through the trees and around boulders.

The sun was getting low when he suddenly heard a voice somewhere ahead. "Go back."

"Is that you, Clem?" Beau asked. "I come to help you in case you got something."

Continuing ahead, he saw the man sitting on a windfall, the rifle standing between his knees. "I ain't hunting."

"I know. I know you aren't hunting," Beau said softly.

"Why did you come after me?" the man asked.

Searching for the right words, the mountain man blurted out, "To bring back the rifle."

"What?" Clem said, turning to look at Beau.

"We need the rifles and I figured you wouldn't be needing it anymore."

Suddenly, as though he was trying to explain his actions, Clem said, "I got nothing to offer her and the kids. Everything I had went over the ridge with the wagon. My whole life's, gone. She'll meet someone that can offer her and the children a new start. Until then Charles will be able to help her."

Feeling a bit angry and guarding his words, Beau said, "You got everything. A wife that loves you. Good children that look up to you. And you got friends."

"We got nothing to start a life in Oregon," the man said. "She'll meet someone that has what's needed to build a farm and a life." He shifted the rifle a bit.

"Before you go and destroy something good, let me tell you what you got," Beau said. "You got two hands that know how to work a farm. Friends that will share their tools and equipment with you. You got a fine team of oxen, milking cows, and a wife that loves you and sews the best clothes on this wagon train. Between the two of you, you'll have no problem building a life in Oregon."

The man sat on the log not speaking. Beau knew this had to end soon. He was going to have to tackle Clem and hope neither of them was hit by the ball if the rifle went off. Then he'd drag him back to the wagons. Telling him he was after the rifle had distracted the man before, so he decided to say one more thing before moving.

"Well, hurry up and do it. It's getting dark and I need to get back."

Beau was about to leap forward when he saw the rifle fall into the snow in front of Clem. The man put his hands to his face and began to weep. The mountain man could hear him say, "You're right. I am a damn fool."

Stepping forward quickly, Beau picked up the rifle and sat on the log next to Clem. "We got to get back. Lucy's worried."

"Sometimes a man's a damn fool," he repeated. "I was sitting here thinking about the plow points, tools, and stuff that went over with the wagon. When I saw it go over the side, it was like everything else shut down."

"You know your son shot the cat," Beau said.

"Yes, I know. I never even told him it was a good shot." Clem suddenly realized. "My boy shot a damn mountain lion."

The two men got up and started back toward the wagons. "What do I tell Lucy and the others?" he asked Beau.

"Tell them you saw a nice deer, but it was too dark to shoot," the mountain man told him. "Or hell, tell them you'd have gotten one but I spooked it."

"Damn, my feet are cold," the man said. "I got them wet coming across the river."

"I know," Beau said.

* * *

Crossing the rugged and narrow trails of the Blue Mountain broke some wheels and tongues. The frosty evenings were often spent repairing wagons and replacing bows on yokes for the next day's travel. Relief was felt by all once they left the high passes behind. While the foothills had their difficulties, the frigid temperatures and fear of snow storms closing the passes were gone.

Once out of the foothills, the wagon train started across the high plains of the Columbia Plateau. It was near desert, with sparse vegetation similar to that seen before they started into the mountains. A constant wind blew from the west. The days were sunny and mild while the nights were bone chilling, with the wind cutting through the thickest blanket.

The cougar skin was proudly displayed on the tailgate of the Williams' borrowed wagon. Young Charles would tell anyone willing to listen about the killing of the cat. The distance of the shot continued to get a bit longer and whether the cat was crouching or attacking became a bit hazy on the telling.

The freight wagon caught up to them a day out on the plateau. The teamster had a good amount of smoked salmon and shared some with the wagon train before leaving them the next morning. With its six mules, the freight wagon quickly became a speck on the horizon.

Despite the salmon gotten from the freighter, the wagon train was eating the pemmican before reaching the Dalles. The pounded meat and berries mixed with fat made a fine soup once a few seasonings were added. At the fire, over a hot bowl, Beau told the story of one winter when he had made soup out of the leather bag holding the pemmican after it was eaten.

The Dalles were a welcome sight for the folks. It promised supplies, news, and a chance to wash clothes and get a hot bath. Before the Barlow Road was cut around Mount Hood, the wagons would be brought down the Columbia River on rafts for the last leg of their journey, bringing another host of dangers with white water and hidden rocks.

They were now 90 miles from the end of their 2,000-mile trip. It was the beginning of November and by the beginning of December they would be on their farms. After a hot bath and some clean clothing, Beau and Jocko stopped into a brightly lit saloon. They ran into Hoot and his brothers being entertained by some sweet-smelling ladies.

Slim had had a few drinks and leaned over to Beau. "Don't tell Otto you saw us with these girls. We'll become the subject of his next sermon."

"The night is young," Beau said. "Maybe we'll all be keeping the secret."

"Not me," Jocko said. "I am almost back to Lisa."

"That's right," the mountain man said. "And you got a young'un."

The Johnson boys raised their glasses of

whiskey. "To Jocko's family."

From there the night went south and Beau woke up the next morning with a heavy head and a brown-haired gal next to him. He felt his waist. His money belt was gone.

"Where . . ." Sitting up quickly, the room spun and he held his head waiting for it to stop.

A sweet voice next to him said, "If you're looking for your money, it's on the table beside you." Reaching out to press her soft body against him, she added, "I don't steal a man's money, I earn it."

After a little more comfort and a good breakfast, Beau headed back to the wagons. He found Jocko drinking coffee. "Did you spend all your money on foolish pleasures?" he asked, kidding his friend.

"You were supposed to make sure I got back here," Beau said.

"Even though I tried, that brown-haired beauty had more pull than I did," Jocko explained.

The mountain man counted his money and went through his packs to see what he needed to get before leaving the Dalles. He had over $200 which should be enough to get started on a small farm. Once he had made a list, he headed for the mercantile, keeping clear of the saloon and its pleasures. Last night had cost him a half-month of pay at most jobs.

After four days at the Dalles, the wagon train took the Barlow Road, heading for Oregon City. The road was cut around Mount Hood through heavy timber and crossed the Cascade Range. While crossing the Cascades, the wagon train hit more snow. These mountains were much lower than the Blue Mountains. It offered challenges with the trail winding through the trees, narrow passes, and had ridges to go over. The final descent into Oregon City required using ropes snubbed to trees to lower the wagons.

The wagon train camped outside the city. After months on the plains and mountains, seeing a modern city was almost intimidating. A few had kept special clothes to wear once they arrived, but most had only trail-worn pants, shirts, and dresses. Clem had gone into the city leading four oxen the day they arrived, and returned with a wagon to replace the one lost and a sewing machine for Lucy. By the next day she had set up shop out of the back of the wagon, repairing and making clothes for the ladies.

As if it had waited, the pregnant milk cow had a calf. It was a heifer and the beginning of their herd. Each wagon was to keep four oxen and the remainder were driven into town to be sold. The money was split between each wagon owner, with an equal share going to Beau and Jocko. All the men except Beau and Jocko filed for the 320 acres of free land offered to each emigrant. The mountain man chose to wait and see where Jocko and Lisa were before doing so.

The men returned with supplies and whiskey. That evening all available Dutch ovens were on the fires with sweet bread, pies or cobblers, and corn bread. One of the oxen hampered with swollen leg joints was butchered and the hind quarters were roasted on spits for the end of the trip celebration. There was music, singing, and dancing that night. Beau sat back with a bottle, watching the people interact. They had become close over the six-month trip, each depending on the other.

When the last team of oxen had been unhitched from the wagons, Beau's position as leader had ended. At that moment, Beau had felt relieved from having the burden of leadership lifted. From the first step west until the last, he'd been responsible for the lives of those with the train. The loss of Jon at the North Platte River was still with him. Beck Graf being killed fighting the Shoshone had him wondering if he should have tried running instead of taking a stand. He wondered if he had saved lives or had caused a death.

Holding up the bottle, he took a mouthful and swallowed the amber liquid, feeling the bite on his throat. Whiskey helped him with these things for a short time, but once the headache was gone and his stomach had settled, the problems were still there. Tonight, he was happy for everyone who had come with him from Missouri. They all knew what they were going to do and where they were going.

Some of the people had friends or family whom they had come out to meet and had a destination in mind, while others were starting fresh and just picked an available spot in the Willamette Valley. Within the next week, most of the wagons would be heading for their future homes with tearful goodbyes and promises to stay in contact.

Beau was going with Jocko, but not as part of his and Lisa's family. The mountain man's job was over and he just needed someplace to be going. He still thought about getting his own farm, but again, he'd be alone and the farm wouldn't be a home.

The Hansons and Williams were the first to leave the next day. They had chosen farms alongside each other. Aarno led his wagon near Beau's and Jocko's fly tarp. The four oxen stood patiently, tearing at the grass, their tails swatting flies off their backs.

The old man handed the lead rope to Beau. "We got an extra wagon and only need one. Nobody's forgotten that you and Jocko gave up the money we was to pay you in exchange for what you got selling the raft. I only wish I had a wagon for each of you. The other folks wanted you to have some things and they're in the wagon."

As Aarno turned away to return to Kimi and Helena, Beau could have sworn he saw a tear in the old man's eye. "Thank you!" Beau called after him. Aarno waved as he continued walking.

Jocko had been watering the horses and returned, stopping near the wagon. "Is Aarno here?"

"He was," Beau said. "He brought you and Lisa his wagon. He said there was stuff inside from others."

The two men stood at the back, looking over the tailgate. Their jaws dropped upon seeing the bags of flour, cornmeal, beans, coffee, and tea. There was side meat, a block of cheese, hard bread, lard, and even some eggs.

Beau felt his throat tighten as he was overwhelmed by the generous gifts. He watched as their wagons left the camp. Shortly after, the Thompsons and Wards left. Hoot and his brothers had gotten work at a sawmill to earn money and meet women to eventually settle down with.

Peck and Carrie were the next to leave. Beau and Jocko thanked them for the gifts. "I only wish it could have been more," Peck said.

"You were a Godsend on the trip," Beau told him. "You kept things repaired and never asked for a thing in return."

Again, emotional goodbyes were said, making everyone feel awkward. The Wilsons had relatives near Salem and chose property near there. It was only 15 miles from where Lisa had the farm and Beau was sure they would see them again.

The Tuckers, Edwards, and Wolseys got farms adjacent to each other. Cora planned to start a school if one wasn't available in the area. Beau let Tano and Herb know that he would miss their fiddle music.

Otto and his son were the last ones Beau said goodbye to. Ludwig was going to farm and his father hoped to start a church in a village near the land they'd chosen. They sat near the fire sharing a meal the night before heading out.

"You taught me a lot," Otto told Beau. "I figured I could lead the wagons to Oregon without anyone's help. Just ride west I thought. I thank God every night that he sent you to me."

"I am not sure who he sent to who," the mountain man replied. "I depended greatly on your ability to keep everyone together. Those Sunday sermons gave everyone hope."

The next morning, the Grafs pulled out and that left Beau and Jocko alone. "I figured you'd be the first one to pull out," he told his stocky friend. "All you talked of is Lisa and wanting to see her."

"I did do that," Jocko said. "I have been waiting for you to be ready to go. I am afraid when I get there she won't want me no more, and I'll need your help to get over it."

"Well, it ain't possible that she wouldn't want you," Beau said. "Why, you got everything a woman could want except maybe money and . . ."

"Oh, shut up," his friend snapped.

The farm Lisa had gotten was in Silver Creek, three days south and west of Oregon City. With their pack horses tied to the wagon and Beau holding the lead rope of the oxen, the two friends rode south. Beau could see the strain on his friend's face and tried to keep things light. They passed farm after farm as they rode.

One night they stayed in a small inn owned by a German and enjoyed the stout brew he made. He knew Silver Creek well. The area had good timber and rich soil for farming, due to the tribes that had lived there in the past and had kept the area open by burning the brush and trees.

Early the next morning the two men continued, knowing that they would arrive at the farm by early afternoon. Jocko walked, driving the oxen. He said it would help with his nerves. Silver Creek was a small town situated on a river with the same name. Jocko went into the mercantile and got directions to the farm.

When he came out, Beau pointed to a steeple. "They got a church that you and Lisa can use to get married."

The farm was two miles south of town. To the west, Beau admired the peaks of the Cascade Range as they appeared through openings in the trees. The first chance he got, and weather permitting, he'd have to do some exploring in them. The rutted, tree-lined road opened into a four-acre clearing. In the middle there was a small log cabin with smoke coming from the stone fireplace. Jocko's jaw was set and his eyes showed worry. As they stopped in front of the building, the sound of a crying baby could be heard.

"Your young'un has good lungs," Beau told his friend.

As Jocko handed the lead rope to Beau, the door of the cabin opened. A pretty woman in a faded gingham dress came out. "Can I help . . ." Then she screamed, "Jocko!" and ran into his arms.

I guess she hasn't forgotten him, Beau thought.

The protesting baby continued to demand the mother's attention. "Come in and meet your son," she told Jocko, taking his hand and leading him into the cabin.

"What is his name?" Jocko asked.

"I call him baby boy," she said. "I was waiting for you to name him."

Lisa was leading a spartan life in the Willamette Valley. The small cabin had two rooms and a dirt floor. The door swung on leather hinges and the single window had greased paper in lieu of glass. A fire place was used for cooking and warmth. There was a double bed with a straw tick mattress in the second room. Everything was as clean and neat as possible, with rough log walls and packed earth floors.

There was a lean-to on the back side of the cabin. It was not large enough to hold their horses and oxen. Beau noticed that Lisa did not have any animals at the place. She told them that the cabin had already been on the land when she'd gotten it. Its prior owner had given the farm up and headed for the gold fields of California.

The animals were picketed behind the cabin. The supplies from the wagon were carried into the cabin and piled in the middle of the floor. Lisa would have a challenge finding places to store them. Beau and Jocko put their blanket rolls into the wagon. The mountain man had told his friend that it would have been okay if he'd have slept in the cabin.

Shaking his head, Jocko said, "Lisa and I both think it best if we get married first. Besides, how could

I explain it if Otto suddenly showed up?"

Laughing, Beau said, "It is unlikely that would happen, but you do have a point."

The next day they hitched oxen to the wagon and the two men walked with them while Lisa and young Jon rode in the wagon. Dressed in their best, Jocko and Lisa found the preacher's house. The man was near the wood shed, splitting firewood.

"You all will have to wait until I get the rest of this wood split and stacked," the preacher told them. "The Lord's work will wait. It appears you two didn't," he said, looking at the baby. "We'll baptize the child at the same time."

Rolling up their sleeves, Beau and Jocko went to work helping the preacher with the wood. In no time they were all headed for the church and the wedding. A few of the town folks wandered in to see what was going on and were treated to a fine sermon about sinning, followed by wedding vows and a baptism.

A few years earlier the preacher had come over the Oregon Trail and quickly took a liking to his new church members. He invited them to come to his home to celebrate their marriage. Lisa offered to help his wife with the meal while the men sat on the front porch with the baby in Jocko's lap. Stories were shared about experiences over the trail and a bottle of whiskey was opened.

The night was spent at the preacher's house, with Jocko's family sleeping in the extra bedroom and Beau on the parlor floor. The next morning a used set of harnesses was purchased from an old gentleman operating the livery. A keg of nails, a broad axe, a draw knife, a pane of glass, and metal hinges were gotten from the mercantile, along with new boots for Beau and Jocko.

Beau had never seen Jocko as happy as he was when they were leading the oxen and wagon back to the cabin. "I am finally home, Beau," he said several times.

CHAPTER SEVENTEEN

The winter was busy. While the Cascades were snow-covered, the valley had little accumulation, with bare ground for much of the winter. A stand of spruce was cut down, limbed and peeled for material to build a barn. The frame was made from squared pine logs. The oxen were used to skid the logs and bundles of the spruce. The spruce poles were placed vertically along the walls and nailed to the frame. Birch trees that were cut for firewood had the bark peeled to be used to cover the barn roof.

They would all work Monday through Saturday on projects to build the farm. On Sundays Josh and Lisa would take young Jon to church, using the wagon drawn by his mustang and gray. Beau would head into the Cascades, figuring the higher he climbed the closer he'd be to heaven.

Beau was lonely. Tramping through the high country had temporarily pushed the feeling to the back of his mind. When on the farm, or in the town, everyone seemed to have family to share their life with.

Most were building a future together. Beau felt he was just existing.

In the quiet hours before going to sleep his mind would be filled with thoughts of those he had known. Friends he had trapped and hunted with and the women he had become close to. They had all gone their own way and he had always felt a kind of freedom being back on his own again doing what he wanted and going through life without any commitments to anyone.

It bothered the mountain man that his thoughts kept coming back to the women that he had known. Ana had been the first, but he had chosen not to take the risk of traveling to Mexico with her. There was Ellie who willingly gave her affection to him, but would require that he give up life in the high country should he choose to be with her.

Then there was Hanna. She was frequently on his mind and he was sure it was her in his dreams with the dark-hair and smiling eyes. Beau knew that he would do most anything to win her hand. He regretted having not told her that he would be coming back to Fort Laramie to see her, after the winter snows melted. Instead he had left, hoping she would follow him to Oregon. Beau also realized that she might not share any of the feelings for him that he had for her. Since he had left her weeping at Jon's grave, the mountain man had created a relationship that might only exist in his mind.

Hard work and climbing around the Cascades had helped him keep his sanity and prevented a risky winter crossing of the Rockies. Now the warm winds of spring were blowing, the barn and a corral were built, two more acres had been cleared, a well was dug and a plank floor had been put into the house. There was a small cot built along one wall, to serve as a place to sit during the day and a bed for Beau at night.

A porch had been built on the front of the cabin, with a couple of benches. They would all sit there in the evening drinking coffee and watching the sun set. One evening, Beau suggested they start the plowing.

"That needs to be done," Jocko said, "but even more important, you got to get your piece of land and Lisa and I will help you build."

"I have been thinking about that," Beau said. "I have never seen two people happier than the both of you. It felt good helping you build over the winter."

"Now it is our turn to help you," Jocko said.

Lisa came out with coffee to join them, her stomach growing large with their next child. "Young Jon is sleeping," she said. "Now, what are you two men talking about?"

"Beau's farm is what were talking about," Jocko said. "It's time I helped him build his home."

"The piece right next to us is available," she said, sipping the steaming brew.

"You two only have 320 acres," Beau said. "You can pick that up for yourselves."

"There's the abandoned place just south of us that would be a good place for you," the stocky friend pointed out.

"You know what has been the happiest times for me here in Oregon?" Beau asked. "Other than being with the two of you?"

"Building things?" Jocko guessed.

Lisa looked at their friend, her brow furled. "What are you getting at, Beau?"

"I will always value your friendship and I've looked forward to being in the Cascades on Sundays," he told them. "But I need something more. I am going to go back east over the Rockies."

"Does going over the mountains end at Fort Laramie?" Jocko asked.

"It could," the mountain man said.

"Hanna will be long gone," his friend replied.

Beau blushed as Lisa asked, "Who is Hanna?"

"She's someone that was with the wagon train for a while," Jocko told his wife. "Beau dreams about her."

Beau appreciated his friend not telling her about Hanna's husband drowning. "I think she will be there until her brother gets out of the army," he said. "Her face haunts my dreams."

"Are you sure it is her in your dreams?" Jocko wondered. "One night, when we had had a few, you told me she stays just out beyond your reach as you chase her."

Beau, smiled, chuckling softly. "I guess I should watch what I say when drinking."

Lisa scolded Jocko for sharing such a personal conversation. "I'll have to watch what I tell you."

Beau stood up and tossed the dregs out of his cup. "I have made up my mind. I am going back east. Truth is, I am not a farmer. I have enjoyed helping you build and haven't met two happier folks than you. You belong here in Oregon, but I don't."

The baby started crying and Lisa went in to check on young Jon. Jocko looked at his friend. "There is no way I can pay you for what you've done for us. Half of the wagon, the oxen, all those supplies, not to mention the work you did."

Smiling, Beau told him, "You already mentioned the work. I am happy and feel we are square with each other. I'll leave with memories of the two of you and if I ever have children, I'll name the first boy Jocko."

His stocky friend tried to smile but didn't do it justice. "If things don't work out for you back there, you will always have a home with us."

Lisa came back out. "Did you talk him out of going?" Jocko shook his head no.

She threw her arms around the mountain man, her pregnant belly pressing against him. "We will miss you," she said, tears streaming down her face.

"It's late," Jocko noted and the two of them went inside to go to bed. Beau sat on a bench and clasped his hands around his empty cup. For the longest time he stared into the dark, listening to the night sounds of frogs, an owl, and the oxen chewing their cuds.

Beau didn't sleep much that night. He was up early and started putting his packs together. Jocko was surprised that he planned to leave so soon. "I was hoping you'd spend a few more days with us."

"Goodbyes have always been hard for me," Beau said. "We said most everything last night and it don't make sense dragging this on."

Lisa came from the back room carrying young Jon. Seeing Beau filling his packs brought her to tears again.

"When I get settled, I'll send you two a letter letting you know how things worked out," he promised her.

She handed the baby to Jocko. Wiping her eyes, she said, "Well, you'll need a good meal before you get started."

* * *

Beau rode away from his friends without looking back. He knew they were on the porch watching. If he looked back, it would only prolong the feeling of loss. Beau planned to travel over Lolo Pass on the north side of Mount Hood. It would save him the tolls on the Barlow Road and on horseback, the 3,400-foot pass was an option. As he had hoped, the view of Mount Hood from the top of Lolo Pass was spectacular with its snow-covered top.

It felt good to be traveling the mountains again. The freedom he had so often experienced was with him. With the covered wagons, they could only travel 12-15 miles a day. On horseback, he would travel twice that, or even more if he had to. Crossing the Columbia Plateau, Beau caught sight of a lone wagon heading east. Suddenly, a smile of recognition broke out on his face. It was the freighter he'd met coming to Oregon.

Pulling alongside the wagon, the freighter looked over. "Are you lost?" he called over. "Last I saw you were heading for a farm in the valley."

"I missed the mountains," Beau called back.

The teamster pulled the mules to a stop. "Time to give them a breather." Pulling a tobacco twist out of his possible bag, the man tore off a chew and then handed it to Beau. After a couple of chaws, he spat.

"If you're heading for Fort Boise, you're welcome to ride on the wagon and give your animals a rest," the freighter offered.

Missing talking to folks after being with people for so long and having enjoyed the company of the man when they'd last met, Beau accepted the teamster's offer. Tossing the packs onto the wagon and loosening the chinch on the sorrel, he tied the horses to the back of the wagon. He had barely gotten seated on the wagon when the teamster cracked his whip over the mules and the wagon was on its way.

The spring floods had not been kind to Fort Boise and they were busy doing repairs. Beau helped the teamster unload his wagon after the mules and horses were put up. They then headed for the saloon. The two men shared most of a bottle after a meal of thick stew and slabs of bread. There was a new girl serving the meals and hustling drinks. She had a wide smile and precocious wit, but the mountain man noticed that her eyes remained serious. Late in the evening, the teamster disappeared into the back with the young lady and Beau set his blanket roll out near the fireplace.

Maybe it was the dark-haired girl's smile that caused him to dream of the one he could not catch. He would get only a glimpse of her smiling eyes and then she was gone. His head was groggy the next morning and he sat up on his blankets with his eyes closed, trying to see a clear picture of her face, but could only picture the eyes. "It had to be Hanna," he told himself.

The mountain man was gone before the teamster got up. The sorrel was anxious to be off and set out at a trot without any urging. Beau stayed away from the top of the rolling hills, not wanting to skyline himself to anyone watching. Again, he was in Bannock and Shoshone territory. Young braves out marauding would find his horses a prize worth trying to take.

Beau met a wagon train shortly after he crossed

the Three Island Crossing. They had wintered at Fort Hall, having been late in their departure from Missouri. It was mid-morning and they were just finishing up repairs needed on two wagons. The people reminded him of those he'd led. The folks had mixed feelings of wonder and fear about what lay ahead. For an hour he answered questions about the river crossings, trail conditions, and the mountain passes.

It felt good as he rode away from them. Many of the memories of responsibility flooded over him as he sat within the wagons. Reaching the plateau where they had fought the Shoshones, Beau opened one of the packs. It held a small, stone marker. He was glad to see that wild animals hadn't dug at Beck's grave.

Over the winter, Jocko had made the marker with intentions of bringing it to the Graf farm. Realizing that Beau would go by the plateau on the way back east, he'd asked him to put it on the grave. At some time in the future, his stocky friend would see Otto and let him know of its being placed.

It was early June when Beau stopped at Fort Hall. There were several wagon trains on their way to California, camped on the rapidly disappearing grass. There was a festive mood in the camps, with talk of the gold just lying around to be picked up. Again, the trains were mostly made up of men. Those who were married had plans of sending for their wives after they had gotten rich.

Spending only one night, Beau added a few things he needed to the packhorse before continuing. He cut north to the Green River, crossing where they'd built the raft. The winter ice and floods had washed away any sign of the work they had done. After swimming his horses across the river, he rode south a bit and did see that another ferry was being set up. Several young Mormons were busy working on it.

The mountain man passed several wagon trains each day. He checked with the leader of each one to see if David or Hanna Scott were with them. After answering a few questions about the trail ahead, he would move on, riding wide of the rest of the wagon train.

Beau spent the night camping with some Flathead braves, who told him where he could find Elijah. The Flathead friend was surprised to see him. "I did not expect you to come back from Oregon."

"I stayed the winter to see it if would grow on me," Beau told him. "It did not."

"The gold in California didn't tempt you?" Eli asked.

"The only reason a man would want gold was if he wanted to settle down in a city," the mountain man said. "I would choose farming in Oregon before living in a city."

"The mountains have a hold on both of us," the chief agreed.

"Your people believe in visions and dreams, don't they?" Beau asked his friend.

Smiling, Eli said, "They can tell of the future. It can be of a good hunt, or of danger."

"I dream of a dark-haired girl with smiling eyes," he told his friend. "I go after her but she stays just beyond me. I can see her but I can't tell who she is."

"If it has been for a long time, it may be Ana," Eli replied. "Maybe your future is in Mexico."

"They started after leaving Missouri," Beau said. "I think it is the wife of a man that died crossing the Platte."

"We have an elder that talks to the spirits," the chief said. "I can ask him to look into your dreams."

Unsure that he wanted to know the future, Beau shook his head. "I am sure it is the man's wife, Hanna. I hope to find her at Fort Laramie."

Beau had brought powder and lead for his friend to help with the summer hunting. For three days the two friends talked of the past and worried about the future. Both depended on the mountains and plains for their livelihoods. The emigrants from the east would change their way of life.

Leaving the Flathead camp, Beau traveled along the north side of the Sweetwater. Not far from Crossing Five, he saw a lone man at a campfire. The sun was getting low in the sky behind him, so the mountain man hailed the camp.

The man waved to him. "Come on in. I got coffee on."

The voice was familiar. "Is that you, Claude?" Beau called back.

"That it is," Mr. Dingle replied. "Come on closer so I can see who you are."

As he rode forward, the mountain man called, "It's Beau Levesque. We met last spring."

"Why, if it ain't you still kicking and breathing," he said, extending his dirty hand.

As they shook the soft breeze brought Beau a whiff of the man. Nothing had changed. He still smelled like a hide wagon. Stepping away to take care of his horses, Beau asked, "Did you have that cold drink from them mountains in the Montana territory?"

"I got there, but the clouds hid the damn place," Claude complained. "I shore enough found ice, but couldn't enjoy the view."

"Back to hunting buffalo?" Beau asked as he took a seat upwind of the old gent.

"Got another month before we start hunting," Claude said. "I figure to do some fishing and maybe wander up to the Badlands."

Beau held his mug out and let Mr. Dingle fill it. Taking a taste, the mountain man had to admit that the old buffalo hunter did make good coffee. Suddenly, the old man got the look of a weasel that had gotten the chicken on his whisker-covered face.

"I got a surprise for you," he said.

"What could that be?" Beau asked.

"We're having sourdough biscuits with supper tonight," the old man said, chuckling.

The mountain man remembered the man's hands being cleaned on the dough last spring. Smiling, he replied, "I am looking forward to them." He figured that the dirt might make them taste better.

The old man was likeable and Beau spent a couple of nights with Claude, the two of them telling stories and chewing tobacco. After enjoying his time with the old man, and a final breakfast of day-old sourdough biscuits and coffee, Beau headed east, squinting at the sun. For several miles the mountain man could still smell Claude and he began to worry that some of the odor had clung to him. Rain began to fall, and for a change Beau was thankful for the cleansing, bad weather.

The mountain man was dozing in the saddle when Fort Laramie came into view. The sorrel suddenly stepped quickly, making Beau look up. His heart began to beat a little faster as he looked at the end of his quest. Then a flash of worry went through him.

Maybe she had gone back east or was on a wagon train he hadn't visited.

Several wagon trains were camped near the fort. They would be some of the last wagons heading west that could hope to get through the mountains before snow closed them up. Riding in through the gate, Beau was surprised at the number of soldiers visible inside. He'd heard that there were more coming, but he hadn't expected so many.

He stopped in front of the hospital. He wanted to find out about the man he'd brought in and he also figured the doc would know if David Scott was still at the fort. A man was sitting on a bench in front of the hospital, humming a song and enjoying the sunshine. The mountain man nodded to him as he went in.

The doc was sitting at a small table, looking through a book. "Excuse me," Beau said to get his attention.

"You bleeding or got a broken bone?" the doc asked, not looking up.

"Nope," the mountain man said.

Turning the page, the doc said, "Then I will be with you in a moment."

Taking a seat on a chair near the door, Beau prepared to wait. The doc glanced at him and then went back to the book. Then he looked again. "You brought in the fellow that was almost dead a year ago."

"I did," Beau said. "I was hoping to find out if he made it."

The doc turned and smiled. "He's the man sitting out front. His name is Walter Hask. He ain't all back yet and still don't remember the attack, but with a little more time, he should be on his way."

The doctor led Beau outside. "Walter, I got

someone that wants to meet you."

Looking up, the man smiled. He came over and reached out his hand. "I'm Walter Hask."

"You can call me Beau," the mountain man said, accepting the handshake.

The doc then told the man, "This here is the man I told you about. The one that brung you in from the attack."

There was a bit of confusion on the mans face. "I don't remember the attack. I remember being in St. Louis with my brother, Everett. Was he with the wagon?"

The mountain man paused before answering. The doc spoke up. "I think he was, Walter."

The man's gray eyes filled with tears. "He is dead, ain't he?"

"I buried him deep and prayed over him," Beau told the man.

"I want to go there some day," Walter said and then he sat back on the chair, staring ahead.

The doc nodded to Beau to follow him. Once inside, he told the mountain man, "His mind isn't all there yet. He can't remember things I tell him. I have told him his brother Everett was killed many times. It is always like he's finding out for the first time."

"I want to thank you for what you've done for him," Beau replied.

"He helps me around the hospital, cleaning and moving stuff," the doctor told him. "I keep hoping he'll come all the way back, but in the meantime, I'll keep him dressed and fed."

"I have one more thing to ask you," the mountain man said. "Are David Scott and his sister still here at the fort?"

"They are," the doc said, as a smile came to his wrinkled face. "That sister of his is a bright spot at this drab, old fort."

"Where would I find them?" Beau asked, feeling his heart beating faster.

Pulling out his pocket watch, the doc checked the time. "They would be at the officers' dining room right now. His sister eats the evening meal with him every night."

Turning to leave, the mountain man stopped and said, "Thank you for taking care of Walter."

Walking across the parade ground, Beau got directions to the adobe building that housed the officers' mess. He suddenly realized that the clothes he was wearing had several days of sweat and trail dust on them. At their cleanest, they were worn and patched. His beard needed a trim and his hat drooped around his shoulder-length, curly hair.

He was about to change his mind and look for a barber and bathhouse when the two of them walked out of the building. David saw him first but did not place him. Then Hanna looked up. A wide smile broke out on her face.

"Beau Levesque! Is that you?" she cried, rushing up and throwing her arms around him. Stepping back, she looked him up and down.

"I . . . I hoped you'd still be here," the mountain man stammered.

"You aren't in Oregon," she said, concern crossed her face. "Did you . . . did everyone make it there?"

Beau's nerves jump inside and he wanted to say, *I came back for you*, but instead replied, "Everyone made it, except for one of the Graf boys we lost in a fight with the Shoshones."

Hanna was suddenly sad and she looked away for a moment, no doubt thinking of the loss of her husband. Beau was about to tell her why he had come back when another officer joined them. Hanna looked up at the captain and broke back into a smile.

Turning to Beau she told him, "I want to introduce you to Captain James Taylor." Then to the captain she said, "This is Beau Levesque, my best friend."

Reaching out, Beau shook the captain's hand, "It is a pleasure meeting you." Inside, the mountain man felt dread.

Hanna took a step closer to the captain and smiled, "James and I are to be married. After the wedding, we will be taking my mother back east. The captain will be stationed at Fort Washington."

Beau looked at the slightly overweight officer, wearing a crisp, clean uniform, and sporting a thick, black moustache. The mountain man felt sick and fought to hide his feelings. He needed a barber and a bath and would still show poorly next to the soldiers and Hanna.

Forcing a smile, Beau replied, "I am happy for the two of you." He felt desperate to get away and told them, "I have to take care of my horses."

It was two days later when a knock on the door woke the mountain man from a drunken stupor. Beau groaned, rolling over on the bed, his head pounding. "Go away," he said in a raspy voice.

Again, there was a knock. This time more insistent. A voice told him, "Mr. Levesque. Please open the door."

"If that's you Louie, go away," Beau begged,

his dry throat hurting as he spoke. He pulled the pillow over his head to shut out the light of the window.

There was the sound of the door opening and a creak of the floor boards as someone entered. Anger filled the mountain man due to the intrusion. He threw the covers off and spun around on the bed, slamming his feet on the floor, ready to dress down whoever it was.

He looked up at David Stiles. The lieutenant took a step back from the angry mountain man and held his hands up ready to defend himself. "I am sorry to disturb you, but I had heard from Louie that you were here and had been drinking hard since leaving us at the mess hall."

Beau suddenly grabbed his stomach. "Move," he groaned, pushing by the lieutenant. Dressed only in his long johns, Beau stumbling down the stairs, and went out the back to the little house.

David followed him and stood out side the small outhouse as he listened to the mountain man heave. The lieutenant had not told Hanna that he was coming to the boarding house, but the brief look on Beau's face when his sister had told him of her upcoming marriage had haunted him. Finding it odd that the mountain man hadn't come back to visit the past couple of days had prompted David to make inquiries of his whereabouts. That was when he learned from Louie that Beau was at the boarding house and drinking heavily.

The door on the little house creaked as Beau came out. He was wiping his beard with the sleeve of the long johns. The underwear was torn wide open in the front. "I damn near pissed myself while throwing up," he explained.

While his stomach felt a bit better, Beau's head still pounded and the bright sun hurt his eyes. The mountain man staggered back into the back door and sat heavily on a nearby bench. David followed sitting on a chair on the opposite wall. "Can I get you anything?"

Beau shook his head and then, changing his mind, he looked up, "Some water, maybe."

Getting up, David said, "You best button up. I'll be right back with some water."

Re-taking the seat across from the mountain man, David was thankful that Beau had buttoned the sweat stained long johns. After finishing the water, Beau rubbed his head vigorously, trying to clear the cobwebs.

Finally, the lieutenant began. "Hanna doesn't know I've come to see you. She thinks you left the fort without saying goodbye."

"I've been busy since I got here," Beau told him.

"That I can see," David replied. "I don't think my sister knew how you felt about her. For most of the winter she has been in a bad way after loosing Jon. Neither I nor our mother could bring her out of it. Then she met James. He was kind and gentle. He was able to draw her out of the unhappiness she had sunk into."

"She seems to . . . to like him," Beau replied, hunting for the right words to say.

"She introduced you to James as her best friend," the lieutenant told him. "During her worst times after losing Jon, her mood could only be broken when our mother talked of something you had done on the wagon train. When the conversation was over, she would slip back."

"I missed her when she left the wagon train," Beau admitted. "I should have come back with her."

"You had a job to do," David pointed out. "The people on the wagon train depended on you."

"Maybe so, but it was wrong for me to leave her," Beau replied, wanting to add, because he loved her. Instead, he kept that to himself.

"My fear is if she sees you like this, Hanna will think it is her fault," David told him. "I need you to come and see her and . . . and if you could, give her support in her decision to marry James."

After David had left, Beau sat on the bench, staring at the floor. He thought about what the lieutenant had said and his own thoughts during the past few minutes. He had never thought of his attraction to her as love. Beau knew it was not love when they had parted at the Platte. Dwelling on her over the winter had advanced fondness to love.

Leaving the glass on the bench and wishing he had another filled with water, the mountain man slowly climbed the stairs back to his room. An empty whiskey bottle lay discarded next to the bed. He caught a glimpse of himself in the small mirror above the side table.

"You look like hell," he muttered.

Hanna and her mother had just sat down to a midday meal of warmed up soup, when there was a knock on the door. Mrs. Stiles set her spoon down and went to answer it. Pulling the door open she saw Beau, freshly bathed and barbered, dressed in a clean set of clothes.

"Please come in, Mr. Levesque," she said. "We have just set down to eat. Would you like to have some soup with us?"

* * *

It was the end of July and the flowers were in bloom across the plain. The mature grass waved in the wind. In the distance a rider leading his pack animal slowly moved toward the Big Horn Mountains. For the next several hours he would be climbing to the high meadow with the shanty. There was the lonely sound of a wolf calling to its pack.

"Are you telling them I'm back?" Beau shouted. The mountain man was in no hurry and stopped at a stream to do some fishing. Leaving the stream, his attention was on the game trails leading to the water.

He was dressed in new buckskins and low-heeled boots. A flat-brimmed hat sat cocked covering his brown, curly hair that was cut just below his ears. His beard was cropped short and his knife and Colt were in the wide belt around his waist. The Hawken was balanced across the front of him.

Disappointment showed on his face as he approached the shanty. The winter snow had taken the roof down, leaving only the walls standing. Swinging down from the sorrel, he grabbed hold of the door and gave a pull. Slowly, he dragged it open, with the bottom knocking down the grass growing in front of it.

There was a racket once the door was open, as three raccoons scrambled to exit over the walls of the shanty. A quick survey of the dilapidated structure told him he'd be sleeping under the stars tonight.

Looking at the sorrel pulling at the thick grass

covering the meadow, Beau said, "Another fine building that has fell to the snows of winter. There's only one thing to do with it."

Reaching in, he pulled some of the roof poles out of the doorway and broke them up for his fire. Tossing them into the grass-covered firepit, he used dried bark from the walls for tinder and started a fire. Hanging from the saddle horn were three plump cutthroat trout.

With the trout broiling over the fire and a pot of water heating for coffee, he looked at the sorrel and pack horse that were grazing a short distance away. "I hate to say it, but we can't stay in the shanty. We'll have to head back down the mountain."

He took one of the trout off of the fire and, holding the green stick used for broiling it, he pulled at the hot skin with his knife. It peeled off, revealing the juicy meat underneath. He removed some of the meat and stuck it into his mouth. As smile came to his face as he enjoyed the sweet tasting fish.

Beau had hoped to spend the next month living in the shanty and doing some hunting in the area. This was one of his favorite places to relax and forget memories like the one of Hanna climbing into the wagon with the help of James, and smiling with anticipation of the trip east.

Attending their wedding had torn him apart inside, but he'd sat with a fixed grin on his face, masking the pain he actually felt. Beau had decided being successful in love was all a matter of timing, and his had been damn poor.

Wiping his mouth and beard with the back of his hand, he told the sorrel, "I guess we could head for the Wind River or the Yellowstone. I've hunted this place out anyway. We can leave it to the wolves."

After finishing the first fish, he added coffee to the pot. Taking the second fish while the coffee brewed, he looked at the horse again. "Maybe the easterners are still looking for a hunting guide. We could go down to the Mormon Crossing and find out."

The mountain man had been avoiding the Red Buttes and the crossing due to the bad memories of Jon drowning and riding away from Hanna. But the money would be good if they shot elk and buffalo. It would be useful come winter.

"I been thinking of going north," Beau said.

When the meal was finished, the sun was just over the mountain tops to the west. Not wanting to be stumbling around in the dark, he led the horses to water and then rolled out his blankets in front of the derelict shanty. Pulling off his boots, he crawled under the blankets, putting the Colt under the saddle and the Hawken beneath the edge of his blanket.

Beau was up at first light. He got the horses ready and then, with great effort, pushed the shanty door back shut. "Got to make it comfortable for the critters," he told the horses. Beau had no intention of spending time to rebuild the roof. He rode back down the meadow, leading the bay. "That damn Tolliver will take advantage of me. Probably charge me double for the supplies I'll be needing."

The sorrel bobbed its head, snorting as though agreeing with the mountain man. The sun was low behind him when he reached the trading post. No one was in sight. He knew the boys had left to bring furs north. His mouth was set for some of the Scottish whiskey. He took the horses to the stable and pulled the gear off them. They needed a good brushing and he promised that he would do so in the morning.

Old Tolliver was sitting in the trading post. "You back so soon? Did you get lonely?"

"Damn shanty roof came down," Beau told him. "Didn't see any sign of elk in the area, either. I'm thinking of checking on some easterners at the crossing."

The old man grabbed the cards and a bottle from behind the bar. With two drinks poured the men toasted each other and tossed them down. Beau always enjoyed the bite of the first drink as warmth spread through his stomach.

"Do you have a contract with the hunting party?" Tolliver asked.

Tossing the last drops of whiskey from the bottom of his glass, the mountain man then replied. "I was told to be there by mid-August. Otherwise they'd find someone else."

The old man poured another measure into their glasses. "It will be a week of hard riding to get there in time."

"My horses are in good shape for the trip," Beau said, taking a sip from his glass.

'If you make enough money on the hunt, do you plan to winter in this area?" the old man asked.

"I been thinking of going north," Beau told him. "So far north that I hear the bears are white as snow. I ain't never hunted a white bear."

"Damn long way to go to hunt a bear," Tolliver replied. Dealing out the poker hand, the old man got back to business. "Taking the hunters means you will be needing supplies."

"Only if I can afford them." Beau said, throwing in three cards.

"You know I don't set the prices," the old man reminded him, giving Beau three cards and taking two himself. "You got to take that up with Ellie."

"How come you decided to let your children run everything?" he asked Tolliver.

"I'm getting old and got tired of dickering," the man said.

"You know that ain't true," Beau replied. "I could get you to budge on prices if I got in a pinch, but she is one stubborn lady."

Ellie came out from the back and stood behind the bar. "Did I hear you say you'll need supplies?"

Appreciating the way her gingham dress hung over her supple, breasts. Beau told her, "Only if I decide to take the easterners on the hunt, and I won't be able to if I can't afford supplies."

She laughed as she came around the bar. "We can discuss the cost of supplies later tonight."

Looking at the young woman, Beau replied, "You know how to put me in an awful weak bargaining position."

* * *

The late morning sun found Beau on the sorrel, leading the bay south, packed with supplies needed for the hunt. Old Tolliver and his daughter watched him crossing the Tongue River.

"I don't understand why you let him ride away each time, Ellie," the old man said. "It's not my whiskey or the price he gets for his furs that brings him back here, it's you."

A sad smile came to her face. "Beau is like the sands of the plain. You can scoop it up in your hand

and hold it for a while, but a grain at a time, it falls out and the wind catches it and it drifts away. Before long the hand is empty."

"He must have feeling for you, daughter."

"Oh yes, father," she replied, tears shining in her eyes. "He likes, maybe even loves, being with me, but . . . it's not me he dreams of."

CAST OF CHARACTERS

Beau Levesque – The Mountain Man
Jocko Wells – The Scout and Friend
Wagon One – Otto Graf, Beck Graf, Ludwig Graf
Wagon Two – Clem Williams, Lucy Williams, Charles, Hazel, 2 more girls.
Wagon Three – Alvin Thompson, Lilly Thompson
Wagon Four – Robin (Rob) Tyler
Wagon Five – Edsel Ward, Mary Ward
Wagon Six – Hoot Johnson, Web Johnson, Slim Johnson
Wagon Seven – Peck Wilson, Carrie Wilson
Wagon Eight – Quinn Rogers, Molly Rogers
Wagon Nine – Art Rogers, Ava Rogers
Wagon Ten – Sean Rogers, Duncan Rogers
Wagon Eleven – Tom Wolsey, Beth Wolsey – Sam Wolsey, Cora Wolsey
Wagon Twelve – Aarno Hanson, Kimi Hanson
Wagon Thirteen – Herb Tucker, Wife
Wagon Fourteen – Tano Edwards, Wife, 1 child
Wagon Fifteen – Jon Scott, Hanna Scott, Ruth Stiles
Wagon Sixteen – Helena Burns, Theo, Lilith
Fort – David Scott Lieutenant
Fort – Louie and Lucy Trading Post and Buffalo Hide

Saloon

Trading Post – Old Man Tolliver, Emma Toliver, Children Ecgbert, Randolph, Elllie

Claude Dingle – Smelly Buffalo Hunter

Ana Garcia – Past Sweetheart. Father was Emilio

Doo Doolittle – Old Trapper and Prospector

Flathead Chief – Elijah (Eli) Weber, Saka'am his wife

Bull – Mean Bruiser

Hal Rinker, Mick Rinker – Prisoners, Cousins

Attacked Wagon – Walter Hask (Survivor), Everett Hask, Albert Goodin, William Johns